LETTERS
TO AN
ANDROID

WENDY RATHBONE

Letters To An Android

by

Wendy Rathbone

Letters To An Android

ISBN: 978-0-9896938-7-5
TITLE: Letters To An Android
Author: Wendy Rathbone

Address all inquiries to the author at:
wrathbone@juno.com

Description: *Cobalt is a created human, vat grown and born adult, with no human rights and indentured to serve others for the duration of his life. Liyan is a young man with wanderlust in his eyes, embarking on a career that takes him to the furthest regions of space. The two become unlikely friends and create a memorable long-distance correspondence. Through Liyan, Cobalt gets to explore the universe, living vicariously through his friend's wave transmissions. A strong bond develops between them that not even the stars can put asunder.*

Length: 66,500 words

For Della

Letters to an Android

by

Wendy Rathbone

(Warning: this novel contains starboats, spacesickness, poisonous green skies, emotional androids and haiku)

Part One

1. Liyan

Liyan had just finished repairs on a coupling unit in the spaceport's huge workshop. A job well done. He threw off his work gloves for the last time and did not look back.

He went outside to breathe the ion-laced air of the tarmac, and looked up at the dark green, force-field encased sky and the space tunnel where a line of hovering round-ships waited for orders to set down. Laser repair lights winked scarlet on the landing field. A rare rocket stretched its white fume into the emerald atmosphere. It would create its own tunnel to escape the force-field without an atmospheric breach. What they were testing with it he had no idea. Nor did he care. This was his last day of work here.

Earlier in the week he'd gotten his flight posting. The one he'd dreamed of and worked toward, attending school 25 hours a week as well as holding down a first level mechanic's job.

At age 20, he would be entering the world of C&C Starlines at full ensign ranking. He'd gotten the go-ahead seven days ago. Barely enough time to give notice to his landlord and pack his small room and the few personal items he wanted to take with him.

Adrenalin rushed through him. He gasped a deep breath of the ashy air and realized he was grinning. A co-worker clanked by him in a black-scarred, bulky silver protective suit. The helmet made a square silhouette against the backdrop of the river-hued sky. Evan looked like some old fashioned robot from the cover of an ancient Earth magazine about aliens and metal men. Evan said, voice muffled from the helmet, "We're gonna miss you around here."

Liyan wasn't going to miss any of this. But he said, "Thanks. Me, too."

"Come by the Aurora later." He sounded like he was speaking around a wad of tissue from an echo chamber. "We're all going to Rory's. We'll buy your drinks."

The Grand Aurora was the port's only five-star hotel with the biggest and most popular bar called Rory's Bar.

Liyan said, "I'm staying there until tomorrow when we get shuttled to the starport. My apartment's already rented to someone else."

"Good, then we'll see you at Rory's!" Evan clomped across the threshold and disappeared inside the workshop.

*

Even the cheapest room at the Aurora dripped luxury. Silk and damask. Real oak furniture. Satin comforters and tapestried walls.

For a few minutes, Liyan rolled on the bed in soft euphoria. A crystal chandelier sang its refracted violetpinkgold essence into his brain. He smelled a fine mist on the air, something like spice and fresh grass and a kind of creamy soap used only in bubble baths. He actually intended to have one of those. But later.

Now, he got up and changed into more trendy clothing: a furnace blue button up shirt and black trousers with low-heeled, newly polished work boots. He would have a uniform at his new job, but tonight he could still choose his own colors. He combed his smooth brown hair which was a bit long to the shoulders now. He figured C&C would take care of any hair style they required from him, so he hadn't rushed for a haircut.

When he felt presentable enough, he grabbed his key and moneycard and headed for the bar.

His friends greeted him with high enthusiasm. Liyan smiled until his cheeks ached.

Beer. Whiskey. Expensive wine. His friends offered him anything he wanted. Such good men and women. They had been fine co-workers, but he hadn't gotten close to any of them. His schooling and his dreaming got in the way of any social life. But they were still generous and they all clapped him on the back as if he were some hero going off to save the universe.

In fact, he was going further than most of them ever hoped to get in a lifetime.

The bar-light was warm and gold. The drinks weren't as watered as usual and packed a punch.

Not wanting to be hung-over on the shuttle ride the next day, Liyan slowed his drinking pace. He wandered away from the crowd toward the shadows by the end of the long, curving counter, and asked the young man making tall, fizzing concoctions of something purple and glittery for a glass of water.

The man turned, slim and graceful, hair the hue of Technicolor seas on old 'wave' programs about true-Earth when it still supported life. He had to have been supremely distracted not to have noticed this man until now. His face had such a fine-tuned edge to it, angled and curved in just the right places, the eyes wide and down-turned enough to be coy but still masculine. Even more shocking, perhaps: the irises were the same shade as the violet fizzing drinks he'd been preparing.

The man placed a glass of ice water in front of him. Liyan hadn't meant to stare, but the man didn't appear to mind. The bartender asked, voice a low tremor on the air, "Is the celebration going on over there for you?"

"I'm leaving tomorrow, a job on a ship with C&C Starlines."

"I see. New realms. New experiences. A new life."

"That's about right."

"Then I, too, would like to wish you all fortune in your travels."

Liyan blinked, oddly pleased though this man was a stranger. "Thank you."

"Where to, first, if I may ask?"

Before Liyan could answer, a waiter came to pick up the three purple drinks. Soon they were alone again. Liyan had completely forgotten his friends. He said, "When the crew are settled and the ship readied, I'm told the first destination is Fair-Orb."

He nodded, his eyes going from mauve to gray in his neat attention. "That far. You'll be a true star-man, then."

"Technically, yes. I passed the tests in the top fifth percentile in nav. I'll be going on the long-hauls." Most people didn't pass them at all, not their first time or their tenth.

"Impressive," the bartender said.

"For as long as I can remember I've wanted this. It's been all work and no play for me." He sighed, finally remembering his friends, looking over his shoulder. They hadn't missed him yet. They were all occupied with their drinks and their jokes.

"They say on Fair-Orb the stars meet the sea," the bartender said.

Liyan raised his eyebrows at such a beautiful but true statement. "It is made of mostly water."

"And at night the towers that jut out of the sea look suspended in space. You truly cannot tell where the seas end and the stars begin. Alas, I will never see it."

Liyan lifted his glass and took a sip of the cold, plain water. It cooled him, but the heat of excitement did not wane. He set the glass down and held out his hand. "My name is Liyan."

The man raised his hand to meet his palm to palm. "Cobalt. I am at your service."

"At my…?" It was a confusing line, one Liyan had not heard before.

"Perhaps I should explain. I will never see Fair-Orb in my lifetime. I am locked into my work contract here. Forever."

"Work contract?" Liyan frowned. "Oh. I didn't realize…you're an android?"

"It is a compliment that it was not obvious to you."

"I thought you were a really pretty…human." He chuckled. "That's all."

"Thank you," the android said. "Of course now that you know this fact about me, you know I have no rights. Despite the longing in my thoughts." His full, pink lips curved into a tiny smile. "I can only travel in other people's stories. And I travel in my dreams."

Liyan did know that androids had no human rights. But he knew little else. "You dream?"

"Of course. All beings dream."

Liyan said, "I've always been taught that androids are machines and that it's wrong to think they aren't. But I know you have organic components."

"Yes, all my components are organic."

"So you're just like…like a person."

"I am."

"It's sad, then."

"What is?"

"That you can't leave." Liyan looked at the purple eyes and blue hair of his bartender. The skin of the face was such a perfect, smooth bronze. He should've guessed. But he'd never met anyone like him before. All he knew was that androids were bought and owned by the extremely wealthy who were the only ones who could afford them. So why was this one working at the Grand Aurora? "The hotel bought you to tend bar?"

"I do whatever is required. All jobs here. The owner inherited me five years ago."

"Oh." Liyan watched as a drink order came in and Cobalt began preparing it. The android had not dismissed him, so he waited. It seemed such a waste, someone with the capacity of Cobalt in mind and body mixing beverages in a hotel bar. Android brains were grown for obedience and brilliance. He would've passed the C&C company tests in the first percentile.

When Cobalt turned his attention back to him, Liyan said, "I have an idea."

Cobalt shifted his head in question.

"Maybe you can't leave here, but I could write you on the wave. Tell you firsthand of my adventures."

The android managed to look authentically wistful. "I would like that."

"You're thinking maybe I'll forget as soon as I leave here, but I won't. I will write to you. I promise."

Cobalt said, "I'll be waiting to hear from you, then."

Liyan watched the long, perfect fingers of the android drum the countertop as if in human anticipation.

"Do I wave you here at the hotel?"

"Yes. My name is my address on the hotel's system."

"Cobalt," Liyan said. "I won't forget it."

2. Cobalt

Cobalt waited two weeks and heard nothing from Liyan. He did not expect any correspondence, but he had hoped for it. Just a little. As much as he allowed himself any hope in his life of menial servitude.

Sometimes he looked toward the green-storm harbors of the shipyards, watching the agate skies roil and roll in the vapors the ships left in their wakes and he would recall his conversation with Liyan verbatim. He would remember the young man's hands, how they trembled against the water glass in excitement and maybe even a little anxiety. He would remember the exact shade of his hair, autumn-leaf brown, and how deep that youthful, brown-eyed stare.

It made him content to know Liyan was out there somewhere beyond the port, moving into the enchanting embrace of other worlds and beyond, into the darkrush of driftless void.

He really didn't expect Liyan to ever keep his promise. But if he did, Cobalt wondered what he would do if he received a wave. Should he respond? What did he have to say, to give? His life consisted of work. He wanted beauty, too, but he had never really found it. Was there any point in describing the fine suits he wore when he was concierge, or how deftly less-than-gentle men took them off him when they rented him from his owner for a night?

And what about his owner? An old man who couldn't care less about him except that he earned. Cobalt did everything he was told. A letter attesting to that seemed, to him, a very boring one indeed.

Sometimes, when he tried to see the stars through the oily gaseous skies of the port, he actually hoped Liyan would not write, that he would stay away and never look back. Just go. Go.

It was what he wanted to do himself. He could only imagine it. But now he had a face to put to his imaginings. He could live vicariously through Liyan.

*

One particularly unfortunate and annoying night, as Cobalt bathed in a lilac-scented tub and attended to handprint-shaped bruising on his thighs, he heard his wavescreen chirp.

His wavescreen only did that when his owner wanted him for a job. But he'd done his job for the evening. He'd been given the rest of the night off to repair and sleep.

What, then, could this be?

Slowly, he rose from the tub. He dripped onto the bathroom rug, delicately drying his sensitive skin, then put on a robe and went to see what it was.

The amber light blinked: *Message. Message.*

He lit the screen and read the odd address. Unfamiliar. His heart twitched in his chest.

He reached out, hesitant at first, and touched the address.

The message appeared.

Dear Cobalt:

I have not forgotten you. Not for one moment. I even hope you might have missed me. I don't mean to be cruel in saying that, only hopeful because we have only met once and I think I am presuming far too much. I may have passed C&C requirements at

13

the top of my class, but I'm still a bit remedial in social interaction. But I made a promise to you. And I want to keep it.

Also, you made an impression on me. I can't forget your face. I think I miss you more than the friends I worked with for two years. Isn't that strange?

And now I want to erase that last paragraph. But I won't. I am very young compared to a lot of my ship-mates, so I think you should allow me to be a bit dumb.

I want to tell you where I am. And I want to make it good for you. You might be able to see a picture on the wave, but it's still not the same as being here.

The starport for the liner, and other stop-over ships, is a giant cube with fifty floors. Inside that cube everything is uniform, the rooms and offices square and all the same. It isn't much to speak of. But looking at the port from outside is like looking at a black metal square window floating against the immortal dark. It's a blank, dark page in space waiting for words. And there are starships in the margins. They hang there as if doodled by some insane, giant hand.

In every distance are tiny swarms of stars.
I hope these words help you see what I see.
The starliner is almost ready. I am well.

Your friend,
Liyan

Cobalt let the milky light of the wave bathe his face as he read it a second time. And a third.

This was a first for him. Never before had he received a wave from anyone who did not want something from him, but only wanted to give.

He touched 'reply' though he had no idea what to say in return. He began slowly.

14

Dear Liyan:

From my room in the Grand Aurora I sit and read your words. They give me a unique vision that I greatly welcome. I will take that vision with me to my work.

Now when I look at the green-marbled skies of this port I will not be as sad.

And I will keep seeing your starships in the margins.

You fulfilled your promise to me. I thank you.

Your friend,
Cobalt

He brushed the 'send' light with the tip of his forefinger.

When he went to bed, he'd forgotten all about his pain.

*

The next night he saw another wave message light flashing in his room.

Dear Cobalt:

We leave tomorrow. While in foldspace there will be no waves. Navigation in this instance is always unpredictable. It could be days or weeks before I can respond.

In the meantime, I wanted to say I had no idea you were sad. But of course this is my oversight. You are trapped at the Grand Aurora for your lifespan which, in the research I have done on androids since I met you, appears to be quite long. The unpleasantness of your situation affects me. I wish I could do something to help. Instead, I will write you when I can. I will tell you of my journeys. That I can do.

I am packed and ready to leave. My uniform is stark white trimmed with black ribbing. There is an optional hat, like a flat cap. I refuse to wear it. My boots are black. The C&C logo is embossed on their sides, the Pegasus image a silver brand we wear there and on the cuffs of our shirts.

I will be working in navigation but not up front. I'll work in the chart rooms at the center of the ship. The computers do the math until the charts look like intricate designs of castles, or pyramid piles of leaves, or the bone structures of indescribable monsters. Equation sets are often differentiated by color. The chart rooms resemble galleries of modern art made of tiny numbers.

I fall asleep dreaming of those numbers.

Please write back. Speak of any subject. If I don't receive the wave tomorrow, it will be waiting for me when we get to Fair-Orb.

Your friend,
Liyan.

Again, Cobalt read the message three times, just as he had with the last one. He memorized every word.

He opened a fresh page.

Dear Liyan:

I don't know how to tell you that I long to see indescribable monsters on navigation charts. It is strange to write that. But it is the truth.

If possible, I would next like to hear your experience in foldspace. I have heard it said that no two experiences are alike. Some say time moves slower or faster. Some say inanimate objects appear to shrink or grow before your eyes. Some suffer a kind of spacesickness for the duration and must remain in sleep mode. As you well know, out of foldspace have come revelatory scientific theories, award winning novels, master symphonies, among other amazing human feats of genius.

Do share whatever revelation you may receive, even if it's only one word.

I continue in my duties. There are many I can enjoy and many I cannot enjoy. This is not a complaint, simply a fact. The sadness in me comes, I believe, from the implanted childhood

16

*memories that are unreal. Because they did not, in fact, happen, I
often wish I did not have them. The theory is they create personality
because we are born 'adult'. I can say perhaps they do that, but they
cause more pain than pleasure because of developing tastes, likes and
dislikes, judgment and subjectivity. If one is going to create a tool, it
is cruel to give it emotion, do you not think?*

The tediousness of my words appalls me but I leave them.
I look forward to your next wave.

Your friend,
Cobalt

Two weeks passed. In that time he did accounting,
reservations, and more bartending. He was also forced to
make his body available to two male clients who were selfish
and unfriendly. But unlike the last client, they did not leave
bruises.

Every night he looked for a message light. None
appeared.

He dreamed of watercolor starcharts. He wanted to
dream of Liyan. It simply did not happen.

He thought of him often, though, in his white uniform
standing on the polished decks of a behemoth ship that
cruised the ancient star-lanes. In the image he conjured,
Liyan's leaf-hair fell against his brown eyes as he read the
math of the stars.

*

3. Fair-Orb After the Storm

Dear Cobalt:

Our first foldspace path grew sluggish the further in we went. There was nothing to do but wait it out. I'm sorry it has been a month since my last wave.

Despite the unexpected thickness and soupiness of our route, the experience was nothing short of enlightening.

I tried to keep a journal. It became impossible when my sentence structures fell apart and I was left with pages containing lists of words only, meaningless without a context.

Here is a sample:

lore silver forest portrait pulse rook bracelet collar pillow stealth music-box ink audience luck mother candle underline sawdust

It only got worse from there.

Here is another sample:

The onetwofour multilingual Doppler mountain laurel must event itself in the sullen range of microwave believability.

No great novels or symphonies came from me, I assure you. Any scientific discoveries I might have made are delusional at best. At least I did not suffer the space sickness. I spent a lot of time in ecstasy believing the birth of myself had only begun. I recommend it.

I have made friends aboard this ship already. They are smart and loyal. More on that another time.

Fair-Orb awaits. I am needed at my post.

Your friend,
Liyan

Liyan poked the 'send' light, then realized he had not addressed Cobalt's more serious issues of being indentured and utterly alone. Cobalt had mentioned childhood memories that did not exist and Liyan had not even asked him about them. Guilt flared, tinged with nausea. He wasn't to blame, but he cared. And he wanted Cobalt to know it. But the busyness of his new life called.

He went to work through corridors of living light. He moved inside a silver being that mixed with stars. He helped to send it and its crew to deliver passengers, cargo and goods to far-flung colonies at distances the mind could not truly perceive. He was happier than he'd ever imagined he could be.

*

Once orbit was secure around Fair-Orb, the deliveries began. Cargo and people exited. More cargo and people entered.

The crew took shore leave in shifts. This gave them 12 hours each. After two days and everyone packed aboard, the starliner would move on.

Liyan shuttled with three friends to the surface. One was a new officer, like Liyan. Two were seasoned travelers who had been to Fair-Orb many times and knew which towers housed the best restaurants, bars, casinos and views.

The shuttles streaked like arrows through the atmosphere leaving copper contrails against a pink sky. On this side of the world, night approached. Lark, one of the experienced men, confirmed that Fair-Orb's impressiveness increased at night. He'd chosen the place and time perfectly. If you wanted to get lost in the stars reflected in Fair-Orb's vast and silent seas, you had to be there after sunset.

The shuttle circled Tower Probable before setting down on a tarmac very much like that where Liyan had worked for two years.

Under red clouds they disembarked. The stars remained in hiding.

Tiri, one of the inexperienced officers, asked Lark, "Will the clouds mar the view?"

"The storm just passed. I made sure of it when I studied the weather reports. Look, they're already breaking up, blowing away."

The tower looked as if it were a huge wax drip-candle. In fact, it was made of the crystallized liquid of a native mineral mined from undersea, and it was harder than titanium. The liquid shone gold with an opal sheen. The city-sized tower housed a million souls and ten thousand visitors a day. Lark told them there were even parks within, complete with grass and trees.

The landing strip made a flat semi-circle around the tower. The sea drifted around it, serene and royal and blue. There were lights upon it, but they were from fishing boats, not stars.

Once inside, Lark pointed out the vertical transit system that ran up and down the tower at various points. Lark wasn't sure of the number of trains that existed within, but he guessed at least one hundred.

Liyan looked up and saw the distant ceiling of firstfloor made of glowlight. He saw clear, glass enclosed trains moving up and down, one at their entrance point and others at more distant entrances. They looked like glorified elevators. Everything was bright and new. The scents came one after another, first the sea, brine and salt, then the indoor humidity of teeming life, raw, sweet, tangy. Firstfloor was like a vast mall and business district. They started there. Lark promised they would go to the topmost level, but not until after dinner.

Everywhere Liyan looked was something new. An orange fountain that made spirographs. A floating, bare-branched tree with a thousand blinking lights. People singing on a quay. Children rushing about a giant, fish-themed playground.

Lark led them many blocks through throngs of bustling people who were on foot or on bikes to Morry's Fishhouse which he swore made the best fillets he'd ever tasted.

Liyan's mouth watered. He was starved.

He tried to remember what he saw so he could describe it all to Cobalt when he had the chance, but it was too much. His senses were overwhelmed.

After the fantastic treat of dinner, they all boarded a train which took them straight up to the top floor to a bar with the most expensive cover charge Liyan had ever heard of. Lark, wealthy and connected, got them in.

"This is the million dollar view," he said.

Liyan saw that the bar was made of giant windows. Even the ceiling was glass. Night had indeed come. The four of them moved to one edge of the room and there it was. Everything Cobalt had told him, and more.

A world made of stars within a realm of stars. The stars, real and reflected, engulfed each other.

They all stood poised and humbled, surrounded, captured, suspended in galactic glitter.

Later, lost in drinking and youthful exuberance, one could say they all had the time of their lives.

They returned to the tarmac at dawn, when the stars began to fade and the sea was pink. The voices of fishermen called through the waning night.

Liyan left Fair-Orb as if encased in a dream.

*

Dear Cobalt:

I made it to Fair-Orb. I have just come from the surface having spent the night drinking on a top floor bar with three friends.
Dawn was drowning the world when we left and the sea-boats were all heading out to their favorite spots. On the salt wind of

21

azure tears and pink seas, I heard fishermen call to each other as their boats wove through their fishing lanes.

I can't tell you everything I saw. It's too much. But you were right about the stars meeting the sea. Their oceans are mirror-still, the tides slow. When a million stars wink on at dark, a million more are reflected. Thus, one million becomes two million—so many prickles of light they sting the eyes. Other oceans on other planets are too choppy to minister this effect.

I don't think people could sleep with open windows at night on this world. Those armies of light would invade their sleep. Everything's so liquid and reflective. An endless fever of mirrored flame.

I want to tell you all of it. Inside the tower: the whispering spiral fountains, the scents of ocean dew and frying fish, the sparkle of the tower itself as if made from frozen moonlight.

I am restless as I write this, and still quite drunk.

Lark, our leader, took us to the nightside and his favorite tower, Tower Probable. A funny name. I never learned where it came from. He led us to a fantastic fresh fish dinner and a bar with a cover charge you would never believe. We grew drunk on beer and starlight.

I am listening to quiet music now, alone in my room, too tired, too drunk to sleep.

I think of you intently, and I am afraid I have not addressed you properly, that I write too much of myself and never ask you questions.

But I don't know what to ask. You are trapped. I can't ask how that feels. I can only imagine. And I agree that false childhood memories may be cruel. But if you did not have them, or any emotion at all, would you even care about this letter?

I took you with me in spirit tonight. I thought a lot about how I would write to you of Fair-Orb, about Lark and my other friends. I knew I could never do the experience justice with my mere words. But you can at least know it is for you that I'm trying.

It is the best I can do for you, though not enough.

I am so drunk I want to cry with happiness. How can I explain that?

I won't try. You are spared for now.

Write me of your deepest thoughts any time. Write me about the weather. I don't care which. I just want to hear from you.

Your friend,
Liyan.

He felt foolish but he prodded the send light anyway. Better any letter than none for a lonely android who would qualify with the best of them to travel the cosmos, but would never be allowed.

Finally he collapsed on his bunk. He dreamed of stars and fish and fish-stars and star-fish.

*

Dear Liyan:

I can see the tower. I can smell the sea. I can hear the voices of the fishermen. Thank you for that. Perhaps your true calling is poetry and not navigation? Perhaps they are not mutually exclusive.

But of course one can also have more than one calling in life.

I am great at many different things myself. I say that without pride. It is my prime function to be good at whatever I am hired to do. Perhaps it is more accurate to say I am a good learner.

As I spoke of in my last letter, I have preferences. I am good at accounting, but I prefer my concierge duties. I like seeing the people come and go. I like looking at them, listening to them. The bartending also allows me this pleasure.

I don't mind my work. Honestly. But I can say I am the most fortunate to be able to travel with you, if only in words.

I am glad you have friends. They sound like good ones.

May I ask your next destination?

The port's false moon is beaming through my window right now. The decoration serves only to remind me there is no moon. And that the moss and lichen hued atmosphere of this asteroid is due merely to toxic gasses emitted from the constantly humming vessels at the landing site.

I know you do not miss this place. But when you think of me, this is where I'll be. Always.

Waiting for another letter.

Your friend,
Cobalt

*

4. The World of Floating Cities

Cobalt had to wait two months before receiving another wave. It was worth it.

Dear Cobalt:

Two months in foldspace. We didn't even realize that length of time had passed. Our chronometers displayed a real-time experience of seven days, eleven hours and eight and a half minutes, give or take a second.

This foldspace experience was more coherent than the last. No rhyme or reason to it. I did not smell colors or hear dreams. I never felt the urge to keep a madman's journal. They say it can be that way, sometimes, like normal star-cruising.

There is little navigation to be done once the ship is inside-out of that black envelope of time. But we still kept our normal work hours. The captain gave us tasks and drills. No one got spacesick.

Lark, Tiri, Sekina and I played a lot of cards and watched a lot of recorded wave stories. Of course nothing from real-time waves could get through to us.

I don't believe I've told you much about my friends. I've only mentioned them.

Lark is 25 and was just promoted. He is a full lieutenant now. He has big feet and broad shoulders and likes to talk a lot. And he's loud. No one cares, though, because he's funny. When I first came to navigation I reported to him. But he's moved up. Sekina is my boss now.

Sekina is the smartest person I've ever known. She's only 23 but will make lieutenant next year. She entered the service of C&C at age 22, after spending four years at an ivy university on Dylan studying physics. She has her sights on a ship of her own by the time she's 28. She has wonderful blue streaks in her black hair. The blue color reminds me of yours.

Tiri is 21. She's also very smart and a good worker. She was trained in military combat before acquiring the math skills to be an officer. She's tall, but all willowy muscle and no-nonsense. She and Lark could almost wear the same size uniform, including boots, but are opposites in personality. They have eyes for each other but have not shown awareness of it yet. Sekina and I can see it. Lark likes having, for once, a 'straight-man' for all his jokes, and Tiri seems to enjoy being that for him.

My friends include me in all their activities together. They are generous and kind. Since no one from my classes back at the spaceport came with me, I arrived to the liner friendless and alone. I was also the youngest. For awhile, Lark often called me 'boy' off duty and on. He doesn't do that anymore, though.

They all know I write to a friend back home. When I mentioned your name, Lark's response was, "I do love that shade of blue." I have told them nothing else about you. It's not from shame that I may seem secretive. It is more about this deep sense of knowing that you are a person. The 'no rights' issue aside, where you come from and your label as 'android' is none of their business. You are a friend. You are the person back home I write to. That is all they need to know.

If my behavior concerning this is wrong in your eyes, please tell me. I don't want to think our differences are so big. That's all. If I am making myself appear unclear about you, or conflicted, I apologize. Nothing could be further from the truth.

Our new destination, now that we are out of foldspace again, is Vaera, where the cities float among the clouds.

Your friend,
Liyan

*

In the sapphire shadows of his private room, Cobalt read Liyan's wave three times and, as always, memorized every line. His body ached from recent abuse. A hot drink scented with cinnamon calmed the stiffness of his muscles. And his mind.

Liyan's letter returned a warmth to his veins he did not realize, until now, he'd desperately needed.

He opened a page and began to compose.

Dear Liyan:

I can see Vaera on Galactic Images, and am picturing you there among the rose and tangerine clouds zooming through the neon fog in a grav-cab. I hope you get to do that. It looks as if you will find beauty and pleasure in any city you choose to visit there. I am ready to hear all about it.

I like to hear of your friends. As you must be well aware, people do not befriend androids. You are the exception. Mostly, we make people very uncomfortable. They wish only to use us and be done. I am used to it. I don't know any other way.

I understand that you feel no need to tell your friends of my legal limitations. Whether they know or not does not change the status of my label. I do not wish any part of myself to cause you grief or cause your friends to be perplexed about you.

Your life is lovely. Nothing should mar it. I would go so far as to say it is a grand adventure for me as well. Please do not forget that I appreciate your every word.

Your friend,
Cobalt

*

Dear Cobalt:

We are a day out of Vaera still and I had some time to myself. I went back over our letters and was both pleased and ashamed.

Pleased at our correspondence, which is a wonderful thing for me.

Ashamed at myself. Not you.

Before I say why, let me tell you that I gathered my friends together in the off-duty room, bought them all beers, and told them I wanted their advice.

They all love to give advice (even when not asked) so they came quite quickly and willingly.

While your last letter was polite and generous, showing an appreciation of me and my words, my adventures, I now think it might be undeserved. My decision to lead my friends to believe I had a human friend back home was not to spare you any discomfort but only myself. I realize that now.

And…there was something in the tone of your letter…maybe I'm imagining it, but I could feel—almost—a pain in you. It is more than just the sadness you have mentioned before. You don't speak of it, of course, but am I wrong? Tell me and I will adjust my thinking!

Two word choices from your last wave stood out to me. Your use of the phrase "legal limitations" made me think of what was missing from that description. Personal limitations. You've never talked of those. And then I realized that maybe it is because you have none, that you are human with no limitations on that or your feelings, only those put onto you by the law. Forgive me if I'm ignorant about this, but I don't think I'm wrong in saying you have emotions just like everyone else. Your early memories may be false but that does not mean the feelings aren't real. People can react with intensity to fictions, why not androids to their own fictional memories?

My point is, you have feelings like anyone and I should pay more attention to that.

Also, your phrase: "Whether they know or not does not change the status of my label."

This is true. And whether my friends know or not also does not change the fact that you are my friend.

So after a few sips of beer, I told them, "I need your advice. Cobalt…the friend I write to back home is an android. And I fear I may have offended him."

Sekina said, "You know an android?"

Lark said, "I don't know if I've ever met one. They're so expensive and rare."

Tiri said, "I have met two who were trained soldiers. Cold as fuck."

They all began asking questions at once. How did I meet you? Where do you work? Are you a newer matrix 1001 model, or the older 900 version? What could I possibly do to offend an android?

I told them that I felt it was not anybody's business, really, where you came from, that to me you are just a person, but that I realized this attitude of non-admission, keeping who you are secret, might negate a part of who you are, or it might give the impression I'm ashamed, somehow, to have befriended you, especially when that label confines you, enslaves you, imprisons you. I don't think doing that to another person, created or otherwise, is right. And if I don't even speak of my thoughts, controversial as they may be to some people, then isn't my silence, in a way, selfish?

I'm not sure my question to my friends was completely eloquent but they did grasp the essential predicament.

Tiri, whose entire social environment before joining C&C was combat restricted mainly to one planet, was the only one who'd met androids.

She said, "But isn't it true they are machines? They have cloned brains, yes, but no sense of self, really, and only manufactured emotions."

Lark, always the quickest in wit and problem-solving, said, "It's the myth we're taught. But really, what's the difference between a brain grown in a fetus inside a womb and one grown in a womb-vat?"

"But they aren't clones," Tiri argued. "Their skeletal structure is metal."

28

"That's another myth," I corrected her gently. "Their nervous system comes from the brain, the brainstem, and spine, which are organically grown. Their skin is real cells. They feel it when you touch them. Their bones are real bone although enhanced genetically to be stronger, as much of the rest of their bodies are."

Sekina said, "Only the wealthy own any. They are bought as toys, the same way the rich buy starships to play with. They are symbols of status. In the distant past it was Rolex and Rolls Royce. Now it's Starcore sculpture and Cellex designer humanoids."

"So what you're saying," Lark said, "is if they are made as toys and bought as toys, they amount to nothing more."

Sekina frowned. "I'm not trying to be inconsiderate, or deny emotions that might be real even if misplaced though false memories or programming. But isn't it like loving a bracelet, a pair of shoes, a house, a ship? The stars, even? They simply can't love back. Not humanly. Liyan, this is like writing letters to the liner's computer system. It's intelligent. It can write back. But it's not going to really mean anything. Not in the way you say this android is your 'friend'."

"With the android soldiers I knew back on Raglin, it was that simple," Tiri added.

I listened to my friends. Lark had quieted. The other two discussed my situation as if I'd gotten perhaps over-involved with a fictional character in a virtual game. No harm in it, just no substance.

When they finally stopped talking, I looked at all three. Then I said, "You have never met Cobalt."

Tiri said, "You admit you only met him once."

Lark said, very softly, "You should do whatever you fucking well want." His eyes were softly sheened, golden and nonjudgmental, when they met mine.

I thanked them for their time. Then we talked of other things.

I had to stop writing for a moment and take a deep breath.

I don't know what else to write now. Starliners don't put into our old home port. I know you may never meet my friends. But I wish you could.

Your friend,
Liyan

*

Cobalt read this letter five times, stopping at certain parts to think about the language, its awkwardness from Liyan's youthful struggles to understand new things, as well as its essence which was the heart at the core of the author.

He had fifteen minutes before his services were required at the penthouse top floor which offered the best view of the port's virtual moon as it rose in poison-malachite skies.

He sat back in his chair, careful not to wrinkle his gray silk suit, the velvet cushion flexing beneath him, and pictured Liyan in his mind from the only time they had met, sitting so young and thoughtful at the end of the counter at Rory's Bar.

Slim. Vibrant. Skin like sunlight. And that gleaming face. Dark-eyed with all possibility. His deepest secret was in that moment he'd wanted to *be* Liyan. Trade souls. Never look back.

What would it be like to own his own body? To decide freely how to command it besides daily ablutions, hygiene, sleep? Even his aquamarine hair had been decided for him by the Cellex Corporation before his first owner had come to pick him up.

He decided little things for himself, like picking the color of his shirt for the day. Or moving a piece of jewelry, a silver bracelet cuff given to him by his first owner, from right hand to left.

When he wrote to Liyan, however, things were different. For that time, he was free. He chose to write to him…was not ordered to do so. He picked the words, decided on the length of the letter and the tone. He then sent his words across vast distances of void, freeing them. Words his brain

30

had conjured. Words he'd composed. Words that came from a kind of hollow place inside him he could not define.

He had long ago realized he was a curious sort of being. But what he was doing here was more than that.

Dear Liyan:

Every letter I receive from you enhances me.

If I think about the offenses other humans have bestowed upon me, your name does not come up.

I wish I could meet your friends, too.

It is true you and I have only met once. There are many things about my life you do not know. How can you? Just as I cannot know about you unless I ask.

If you would like me to address your friends' questions, I can do that.

Am I a being only because I think I am? Could not the same be said of you?

There is a very simple statement I can make, but few ever ask it of me.

Yes, I feel. In every way.

You might wonder how I can be sure of "in every way."

Well, I am sure. That is all.

I would like to compose more, but I do not have a lot of time right now. The moon is in full brightness tonight. Real or not, it is a silver, enthralling blaze.

I have my duties under its watchful eye.

Your letters from far-flung reaches where expansion is the rule make me want to fight those duties. But I won't.

I will think of you and be happy instead.

Your friend,
Cobalt

*

Cobalt sent the letter without any hesitation.

He got up and went to his window, parting the silks. In the verdant sky a sterling disk beckoned.

In the elevator, on the way up, he adjusted his jacket's cuffs.

In the rich, draped penthouse he shared a glass of moon-colored wine with the man he met there. He pretended not to notice the hunger in the stranger's gaze.

Later, he let him undress him and touch him everywhere.

The man took his pleasure three times. Cobalt felt everything.

*

Dear Cobalt:

I love writing to you, never doubt that.

Tiri can think I'm a fool and it's okay. You value what I have to offer and that's enough for me. Later for more questions.

But now let me tell you of the past day, and the floating cities of Vaera.

The liner's sleek, arrow-shaped shuttle circled three cities before it came to rest, docking on the tarmac of the one called Glass.

It was the four of us again. Lark, Tiri, Sekina, me.

The clouds sat around us like big pearly marshmallows, and though it was day, some were flecked with mica-glints from the coming-going, blinking-winking city life.

The city may float, but its grav-locks hold it tight so when you are in the middle of it it's much like any city on any world. A constant rain-scent lingers. Knowing you are suspended in the air is the treat.

We took a grav-cab through dewy, shining streets to Glass's most famous club: Try. It was the size of a city block and noisy, shadowy, vapory and twinkling. They served us huge steaks and blue wine. Lark danced with Tiri.

A young couple took an interest in me and pulled me into the swaying throngs. He wore a belt of light around his waist (no, his name was not Orion), no shirt, and pants torn in long strips up to his thighs. His skin was a dark bluish-brown. She wore spring-boots and a leather cloak and very little underneath. Both their eyelids were painted pink.

I realize now the blue wine had 'Enchantment' in it. Later, Tiri did not lie about spiking our drinks. Her excuse: "We did it all the time in the army." Sekina, who outranks Lark now and works for a different department, told Lark that because he was Tiri's immediate boss he had to take care of it. Lark did not write up Tiri for it in the official log, but he took her away from navigation for a day and made her clean the level four portholes of the common rooms top to bottom.

I remember only fractures of the rest of the night. I hesitate to write of what I remember. It's personal and yet I feel more comfortable about certain subjects in a letter rather than face to face. So I'll continue.

The couple took me to one of the club's many private rooms. The outfit I wore had a lot of zippers and buttons and the woman kept undoing them.

When she was on top of me I kept looking at the guy's lightbelt as he watched us through drug-slitted eyes.

I never did anything like that before. The words formed in my brain but didn't travel to my mouth. 'I've never done this before. Please go slower.'

I kept looking at the man's lightbelt with a strange, hungry concern.

Soft breasts against my chest. A hard couch at my back. The flashing belt. A tightness gathered in the bottom of my throat as I stared at him. I really don't recall the pleasure at all. Later, when I tried to put all the pieces of my memory together, I realized what I really wanted was the man.

My point: it was my first time and not everything I'd hoped for.

When I said this two days later to Sekina, she said, "No worries. That's how it is for everybody, honey."

The thing is, I didn't expect to be sad about it.

The floating cities. Orion's belt. Clouds. Rain. Drifting on the wind.

Sorry I can't tell you more about Vaera.

Your friend,
Liyan.

*

Cobalt read as he rested in the surroundchair as it hummed about his body, massaging, comforting. His thick cotton robe wrapped him in warmth. He sipped white tea.

Perhaps he had not fully processed how young Liyan really was until now. His demeanor in Rory's bar and his letters were mature beyond his age.

And yet this last part of the letter showed the vulnerability of his youth. Despite his enthusiasm for travel, for his new job, Liyan was more disciplined than most young men his age. He'd admitted it at the bar; he'd spent his life pursuing his dream job. The wildness of, perhaps, someone like Tiri did not reflect Liyan's own nature. A personal naiveté showed through in his outer maturity. A lack of social experience.

By the fourth time he read the letter he could describe the feeling inside his skin as a bit like anger. But not anger. It was a need as if to tightly crush something to release an inner pressure.

A childhood memory frothed in his mind. In a concrete play-yard a little boy punched him. Heat. Pain. He wanted to cry. Instead, he punched the boy back. A hand grabbed him. Adult and firm. Took him to a dark room. Hit him on the thighs with a wooden stick.

The teacher said, "Go now and stop crying."

He replied, "I'm not crying!" His first fight and his first lie.

34

All unreal. Some other boy's memory.
But the feeling he had now? It was something like that.
He leaned forward and created a blank page.

Dear Liyan:

Your memory slices of Vaera are greatly appreciated.

I have little contact with people in more personal conversational matters. So your descriptions of your travels as well as personal insights and experiences are welcome and very interesting. I can see holos of outworlds and fictions on the wave any time, but my real life is limited. The words you write to me are real. I can hear you, picture you. For me that is a great thing.

Your letter reminds me there is quite a vast difference in our ages. At least memory-wise. In real time we are the same. I have existed for 20 years. But I was born adult and given 20 extra years of memories to ground me. That's what they called it, grounding. While we have both existed for 20 real years, I have 20 years of adulthood while you are still in the process of embarking on it.

I am glad you did not stop writing of your evening on Vaera. Perhaps it is not only words, but the long distance communication itself that makes it easier to write of more difficult subjects than talking about them. In this way, we both benefit.

If you are bothered by your experience with the dancing couple, I can tell you that you will undoubtedly have more, better and different experiences to look forward to, if that helps.

Because of my status, I must know many things. My memories were chosen to educate me in all areas. Thus, I was not really born a virgin. It sounds impossible, but not for me. I was given memories of sex so that I would know everything about it should I be called upon to perform that specific task in all its assortments. It is one of many subjects I was born knowing how to do.

Like you, my first "real" time was unremarkable as well. Put in a position where I have no choice in any matters pertaining to jobs I am hired to do, I am mostly surrounded by selfish humans. The situation is fortunate, perhaps, for them. Not so for me.

Some androids must go through long, harsh training to accept and expect this fact. The rebellious ones are destroyed. Or so they told us. Since we are expensive to produce, I suspect this was a lie. Because we are ingrained with a strong will to live, maybe threatening us with oblivion was also was part of the training. My time at the kennel-yards was brief. I am a quick learner.

I don't know if you even want to hear about these things. So I will stop here.

Know that your letters are some of my most treasured moments. I always look forward to them. That you can share with me the intrigues of your life honors me.

What will be your next destination?

Your friend,

Cobalt

*

5. Quasar of the Bearded Dragon

The ship spun into the smashed backdrop of foldspace. A violent light invaded his skin, a thousand simultaneous needles.

His mind threw itself against the void. Windsong moaned. It was all black stars and burnt sugar.

Liyan struggled to navigate without numbers. He had forgotten the equations of abysses. He could not count a single beat of his heart.

His mind banged, amorphous, the walls of the universe. A deep well of bells.

A year of traveling and he had never gone loopy or spacesick before.

Now all he could do was paint the sound of fire in his dreams with a single, meteorite-gray pencil.

Oblivion licked and laved.

The end came when his friend Cobalt appeared standing at the edge of a long bar-top suspended in mist, mixing cats-eye drinks and nodding. "A glass of ice water to quench your thirst?"

Dear Cobalt:

I woke yesterday in sickbay strapped to a bed and screaming, "The ship is lost!"

The medic on duty, a guy named Dail, had phantom auras dogging him as he came to check on me.

He said, "We're leaving foldspace now. Just breathe."

I pulled at my restraints. "You have to let me up. We're straying! I have to fix the equations."

"Just rest," he replied. "It'll only be a few more minutes."

"You're not listening!" This went on until I felt the ship tremble. The crossover had happened. My body relaxed. The tawny auras surrounding Dail dissolved.

The panic drained out of me.

"See? All done," Dail said.

I looked around. We were alone. I guess I was the only one with spacesickness this time. Another first time for me.

Sweat dripped into my hair. I realized I was starving. This meant I had been restrained for less than a day. Otherwise I would've been force fed. I would have had wires attached to various places on my body. So I knew then I must've gone crazy and been brought to sickbay some time the night before. I did remember being okay for the first part of this trip. But now all was a blur.

Dail began to undo my restraints. I stretched my muscles and sat up, only to have the panic return.

The ship alarm began to wail.

I staggered out of the bed. Dail flipped on the sickbay monitor and sound. The captain was ordering all hands to their stations.

It turned out we'd come out of foldspace into an unknown sector. Our destination remained undetected. No one knew where we were.

Of course navigation would take the blame, even though an error in a single number, or even a string of numbers might not account for such extreme displacement. Any unplanned-for anomalous gravitational event could throw us off course in foldspace without us knowing it until we exited. But navigation took anomalies into account.

This was something else.

Dail looked at me as if I were a monster. "How did you know?"

I shook my head. "I thought it was a nightmare but then I just knew it was real."

"You said you had to fix the equations."

I tried to remember. Foldspace can be like a dream. If you don't latch onto experiences concretely, keep a journal or do any other kind of memory assisting, most of the odder experiences within it will fade. Only the more startling or beautiful events, the ones that fill the body with awe, remain.

"Do you remember what you were thinking when you said that?"

I shuddered. My body was weak, exhausted. Hungry. Thirsty. "I'm trying."

Dail called my team then. "Get someone down here to sickbay with a portable nav-comp."

Word must've gotten out fast, because while I was monitored, fed and watered, heads of nav and command sections came in and out of my sick room. The head doctor came, prescribing stimulants to keep me from falling asleep. Even the captain came. He was an older man who had not taken the youth hormones. His hair was silver, brilliant. His eyes were chips of gray and he was very tall and slim. He was the kind of person who took up a lot of space in a room full of people just by standing, being, breathing. He took one look at me and I knew he saw a mere child. He had forgotten my name. He said, "Are you sure this kid dreamt the way home?"

Lark was there beside me and answered for me. "Liyan's one of the best I've seen."

I worked furiously for twelve hours without stopping, filling screens with numbers, ordering the computer to complete my visions, translate them into new charts. The ship did not know whether to go up, down, sideways, back or forward.

I worked on pure subconscious instinct and a deep inner conviction that had followed me from foldspace. It was like I'd seen something in my delusions and that something was the ultimate image or goal, and my equations were taking me there.

Captain Eccu decided to trust me. The monitors showing the outward void were scary. They showed nothing. The depth of black spun so deep it dizzied. It looked flat and endless simultaneously.

Nothing can make a person realize how tiny and insignificant they are than that view without a single star to fix on. Nothing beckoned. Nothing lit the way. It was emptiness emptied of itself. Oblivion without even a speck of dust.

The crew remained professional. The passengers were told about a delay but nothing more.

I worked for a day and a half with very little rest.

Captain Eccu did not question me when I finally uploaded my number-story and directed the ship.

He let me have the helm from my heavily monitored seat in sickbay.

At 21 years old I took the helm. I kind of like saying that.

It lasted an hour.

My computations took us through endless, speck-less dark. No one said a word as the dark continued deep and long despite our full speed.

Then something that was not nothing was detected so distantly it remained unidentified for another hour. The captain took over.

I was left to merely gaze.

The displacement grew and grew. Identification was made. You could feel the tension on the ship release.

We all watched the monitors.

The quasar swam like some sort of gigantic interstellar being. It had wings, feet, a tail, all mixed with a million different shades and colors, swirls of azure flamed fog, eddies of fuchsia, magenta, carnelian, phosphor. Its body appeared to be made of rivers and wind. The angle of the ship's approach caused the three-dimensional image to appear as if it turned its rectangle head, eyes of scorched suns, to gaze upon us. Horns like spiral galaxies adorned it. A beard of thunderclouds threaded with glints of glistening rainbows wafted from its chin. The tail had a spike of sizzling energy, fizzing turquoise fire.

It was then that I remembered while I was sick in foldspace speaking to a bearded dragon called Crying-In-Echo. But that could never happen, right?

Our conversation as much as I can recall:

"Hello? Where are you going?"

"Cartazia."

"I know it not. I've been asleep and alone forever until now, here, in the ruins where you have awakened me."

"What ruins?"

"Ideas shattered, vanished. No thought. No observance. No end but all the dead and forgotten memories that no longer light the realm."

"What are you?"

"The animation of your loss."

"What is lost?"

"Why, you are, my friend."

"Crying-In-Echo, how do I know your name?"

"I told it to you in my voice-tone."

"How do we find our way?"

"Boldly. Down and then up again. And if you are truly bold, straight into the open jaws of my bearded mouth. I have not eaten…ever. But I will digest you into the starred dimension if you can ride the inner stream. See it in your mind. Write it in the language your ship knows."

I have not revealed this dream-conversation to anyone but you. It is something I could not speak of, until I began this letter.

After all of it, what I have left to say is this: damned if we weren't birthed by a dragon from nothingness back to our dimension of origin.

A true foldspace dream.

My equations sent us through the quasar which contained a curling gravitational phenomenon no one can yet define or understand.

The ship twisted, rocked, churned and turned.

Lark says we went into foldspace again for only a few moments. I think it was something else.

But in minutes the stars synched in to reflect our charts.

Cartazia was a day-trip away.

I am well now.

I long to hear from you.

Your friend,
Liyan

*

Dear Liyan:

An amazing letter. An amazing not-dream. And yet a dream like one I've never had.

I don't want to think what might have happened had you never succumbed to spacesickness.

My life would be troubled without you in it.

You are humble in your disclosure of events, however. I read on the wave of your heroism, and that you were decorated for it. You never mentioned that. People heard this story, wrote about it in the wave journals. You are famous. For the moment. Until something else comes along to distract the many worlds.

How fortunate I am to know you in my drab life.

I hoped for shared adventure from your letters. You have delivered more than I could ever have hoped in less than one year.

I say this now because I write this on the eve of the new year here at the spaceport's hotel in my lush suite sipping crystal wine. Normally I would be bartending but the human bartenders wanted the night's grander tips and shuffled me off my duties. My owner sent me to my room.

I have had a delicious night off and have been relaxing beneath my own home's miniscule version of a quasar: the cityport's firework display to celebrate the holiday.

There were no dragons.

Amidst the fires, the moon fell up to the green sky.

The coolness of my silken sheets and pillows are such comfort. I am lucky on this night to be so unusually content and read a letter of heroism from my friend.

Deep into the construct of my skeleton I can feel an ache of wonder and astonishment and know in this moment the soul they say we androids cannot have.

I rest my head in my upturned palm and scan your words from the beginning of our correspondence.

Even far away you sit beside me and fill in all the spaces I did not know I had.

Your friend,
Cobalt

Part Two

6. Second Meeting

The shuttle came in a spark of syrupy tinted light. Against the marbled sky it slid to touchdown, finally taking on its true shape, a gray-lined wedge.

Its contrail percolated and slowly dispersed.

Cobalt stood by the window impeccably dressed, jacket with coattails brushing the backs of his thighs, crisp white shirt, scarf a scarlet accent about his throat. People stared at him. They looked because he was considered beautiful, and not because they knew what he was.

He remembered the look on his owner's face earlier that morning. Pel was 70 but looked 35. He was the brother of Cobalt's previous owner, Pela, who had died in a spectacular coach crash. Cobalt had been hers for five years before Pel inherited him. Cobalt had done nothing for her when he lived with her. He'd been purchased by her husband for her, a status symbol to show off to her friends. He was like a pedigree pet on a golden leash. Mostly she ignored him even as she made him sit by her feet at social gatherings so others could see how rich she was.

Pela's husband hadn't wanted Cobalt after her death. Pel gladly took him on at the hotel, seeing him as a means to make him more money.

For the first time in fifteen years, Cobalt went to his owner and asked for time off.

Pel's shock wrinkled his old-young face. "What the hell for?"

"I am meeting a friend."

"Since when do you have a friend?"

"He is visiting for a short time. Two days only."

"And you want to show him the sights of this godforsaken spaceport?"

"He's seen the sights. He used to live here."

Pel was a mostly thoughtless owner, expecting him to work long hours despite his need for rest and sleep, discreetly selling him as a sex toy to wealthy visitors, but he was not a cruel man. He never threatened or whipped him. He never spoke with hate or ridicule or disgust. He merely expected him to obey and do the job as one would expect from any useful tool.

"I suppose you met this friend through all the work you do here."

"Yes."

"Interesting. Well, you never ask me for a thing. I guess I can give you two days. But no more than that, understood?"

"Yes."

Pel frowned. "You live here and have all your needs met. Anything you need or wish for is delivered to your room. You've had no need of a salary all these years. Do you need some extra money now?"

"No. My friend has money."

But in a strange, fatherly gesture, Pel forced Cobalt to take a moneycard. "For expenses," he said. "In case you find yourself outside the hotel."

Now Cobalt watched the shuttle come to a stop. He could feel the card in his breast coat pocket, a square of plastic pressing against his heart. The fact that he could offer to pay his own way during this visit quickened him. It was a freedom he'd never known.

A surge of heat washed through him, a kind of thrill, of anticipation.

In a few moments Liyan would be walking through that door. His liner had a stopover close enough to the old spaceport that returning for a visit would not be a hardship.

Cobalt had never expected Liyan to use his short time off to visit the ugly old asteroid of his beginnings, but Liyan had suggested it. Insisted on it.

I want to see you, my friend, he'd written. *After two years, I want to see the face again of the only person who shows an outside interest in my life. I have no other family. My parents are faraway and do not wave me. You are it. Let's communicate this one rare time other than using the wave. Can you get some time off? Will you have dinner with me? Can we have a drink at Rory's Bar like normal friends?*

Of course, Cobalt had answered. *Of course we can do all of that.*

Two years of correspondence. Cobalt felt closer to Liyan than any other human he'd ever met or known. And they had only ever met once.

But words, even across vast distances, were a way of sharing no less than sight, sound, touch, scent. They confided in each other. Friendship bonds did not rule themselves by distance or time. They did not form just because two people occupied close proximities.

Four people left the shuttle. He recognized the third, all in white, his uniform perfectly tailored to his tall physique. The cap he refused to wear was attached to his belt. His brown hair reflected the skies with an elfin sheen. It was styled back from his face but errant bangs still escaped in striped shadows against his forehead.

He came through the glass doors and their eyes instantly met. Liyan rushed toward him, reaching out. Their hands met. A swift shyness shimmered the dark eyes to be replaced by a wide smile. Their hands grasped, more than a handshake. Liyan reached for both of Cobalt's wrists. Cobalt found his own hands pressing up, grasping. It was almost a hug. The clasp of men who aren't sure how well they know each other.

"I can't believe it's been two years!"

"It does seem too long."

"Waves don't do you justice. I've been wanting to see you again since our first letters."

"I expected never to see you again, actually," Cobalt admitted.

"Well you look grand."

Liyan stood slightly taller that Cobalt. He didn't remember the height of the human as above his own.

"Thank you. So do you. Have you grown?" When he spoke it sounded so stupid to his own ears. Liyan was an adult male now.

But Liyan only laughed. "Probably. Space does that if you're gone long enough. Some people add up to three inches. But I was also still such a boy when I left here."

Cobalt acknowledged that at 20, some human males continued to have growth spurts.

Over the past two years, Liyan had been twice decorated. He wore the glistening emblems of his heroics on his shoulder. At 22 he was well on his way to becoming a lieutenant within the new year.

Cobalt turned toward the port exit, the concierge in him as well as the friend taking over. "Are you hungry?"

"Starved. The trip was five hours and the included meal was awful."

The port was not a tourist attraction but remained a popular stop-over and repair station. The lobby was crowded, the bustling air humid. They made their way through weary throngs of travelers.

Liyan paused at a window overlooking the dark tarmac where red lights winked and dusky buildings cowered beyond. "There's where I used to work." In the distance, silver-suited men moved in and out of the old shops.

"Nothing you miss?"

"No. Not for one minute."

*

The steak dissolved on the tongue. The wine glimmered in fake moonlight through wide, crystal windows. For dessert they ate fresh apple pie with real cream.

"I never came here before," Liyan observed, glancing around the ornate restaurant situated on the quay, a force-field enclosed boardwalk on the edge of the asteroid that dipped straight into the green night sky. "I couldn't afford it. Everything I made at work went to my school bills."

"I understand. It is my treat."

"Oh, no." Liyan waved his words away. "I have a lot of money now. This weekend is my treat."

"Pel gave me a moneycard. I usually don't need any money. At the hotel all expenses are paid and anything I need is ordered and delivered."

Liyan nodded soberly. "I know you don't get any salary. I wasn't even sure you could get the next two days free."

"After all my service, it was not too much to ask of Pel."

Liyan's eyebrows narrowed. "Then he is good to you?"

Cobalt went blank for a moment. He finally said, "We are not friends as you and I are. And he expects much."

"But he let you off."

"I have never asked him for any favor before." Cobalt gave a little smile. "I think I caught him off-guard."

If Liyan noticed that Cobalt had not directly answered his first question, he didn't let on. He gifted him instead with the sweet, youthful smile of one who is on a direct path to paradise. That smile alone sent surges of warm pleasure through his android veins. He wasn't sure what to make of it, but decided he could be in this human's presence forever and it wouldn't put him off or make him uncomfortable the way so many humans did.

Liyan's disarming and gentle nature was only partly why. The other factor was that Liyan treated him as if he were a true friend, a normal guy.

47

That had never happened to him before.

Their lengthy correspondence, and now this second meeting, had him utterly bewildered.

For hours they talked. After dinner when they had loitered long, they ended up at Rory's bar.

They talked of Liyan's friends, his job, and Cobalt asked him questions about all of it. They discussed everything from the philosophy of the sea-djinn of Sariha V that death was a cluster of infinite bloomings into infinite lives, to where in the galaxy one could get the best hot dog or pizza. Liyan insisted it was Starsher and Qutnoy, in that order.

As the hours passed, they did not want to leave each other.

But Cobalt could see Liyan was tired from his long flight and the excitement of them finally meeting again.

"You must rest," he insisted.

They agreed to meet for a late breakfast.

Cobalt slept well on the first night off he'd had in his lifetime.

*

7. Second Day

Today Cobalt observed that Liyan did not dress in his uniform. He wore more casual jeans and a black renaissance shirt that billowed at the arms which he said he'd bought at a Doomsday celebration on Palenza, one of fifty orange and ochre moons orbiting the gas giant Zir.

They walked along the star-wharf, past the import vendors and alien collectibles. Rockets rattled in the distance. The emerald dawn of the port's false light lasted twelve hours. The moon only came at night, unlike on real worlds.

Ionized air stung Cobalt's nose.

"I used to come here and walk when I'd studied all night and was too hyped to sleep," Liyan said.

"I came here once when my previous owner, Pela, visited her brother. But after I came to live with Pel, I've never left the hotel."

"Not once in all these years?"

"Not once."

"I grew up on Xatar. It's a farmworld."

"I know of it." Cobalt said. They had not talked much about their childhoods, both real or programmed, in their correspondence. He was interested to hear more. In fact, anything about Liyan greatly interested him.

He had his hands in his pockets. Liyan had mirrored him as they both sauntered, side by side, down the sidewalk.

"My parents wanted to move on to Crim. I didn't want to go. I had big dreams. They didn't have the money to help me. So I was 18, on my own, and needed a job. This is where I ended up. I knew I couldn't stay here forever, so I started taking classes with my eye on C&C."

"And because you're pretty smart," Cobalt said with a smile, "it all worked out."

"Yes, it all worked out."

The human's grin came again, lighting up Cobalt's insides.

They had orange flavored ices as they stood at the end of a pier looking out at the marbled sky above and below them. The double force-field around the port flashed off and on like lightning.

They had hot coffee at a little hut decorated with old true-Earth tikis.

Liyan sipped as steam rose from his cup, and spoke softly. "I love my job, but ever since the bearded dragon incident I've had my share of anxiety. I never told anybody all the stuff I wrote you about it. Maybe I was too naïve when I first started the job to realize how…how big it all is…. Sometimes I dream of the void all around me and it can't hear or see me. I'm utterly lost. As if I've taken a piece of it inside me."

49

"We are in it now, though," Cobalt reasoned, "with only a force-field between us and instant frozen death. All that void."

"That's not comforting." But he laughed as he spoke.

Cobalt continued his thought. "Foldspace has been mastered, but that doesn't change the fact that the stars are vastly far apart from each other. No matter where you travel, it's all the same... a great big nothingness."

"It feels different, though, when you live somewhere stable. Like here. Maybe it's because this port is stationary," Liyan said. "I didn't know how to write this to you, but sometimes I'm very afraid. I don't talk to anyone about it. All my friends in the crew say it happens to everyone. The usual anxiety of space travel. But I don't like to acknowledge that. This job is my dream job. I can't let anything like fear of space keep me from it. I don't want my friends to know, either."

"You feel shame?"

Slowly, he nodded.

"You shouldn't. Fear spurs us on. It's an instinct for survival. Nothing else. If you act on it, you may find surges of brilliance that, in the moment, don't seem extraordinary, but in hindsight you see they are. If you felt nothing, would you try as hard to solve a problem or escape a perilous situation?"

"Embrace fear. That's what you're saying."

"Yes."

"What have you feared, Cobalt?"

He glanced away but still sensed Liyan's heavy gaze on him. "More than you would think."

"I'm sure just like everyone else you fear pain, loss, or being lost." His head tilted.

Cobalt let his gaze move over the steaming cups on the table and back to Liyan's pensive face. "I do. It is the rare human who recognizes that, as you do. Most consider my emotions to be half-baked, rudimentary, or a part of programming that to them is not real and therefore invalid."

50

"Reality is in the eye of the beholder, a lot more subjective than most people think. Reality may appear to contain objective black and white issues. But I've learned that's a pretty...or ugly...illusion these past few years. Travel does tend to expand the mind."

"Your mind was expanded before you left. You're quite unique."

Liyan laughed. "As are you."

Cobalt liked to hear him say that.

A little later, Liyan said, "Sekina, who is a scientist and desires accuracy, still doesn't forget to ask, 'What does your intuition tell you?' She's a very good teacher. 'Follow your heart,' she tells the newbies when they become confused or begin to panic. 'You'll get there'."

"Does she still have blue streaks in her hair?" Cobalt asked.

"Something called plum right now. It catches the light."

"I like hearing about your friends."

"They're all interesting, different. Even amidst human dramas they are good people. Loyal, too. Ship-board marriages are common."

"Yes, you told me of Lark and Tiri. And you? You have not written to me of lovers or similar such experiences."

To Cobalt's delight, Liyan's cheeks actually flushed. He said, "Since that horrible one time, no. I'm busy a lot. And Tiri stopped putting 'Enchantment' in people's drinks after she was punished."

"Then you don't..." He hesitated. It wasn't really his business.

Liyan shrugged. "I haven't found interest in casual contact so far. And I'm young. I have lots of time to fall in love."

"You believe in love, then?"

"What?" He frowned. "Yes! Of course I do. Don't you?"

His fingers caressed the edge of the table. "Sometimes. I don't know."

"You're young, too," Liyan offered.

Nodding, he scratched the table-edge with his fingernail. "In true-years the same as you. However, I have been adult for all of them. You were a child."

"Your memories...the ones they gave you...do they teach you of love?"

"Caring for others, maybe. Not so much love. And not adult love."

"You didn't love your first owner?"

"Pela?" He winced. "She barely said any words to me in five years. She was anti-social and self-centered. She required nothing from me but my status as a symbol of immense wealth, which she thought gave her an identity. But I think I bored her as all her toys did. She would no more try to have a conversation with me than with a fiction story on the wave. I was her doll on the shelf."

"You didn't...weren't required to sleep with her?"

"She was too neurotic to think like that. I don't think she wanted anyone or any thing close to her. She rarely slept with her husband. Their marriage was a convenient stage play for them. She collected expensive toys, played games, saw movies, shopped and had parties. The parties were all show. She did them for attention saying all the right things. But none of it meant a thing to her. Later, before the coach crash, she began drinking to excess. Compared to her brother Pel, she was unhappy. Though she did not like me to respond, sometimes she would confide things to me. Once she told me she felt about as useless as a flower in a vase in a room no people entered."

"But Pel requires a lot of work from you?" Liyan asked.

"I like to keep busy. It's better than doing nothing."

Grinning, "I like my job, too."

Cobalt did not correct him. He didn't say he liked his job. Some of the things he did he hated. Some he enjoyed.

But this time spent with Liyan was the best time of his life.

8. Third Day

"The towers were steepled like rockets. The city looked as if it would shoot up into the sky at a moment's notice. It was a cluster of needles stabbing at clouds." Liyan had described Fellar to Cobalt over breakfast the final morning. Fellar had been his last stopover, where he'd caught a shuttle to the spaceport.

As beautiful as Fellar's goldenrod skylights were, he had not wanted to stay. He'd rushed for the first flight out to see Cobalt. He had not even taken the time to say good-bye to his friends.

Every moment with Cobalt these last two days brought an exhilaration of energy. His skin had been hot for two days. His conversations with the android spun like fever-dreams of intense, persistent pleasure.

No one in his life had ever listened to him with such devotion. He often thought he was talking too much, not asking Cobalt enough questions in return, but Cobalt kept up the interviews until they were both dizzy, hungry, tired, collapsing from too much fun and maybe too much wine.

There were many moments his heart almost lurched from his chest; once, when Cobalt said, "You are my ticket away from here. I travel with you."

The worst time came when he had to leave, his job and his star-faring soul calling to him. Cobalt accompanied him to the shuttle lobby, lips curving up wistfully but lavender eyes grim.

He did not ask, nor did he hesitate as he had when meeting Cobalt again after two long years in space. He simply reached out and hugged him, breathing in the android's soapy, ever-clean scent. He felt a tremble in the limbs.

"You're shaking," he said.

Cobalt's warm, smooth cheek rested against his for almost a second. Matched in height, they came together gracefully. Cobalt's chest rose against his, a tremor in the breath. The android whispered, "Liyan, maybe I won't see you ever again."

"Don't think like that." He had to force himself to step back and grin. "I plan on having my own ship by the time I'm 30. Then I can come here whenever I like…ur, uh, well, within reason."

The flutter of Cobalt's laugh came laced with grief. "I know you will get everything you hope for and more."

He winced. "How do you know that?"

"I just do."

Liyan caught his lower lip between his teeth. "You're one of a kind, Cobalt. Never let anyone lead you to think otherwise." As if the hug had not been enough, Liyan reached out and clasped the slender shoulder. "I have to run. I will wave you."

Then he turned and hurried through the glass doors before the android could see how the warmth in his eyes stung in more than normal moisture.

The shuttle waited in a pool of auburn light.

*

As Cobalt walked through green air and hurrying humans toward the Grand Aurora Hotel, his chest ached. He thought: *I can let you go because it is how I will survive.*

But his hands formed fists as he made his way down the sidewalk, his head bowed low.

Part Three

9. The Swan Boats of Davenda

Earlier in the evening, Cobalt had said to Pel, "I don't like him. I certainly don't want to go with him to some party at the penthouse."

"You don't have to like him. The money is good. That's what matters." Pel had not inherited his sister's wealth when she died and he resented it. Most had been her husband's to begin with. There had been a pre-nup. Pel had his own wealth but it was never enough. He did not own the hotel outright. He had four partners. He always looked to Cobalt to bring in high figures of personal extra cash from specific, wealthy clients.

"But last time he hurt me."

Pel looked up frowning. "You never complained."

"I…"

"I'll make it clear to him. A heavy fine if you are damaged. Will that suffice?"

"The money means nothing to him."

"Let me put it this way," Pel said. "You do this favor and I will let you see your friend whenever he comes in to port. If you don't, my generosity may waver."

It took him only seconds to say yes. But he must've shown some hesitation, because Pel, who was not really a bad man, said, "I'll speak to the client and make sure he understands the rules. He should not hurt you."

Cobalt nodded and went back to work.

When he retired to his room in the middle of the night, a present was waiting for him on his computer.

＊

Dear Cobalt:

I'll set the scene: Under a moonstone sky, picnicking on the copper sands of Seventh Lake and letting the light soak our bodies, skin like sponges in the pools of bronze warmth, all hazy and no clouds and lots of wine. That is what I remember, that and the lake that smelled of distant thunderstorms with its scintillating flashes of liquid amber.

Oh yes, and the huge swanboats, black on gold, parting the lake surface in clean silence. A dozen of them at least. And they were alive! Humungous trained birds bridled and waiting. You climb aboard and literally sit in cushioned down, the black feathers rising up around you as they paddle out on the gleaming water in a gentle glide.

The softness of their backs. The sweetness of the water as it mists up and you breathe the candied air.

Tiri was up front steering with the silver lamé reins...always wanting to take charge. Lark leaned back toward the tail. With my eyes closed, rocking, I could feel him looking at me before he said, "What's wrong with you?"

"What?" My eyes shot open. The tricks of the light and mist against my face made him look as if he had two heads. I smiled and said, "I think I read a poem like this scene...once when I was a kid."

His two heads shook. "We gotta get you laid," was his only response.

I realized the mist was not from the lake. Tears had been trailing my cheeks.

Ever since I was a kid I get this way when I'm happy or extremely moved.

I expected Lark to tease me as others have because my eyes too easily tear up at the oddest moments. He didn't.

I swiped the back of my hand across my cheeks and stared up at the shining sky, grinning.

My very next thought was how to describe all this to you.

I once took a poetry class when I was 14. I managed trite haiku. My teacher said, "Let your mind sink, drown in the view, the feeling, the story. When you come up for air, gasp out the first words that come to your mind even if they are nonsense."

The advice was about accessing the subconscious mind. You can't force it or control it, but you can help it speak if you just let go.

When my shuttle stretched into the tarnished skies of the spaceport, leaving you behind, I let myself sink.

Good advice, because I hated leaving you.

I know you know that.

So, there's that.

But the problem is I haven't come up for air yet.

While composing this, I've already gotten up, walked around my room five times touching things, my walls, my comb, my bedspread.

Sometimes I speak aloud in my waves to you. But this one I spelled with my fingers, a silent tapping.

I feel filled up with the springy air of Davenda.

I will be 23 next month.

Cobalt, do you have a birth day?

Your friend,
Liyan

*

Dear Liyan:

I do the silent tapping, too. I don't like to speak my waves. It doesn't feel right.

Your words made me feel the soft glide of the swans, and smell the amber lake. I saw that translucent, moonstone sky.

How very welcome, the relaxation of your words.

I cannot report anything so astonishing from my own life. You know the port too well from living here. How many ways can one describe a toxic green sky in manufactured light because we have no sun? I deal with glittery, spoiled humans all day long, tourists who have not come here to gawk, but are only stopping on their way to somewhere else. They are always bored, except for the very young who are refreshingly content with swimming pools and free mints.

Adults require more attention and entertainments. You would think it would be the other way around, but not here in the life of the hotel.

I would like to tell you that Pel has made a promise to me, knowing how I valued our two days together, that I may see you any chance you get to come back here for a visit.

That is nice to know. He could have forbidden it. Then I might be forced into thinking of how to break android law, which of course my programming will not allow. Luckily I did not have to test that programming. We made a deal.

I have a birth date. More like a "waking" date. August 1. If that means anything in space.

I am a Leo. And of course that means nothing as well. On true-Earth it meant it was the constellation I would have been born under. Where I was 'born', on the factory planet Yet, no one cared to name the constellations.

Next month brings Pisces. Your sign is well done. You are, I think, a star-fish. A star-fish in the belly of a great starliner that fishes the night for wonders galore.

Tonight I have had too much wine, as you did on Davenda. Pel allows it when I bar-tend and do other certain jobs. Alcohol does not make me drunk like a human. My body handles it well. But it does swirl my mind.

It also dulls resentment.

Oh, but I have no jealousy toward you. Not ever. Your ability to wander the starry seas, and communicate to me from them, brings me sanity you can never know.

Your friend,
Cobalt

*

58

Dear Cobalt:

You are indeed a Leo! In the true-Earth sense, nowadays it's just a descriptive term. They say Leo's are warm and loyal. Make an impression. Stand firm. You are the sign of the Lion, a homonym for my name!

Pisces, on the other hand…focused, emotional, empathic.

That is, if you even believe in that stuff.

I have not gotten my work done for days. My mind is on the lieutenant's test.

And Tiri and Lark have been fighting.

They leave the air in the common rooms black with their words. They're my friends and the tension eats at me, too.

I want to hit them. And talk to them. And straighten them out.

One particularly bad afternoon, after a big fight they both left the room still dogging each other. I ran after them furious because they could not keep all this private. Too much information! Lark accused Tiri of laziness, but also of pushing people around, especially him, making demands. "Demands of what?" she asked him, glowering at him. He answered her saying she tried to tell him what to like even when it came to food. I thought: Food? This is about food? I really expected him to say something like she demanded he allow sheep into their bedroom or something!

When I followed them around a corner and into a bulkhead alcove, there they were, embraced tight, fumbling practically in public with their clothes fasteners.

Tiri glared at me. "Get out of here!"

I was truly embarrassed. But Lark just raised his eyebrow and said to Tiri, loud enough so I could hear, "Or he could join us."

I groaned in exasperation, and gave each of them my wincing stare, the one that makes mice run (I grew up on a farm, remember?) I went back to my work station and looked at stars that were numbers for a long, long time.

As to your wave:

Hey, what kind of a deal did you make with Pel? I hope no extra work for you. I think he works you too hard anyway. And you deserve a personal life.

When I first met you, I saw no resentment in you whatsoever. Just acceptance. But now that I'm older I know I was being crazily naïve. Your jobs require certain behaviors from you. As bar-tender that night, your job was to listen to me, serve me, and not complain about it.

I know better now and I apologize for my stupid short-sightedness in thinking you were ever content at that life. Firstly, you are way too smart. You are whole but unfree. Who wouldn't resent it?

Now I must sleep. Foldspace is tomorrow. Side effects include: spacesickness, boredom, temporary heights of genius, delusion, illusion, hallucinations, an urge to play poker and drink algebraic whiskey until you find even the leftover peas on your plate hilariously funny.

The passengers and cargo from Davenda will be delivered to Quin. Then we take on more. And more. In endless circles and cycles through the universe we go.

And I am happy to do it.

Your friend,
Liyan

*

Dear Liyan:

I wish you well on your test. I know without a doubt you will make lieutenant. Will this make you the boss of Lark and Tiri? Or, at least, in equal ranking with Lark?

This man who is your friend seems easy-going, and fond of you. I am glad. Tiri is a coiled serpent, perhaps, the personality of a decision-maker, a leader. Perhaps she will beat you to the captaincy of a ship? Wonderful that she also has you as a friend and Lark as a husband.

60

Sorry to hear about the arguing.

I know Sekina no longer works in navigation, but does she drop by? What color are her hair stripes this month?

I made a deal with Pel to do extra work. That is all.

It is an unremarkable job I do, actually several jobs as you well know, but I get to meet all kinds of people.

In my hours before sleep I have been reading. You might be pleased to know I investigated haiku after you mentioned it. Like captured images of brevity.

I look at books on the places you visit but none are better than your waves describing them. Knowing that you have set foot on these worlds makes everything personal, immediate. I am happy for anything you may write.

The bored travelers we get at the hotel are looking for merriment and entertainment. They are on vacation, or going to or from a job. They are not looking for deeper meanings. Freedom is taken for granted.

Yesterday an older man died on the thirtieth floor. Natural causes, they say. In the tub. I have seen it before. The lifeless, unanimated person carried from the lobby by the death-techs. All very discreet.

I myself do not age. I have no DNA factors that leave me open to illness. My life span is quite long. Still, a chill rests against my skin to see death. Every time. I think all the souls must be out there somewhere, beyond the void. But I have a desperate feeling inside me when people check into the hotel on their way to some destination where they'll never arrive because they die before they can check out. I feel a slight constriction in my veins often accompanied by temporary nausea.

I state this not because I think you don't believe I feel as any real human being but because I am used to stating what would be obvious in a human because it is unexpected of me.

I have been taught reserve in all things including emotion, opinion, judgment, ego, desire, and having a form of a personal life (such as marriage or traveling or extracurricular activities on my own) and harsh law discourages any contemplation of escape (besides, where would one go without money and passport?) but there is no reserve on dreaming or imagination. And just because a sort of stoicism is trained in us does not mean it ever succeeds in dissolving the heart.

Until I met you, my thoughts were kept secret.

You make me believe it is not presumptive to express them to you.

Thank you for that and please write whenever you can.

Your friend,
Cobalt

*

Dear Cobalt:

I hope I never gave any impression that the universe we live in is fair or just. I never thought it was, even for myself.

But compared to you, I have been born privileged. You may not be starving or homeless, and I have worked double shifts all my adult life to get ahead, but I still have freedom in choices which you do not.

Tell me your secrets any time. I will respect them, honor them always. The struggle of emotional existence is in every creature. Even pets need love. My inorganic bearded dragon was lonely! But you are none of those. You are a human who has been born artificially, and born adult. That is all. As far as I can tell, you are still human, though people will argue it. Those people are materialists and/or bigots.

Also, they have never met you. I have. And I don't pretend not to see the flicker of lifespark in your eyes; some might call it the soul. It's a dimension beyond more than intelligence. I "feel" it in your waves and when I have been at your side.

You confirm it in your every word to me.

If this is all a programmed ruse, tell me now! I still won't believe it.

You live behind a wall because you have been forced behind a wall, that of the home of your first owner and, now, the Grand Aurora Hotel.

And you dream! If anyone ever makes you feel less than whole, always remember that about yourself. If you can't remember that, I'll be here to remind you.

And, ah! The haiku.

You must try to write some. I have. They fail miserably.

winterspace:
a desolate mist
of suns

And such shit. I love it, though. A single breath containing a multi-dimensional scene. And remember the haiku is not about syllable count. It does not translate that way into our language. It is about seasons/nature and an accompanying image/feeling/sound/movement/scent, but then of course you knew that.

Basho, Issa, Buson, Shiki. Eurixiiam of Karvi.

Don't weep, insects –
Lovers, stars themselves,
Must part.

- Issa

That is my favorite of the classics so far. I mean, insects weeping? What a concept! But doesn't everything? My dragon, the ship as it strains through foldspace, my own stupid self.

Or maybe it just sounds like they're weeping, the shiver shrill buzz purr stutter of life. A celebration and a grieving.

There are indeed crickets in the arboretum of the ship.

Crickets in space. A laughable but true concept.

Cobalt, why do you wear the silk-blend coat with the tails (both times I met you?) See? In some things you do have a choice. Or did Pela teach you to dress yourself?

By the way, Tiri would appreciate your reference of her as a coiled serpent. She advocates strength and an ever-readiness to battle, if needed. She would take it as a compliment.

Sekina is wearing peacock green stripes in her hair this month.

The lieutenant's test comes one day after my birthday. I feel ready.

Your friend,
Liyan

*

Dear Liyan:

from Shiki

I am going
you're staying
two autumns for us

I found that very famous haiku for you. For us.

To attempt my own, I went to the second floor balcony overlooking the hotel lobby when I should have been eating my lunch. It was afternoon when the hotel is very busy. I watched the people come and go. I watched them in all colors swirl through the space of the parquet floor and through the hurried moments of their lives on this old port in a backwater star-cluster where the poisonous skies shed a surprisingly beautiful phosphor light.

64

**A girl looks down
at her red suitcase.
The rumble of rockets.**

*

**Through arched windows
entangled stars.
The path you took.**

*That one is a fiction. I can't see the stars through the thick
ooze of bottle-green skies. I wrote more notes but nothing to call a
poem. Not really.*

*Send more of your winterspace poems or anything. That one
was excellent.*

Now you know an android who writes poetry.

*This is all your fault. Did you not read my last wave telling
you extracurricular activities for my kind are discouraged? Of
course this is harmless and strangely enjoyable and does not
necessarily require me to leave the hotel. Pel would not care if I
wrote lines of equations or nonsensical juxtaposed words. As long as
the act does not bring my mental state into question.*

However, in history, poetry is often written by the rebels.

So we can keep this to ourselves.

Let me know about your lieutenant's test.

*And to give you peace of mind, I never believed you observed
me as anything other than human.*

*Some people are and always will be hateful bigots. Most
people are simply uncomfortable in speaking to "property." And
anyway, friendship, like poetry, is also discouraged.*

Your friend,
Cobalt

*

10. The Thunderlights of Nod

Liyan shuffled through his hand-held screen, looking over his notes from two classes he'd completed. He was readying himself for finals. All in his off-hours.

He'd come to one of the less public viewports on the ship for some peace. His own quarters had closed in, far too small and cramped for all-night study sessions. The dim starlight poked through the long windows leaving pools of glittery reflections on the hard floor.

He'd been alone for almost an hour when Lark walked in. Surprised to see him, he said, "Still studying?"

Liyan grinned, nodding.

"My friend, it's not the end of the world if you don't pass the first time. You're only 23."

"What does that mean?" Liyan asked. "You think I'm too young for the rank?"

Lark shrugged, turning until he was outlined in stars. "You're still a baby in many ways."

"You always say that." He tried not to sound irritated but a part of him was. "Are you jealous?"

Lark just laughed.

Then Tiri came in and the tension increased. She wore her uniform but it was open at the chest. Lark wore jeans and a t-shirt.

Her first words were almost thrown from her mouth toward Lark. "What are you doing?"

"I was going for a walk," Lark said quietly. "Look, I found Liyan."

"Good for you!" She walked toward a more shadowed corner where the stars couldn't see. She didn't even say "hello."

Liyan watched her warily. Something was up.

Tiri had let her hair grow. Now it touched her shoulders in gentle waves the color of a coppery sea. She was tall and narrow-waisted. One might've called her 'willowy' except for the extra muscle her previous job had packed on. She'd kept up her weight-training.

She was lovely.

Lark worked out with her once in awhile, and it must've been enough because his arm muscles were nicely defined beneath the short sleeves of his t-shirt. His firm silhouette before the starfield might've made an intriguing holograph.

Looking at them, Liyan did realize how young he was. Though Tiri was only a year older, it was true he was the 'baby' of the three of them.

Tiri motioned to Lark who sighed loudly and joined her in the corner. Rasping whispers turned to raised voices.

Finally, Liyan said, "Are you doing this on purpose? Do you want me to hear you?"

They both looked at him. Tiri glared. "You're free to leave!"

"Hey, I was here first."

"It's true," Lark admitted.

"Fine! Side with him then!"

"I'm not siding with him. It's a fact."

"You always argue, taking everyone else's side." Tiri crossed her arms.

"I don't do that."

Liyan stood up. "I'll leave. It's okay."

"You shouldn't have to," Lark said.

Liyan put the screen under his arm. "It's not a problem." He had come to the viewport to calm his pre-test jitters. Now his stomach churned in even more discomfort. Lark and Tiri argued. A lot. He should have been used to it but he wasn't. Sometimes he could laugh at it all. All couples argued, right? But he was around them while they were fighting all too often, and sometimes his unease made him want to run and run until he dropped and forgot everything. His life was wonderful, everything he'd hoped for. He had grand times visiting worlds most people only dreamed of, taking in alien views live and in person no artist could truly capture. He lived in a dream. But the desolation of utter space was bound to get into everyone once in awhile. And there was his anxiety, his space-fear which he'd confessed only to Cobalt, which had not receded. There was a hollowness inside him. His friends' arguments prodded that hollowness.

Tonight, he could not leave the viewport quickly enough.

In the corridor he moved quickly toward the stairwell in favor of the tube. He wanted to feel his legs moving, pumping, as he made his way back to the level where he lived.

Footsteps rushed up behind him.

He turned.

Lark stood before him, breathing deeply, cheeks a little flushed; he reached out and touched his shoulder. "You'll do fine on your test," he said.

Liyan blinked heavily, took a deep breath. He clutched his portable screen to his chest. "Thanks."

"I don't think you're too young. You're smart enough to make up for any experience you lack in years."

Liyan didn't know what to say. Behind Lark, Tiri moved deftly into the corridor and stood about twenty feet away just watching them. Liyan met her eyes.

She did not smile but held his gaze.

"We both think it," Lark added. Then smiling wide, he said, "It's something we do agree on."

Slowly, Tiri nodded.

"You want to come with us for a coffee?"

Slowly Liyan shook his head. "I really need to get some sleep."

Lark had not taken his hand from Liyan's shoulder. He squeezed. "All right then."

"Good night." Liyan moved away.

He took the stairs two at a time until he felt a satisfying burn in his thighs.

68

When he got to his room he lay back on his bed. He
didn't sleep. Instead he got his screen, held it in front of him,
and brought up something Cobalt had recently sent him.

in the chill green fog
the sound of three-winged ships
moving into night

*

even a force field cannot
hold back the void
only a human embrace

Flecks of diamond stars still prickled his vision. Lark in
perfect form before them. Tiri's stare, her arms crossed.
And now Cobalt's poems.
He opened his keypad.

Dear Cobalt:

A person's dreams can come true and still mistakes lurk
waiting to leap upon the mind and all its choices. The decisions one
makes when feeling strong, relentless, fearless can also be rash.
Strength does not mean wisdom, right?
Perhaps I am making no sense right now.
Maybe I won't even send this. But I like writing my thoughts
to you. The form of our waves allows me an introspection I might
not ordinarily get in my day to day living. Like a form of meditation.
Allow my rambles for now.
Your haiku touch me. In a simple, no-nonsense way, they are
brilliant flashes of insight that prove you have a heart. That sounds
cliché just to write it. But I have so many thoughts and, tonight, not
enough words to contain them. Just know that something of what
I'm feeling right now is captured in those little three-liners.
I'm nervous. My test is in two days.

I have studied and studied.
Lark says I'm too young.
I don't know.

Lark and Tiri were fighting again, breaking in on me in the middle of the night at the ship's lowest level viewport where I was studying, reviewing, in the quiet and the starshadows. Despite my confessed (only to you) space-fear, sometimes I love the strange, desolate peacefulness of the blackness of space through the port windows. The stars are there, but little comfort. They are so distant. But space itself is like a blanket. Cold, though. Yeah. Like your poem that talks of the void, and then the human embrace. You never mention the words 'cold' or 'warm' but I feel them there between the lines.

I'm both cold and warm right now.
The tests. Lark, Tiri. All of it.

I miss you. I really wish you were here and you could meet my friends.

We go to Nod in two days time. My tests are scheduled for the morning we arrive at Nod. I'll finish in time for shore leave. When I return I should have the results. The captain gives the results to each individual personally.

If you pass, and all your other records of work performance are in order, he promotes you.

Lark says I am smarter than my years. Right now, I don't think so.

If in the next two days you find yourself looking out past those poisoned skies of both our beginnings in friendship and adventure, say a wish for me. I will say one in return.

Your friend,
Liyan

*

70

Dear Liyan:

You will pass your tests and your captain's judgment. I have no worries. But I understand your worries. You are the one facing your dreams head-on, knowing they could take on different tones and hues than your very personal visions.

Worrisome, indeed.

I find no responsive haiku from you this time but I understand. You are not in a poetic mood. I am trying myself to find the poetry in the oddest things and often cannot.

Is there tension between you and Tiri? Or you and Lark?

I do wish I could meet them. They seem handsome and brilliant all at once.

If there are brilliant people who pass through this hotel, I meet them only briefly. I do not work with any that fulfill that adjective in any capacity. If they show signs of intelligence, they are usually also dull.

Pel is not stupid but he is a very narrow man with little imagination that I can discern.

My first owner, Pela, showed no signs of deeper thought past the color of her outfits or the scents of her bath. She did not even sleep with her husband, so one wonders about the heart in her case as well.

Everyone must have one, of course, but how it manifests or atrophies is attributed to so many lifelong factors. Insecurities, loves, griefs, illness, broken emotions or healthy emotions…and how can I say it? Sometimes, it is in the difference between the two?

Allow me to ramble, too. I have had a difficult night and very little sleep.

But hearing from you quite suddenly at my sleep hour made everything better.

How can that be? You are one person so far away writing me waves made up of little particles that form words that then make a picture in my mind. How is that possible?

The universe is a strange place. Communication may make it less isolating but perhaps even more strange!

I am lying in bed as you were in your last wave, on soft satins the shades of flame, trying to relax, to sleep.

It comes easier now, knowing you are out there following your longings and still thinking of me.

remembering
the ice chiming in your waterglass
before you left

Your friend,
Cobalt

*

Dear Cobalt:

I took the tests. Two hours each. I feel good now.
Off to shore leave.

I plan to see the thunderlights of Nod. They are like true-Earth's aurora borealis. Only these lights are accompanied by a drumming (thus they are called 'thunderlights') that can cause cognitive dissonance, but not anything more severe than a few glasses of wine might do to the brain.

What things can you not find poetry in? I want to know. Even the ugliness. Because friends share all of it, right?

I have told you about Tiri and Lark and the discomfort I sometimes feel there.

You asked: Is there tension between me and Tiri? Or me and Lark?

The questions confuse me. I thought I was writing of the tension between Tiri and Lark. I do not participate in their arguments.

Lark and I are better friends, yes, but Tiri and I enjoy games together, and we are a great team in nav. I forgave her long ago for putting 'Enchantment' in our drinks at that nightclub in that floating city of Vaera. She never meant anything sinister by it. It was a common form of recreational drug when she worked as a soldier.

We also work out together. I do some weight-training to gather muscle mass for landfalls. In any closed environment we grow soft if we don't move. Tiri is an excellent work out partner. She knows everything about everything when it comes to exercise.

As I said in one of my last waves, Lark joins in, too, but he's lazier. Maybe twice a week he comes. Lark's laziness doesn't show, however. He is trim and strong. Tiri and I meet every day with one day off for rest every six.

Once Tiri said, "How about working out naked today?" I said, "No."

I think something must be seriously wrong with me!

Another time she called me a prude. I don't recall the exact context. Lark told her to apologize. She said, "Are you telling me as my boss?" He said, "No." She said, "No chance, then."

I just stood there trying not to laugh because I wasn't really offended, and especially not by Tiri. I've grown used to her bluntness. She says what's on her mind, that's all.

I don't see any tension between me and her, not really, or me and Lark. There is always that syndrome of being the third wheel when one hangs out with a couple. We enjoy meals together, and games.

They also always invite me when we get time to go planetside at our stopovers. They invite Sekina, too. And sometimes others. If it's just the three of us, we're fine. But yes I am the odd man out, so to speak.

We leave for Nod tonight. We get a full 24 hours there.

By the time I get back I will learn the results of my tests.

I will wave you as soon as I can.

Your friend,
Liyan

*

Dear Liyan:

I do look forward to your next wave.

I am confident you did well on your tests. You studied hard. You are smart. There is no reason to think otherwise.

*Nod is a beautiful planet, described on the waves as **"a fairytale getaway" "a lush and magical realm" "offering exotic tours of alien castles direct from fabled fantasy."***

It is a world still being excavated, the human-like inhabitants long gone. Some say they lived a million years on that world, then vanished mysteriously ten thousand years ago. But no one scientist agrees. Evidence suggests they might have migrated elsewhere for unknown reasons. There is no evidence of war, thus the sites for sight-seeing are intact except from the erosions of climate and time.

I hope you find your stay there inspiring.

I assume when you say "we leave for Nod tonight" you are going with Lark and Tiri.

I enjoy hearing about them and am glad they are your friends. I never meant to actually suggest you had tension with either one; I only wondered. You explained the "third wheel" syndrome quite well and now I understand the relationship better.

Please accept my apologies for when I misunderstand certain social interactions. I meet a lot of people in my jobs, but I am limited in social experience because of my status. People who understand what I am do not respond to me in normal human ways...at least that appears to be the case in a very high percentage of interactions. So I am at a disadvantage when it comes down to discussion of such things as even normal friendships.

I have a planted childhood memory of a friendship with a neighbor boy. It is unreal. It is a poor context, assuming my brain can process that I grew up in a house in a neighborhood of families with other children and went to an all-child, human school.

I remember my more unpleasant adult training at the 'farm' more vividly, where it is emphasized over and over that we are NOT really human. It makes me wonder why they even bother giving us those earlier "human" memories. I understand it is to give us unique personalities, but might we not develop those on our own?

The boy I remember as a child was shallow and un-unique, someone to ride bikes with or play against in real or virtual hockey. I have never ridden a bicycle in my life. I have never actually played real hockey, on a field or on ice. However, because the memory is there, I suppose I could do those things if ever asked.

I have a very vivid memory of sitting in a field of yellow flowers watching bees feed from their centers. I can hear them buzzing and fizzing the air. I can smell the honeyed pollen.

Memory is a slippery thing. Humans assure me it is for them as well. There are many adult humans who say they don't even remember much of their childhoods.

Perhaps I am on a more even level with humans than I've been taught to believe. It is a comforting thought. And also disconcerting.

Have a good time on Nod.

Your friend,
Cobalt

*

Dear Cobalt:

I'm writing this as I still wait to hear the results of my test. No! They are not yet in!

But I am back from Nod with fantastic images wavering in my mind.

Worlds are huge and vast. Each planet has beauty and vistas that might take dozens or hundreds of tours to fully appreciate. We get, at most, 24 hours to choose one place to see before returning to the ship.

You are correct in everything you said about Nod. It is a fairytale world. The inhabitants left it intact but empty. It is a tourist mecca of sorts.

Every person in our group had already agreed we wanted to see the thunderlights. They are best viewed from two locations in the northern hemisphere of the planet.

We chose to go to the territory called The Fairylands of Nod, a thousand square mile stretch of land surrounding the planet's largest city, Nyght.

Taking in all the local geography, you could pretty much choose any point in that thousand square miles and find something fabulous to fixate on.

We decided to take a shuttle to the "Chesslands."

As we approached from crystal, azure skies, you could see in a vast wilderness clearing strange lines of broken columns for twenty miles or more of desert marking the Chesslands. We landed at the edge of that desert where the line of the forest begins. Looking at it from the ground, it seems to go on forever, broken columns like a sea of white bishops from a giant chess set.

I said the clearing was a desert. I only say that because nothing grows there. Nothing but the strange sculptured structures mirroring each other on and on. But the clearing, as I already wrote, is actually surrounded by a vast wilderness, "a forest of marvel and wonder," so say the guidebooks.

A storybook train runs through forest tunnels and hills. There were many such trains that ran east, south, west, north. You could choose your direction. Again, it didn't matter. Every mysterious grove in any direction bragged of rich views. After walking through the bishop-shaped columns of the Chesslands for a ways, we grew bored and took the northern train. It wound slowly through draping greenery, making frequent stops at tiny touristy villages that looked like pictures from a children's fantasy book. We decided to stop at one called Beauty's View because it had a floating hotel that advertised the best view of the thunderlights.

The Beauty's View hotel had every amenity. Its twenty stories floated above the trees. You could take elevators up from ground level that were really little square, glass-box air cars that rose and fell at the push of a button.

Everything became only more amazing after that. Tiri, Lark and I shared a suite. We saw a distant lake from our wide windows, with little rivers and eddies that snaked into the trees. Boats were traveling slowly up and down those flashing, blue waterways.

76

We decided to take a boat trip for a couple hours. Every turn the boat made on the slow rivers revealed ever more beautiful alcoves, secret grottoes, lagoons, caves draped with green lace, hidden gardens.

We came into a larger pond, through curtains of brass and emerald leaves and everyone held their breaths. This little lake, this hideaway paradise assaulted our eyes with a brilliance of color. Where to look first!

The still lake reflected everything, doubling our vision upward and downward. Flowers cascaded from tall bushes, everything against the backdrop of darker trees. Before us was a lavender beach. On the far edge of the little lake the forest gave way to soft orange cliffs glinting in the bright sun. And in the very center of the lake was the head of a giant sculpture rising from the water about 50 feet high. The face on the head was female, a young humanoid woman carved of soft-hued roses and pinks, with dark eyes and detailed lashes, a straight nose, peach lips. Pale red flowers adorned her forehead like a summer garland. On top of her head draped a full-plumed crane, white with blue-feather accents. She wore it like a fancy hat. The crane's head arched downward, the beak of dark yellow almost touching the woman's forehead. The face gazed across the still water like the perpetual but frozen rising of a goddess. The sculpture looked air-brushed to make it stunningly life-like.

Everywhere flowers bloomed, every shape, size and color, lilacking the air with their mingled scents. It was like being drunk, breathing that air. We were truly in a fairytale.

At the forest edge, violets carpeted the pathways. The bended brown trunks of trees arched and framed the lake, the inner forest, the mauve-blue shore.

They served us wine on the boat. We didn't need it. The air was wine itself. But we drank it anyway.

We had no words to say to each other as the little boat circled the statue, the crane-topped goddess, and headed back to our outlandish, Unseelie hotel.

This…this was like feeding starving eyes that have never before seen color, nature, life.

Lark's eyes glinted gold in the fairy-light of Nod, watching me wipe my tears. Again. I've got to stop doing this. Every planetfall lately I start weeping like a baby.

He was smiling, though. And Tiri was snapping holo after holo with her hand-screen…when she wasn't offering to steer the boat.

We ate like kings. Cheese stuffed steaks. Little fish-like things. Burning sweet cream and ices. And more wines of ruby and alabaster, our choice. I prefer the white even though the red looks lush, gaudy, more precious.

The top floor of Beauty's View, like the little box elevator boats, is made entirely of glass. After dinner the sky grew dark, yet clear. The stars popped on, failing to fling their warmth.

And then the thunderlights. We heard them first. A series of rumbles and tumbles of air. A drum. A rum pum. A flurry of staccato. Then they flashed. Crooked lines making tangles and puzzles, a rainbow of spirographs, a new design with each flash. All colors and shapes filled the skies. Colors I can't name. Shapes I've never seen. Abstract but also strangely rhythmic. You can see holos, but they can't convey the feeling of standing under them in a clear dome, looking and thinking yourself engulfed in some immense candy-world's mouth.

Lark said, "This planet belches unicorns and rainbows."

Tiri smacked him. "It's gorgeous. Liyan thinks it's gorgeous, right, Liyan? Stop making fun!"

"If you go for that sort of thing," he replied. But he was taken aback. I could tell. And he got all soft, blurry, framed in neon thunderlight as he embraced his wife.

We stumbled to our suite drunk and in awe of the day, falling quickly into our respective beds, dreaming in fairy-vision for the rest of the night.

Cobalt, I want to tell you I did wish many times that you could be with us. And I always think about how I will do justice to the scenes I see in my waves to you.

And do not think you are at a disadvantage at understanding friendship. You are a good friend to me. And I value my friendship with you.

If you misunderstand something I say, I always believe it is due to my lack of writing skill. This written language is different from the spoken. You cannot see nuances of body language or hear tones and inflections and shifts in the voice. And the eyes communicate so much, too. I want to see your eyes often when I read your waves. Too bad voice and image breaks up on far-distance waves. It's foldspace that blocks us even after we come out of it. It makes me feel so faraway.

Tomorrow I should learn my test results.
Expect another wave soon.

Your friend,
Liyan

*

Dear Liyan:

Your amazing descriptions!
I do not need haiku from you if you keep writing me in this way!

What a breathtaking planet, a miraculous tour. I think the goddess in the lake stands out for me even more than the thunderlights. But I can hear them...or maybe I am hearing the rumbles of the spaceport here...and I can see the crane-hat of a lady rising from a mystic lake forever and ever.

How fortunate I am to hear of the far-off alien world firsthand. A world where inhabitants lived as shortly as ten thousand years ago, only to vanish mysteriously into the night.

I have my hotel and my green skies, a constant image to wake to. But then I have your waves.

And I have my haiku which are like split-second dreams. Perhaps in those split-seconds I actually can travel faster than the speed of light to form my words based on either what I see, or maybe even what I dream. Or what you see and dream and then communicate.

a flooded statue
eyes downcast
a goddess rising

I would love to stand on the orange-cliff shores and observe
so I could write more and more lines of the true experience. For now
I will have to imagine it all, but thanks to your helpful waves it is
easier.
I await word on your lieutenant's test results. Anxiously.

Your friend,
Cobalt

*

Dear Cobalt:

I'm half-drunk writing this. Yes, we were celebrating, me,
Lark, Tiri, Sekina and a few others.
I passed the lieutenant's test. I did very well. The captain
himself ordered me to his office where he officially upgraded my rank.
I have a pin and everything.
Lark is technically still my boss but I was asked to work on
the bridge four hours a day. It's up front. Where discussions that
affect the entire ship transpire, and the big decisions are made. You'd
think it a breeze running a passenger and cargo liner. But it's
complicated and there are a lot of protocols to follow. It's still called
"paperwork" though there's no paper involved. I will now add to my
nav duties, doing quick updates and answer any questions, write
reports on daily and long-term nav calculation programs that the
computer runs.
Right now my words to you face me on my wave-screen and
they're spinning.
My eyes are aching. I don't remember how much I really
drank. I'm usually a person who measures and counts such things as
glasses, if not bottles of alcohol. Not tonight. I really didn't pay

much attention. Euphoria is like being displaced from reality…and the body.

Now I just need to tuck myself in and try to sleep. Although with my vision turning round and round I don't know if I will fall asleep easily.

Or maybe I'll just pass out.

I'm happy.

And I miss you.

Thank you for the goddess poem. More of that please.

Your friend (and new lieutenant),

Liyan

*

Dear Liyan:

Congratulations are due. But I speak the truth when I say I had no doubts you would pass your tests and be promoted.

Working in new areas of the starliner will be very exciting. I can imagine the thrill you most certainly feel. Your passion for this work shows. I know you aspire to have your own ship one day.

I have no doubts this will happen for you.

You are diving into your life full-force, now. You have made a home in a place of space. That is truly amazing.

You have good friends who support you, always an important step in moving forward in life.

I remember the boy in the bar asking for a glass of ice water, stars in his eyes, how exuberantly he embraced the idea of a conversation with me that ended in a promise he kept: to write me of his adventures wherever he went.

I admit I was unsure if I really would hear from you.

After we did connect, I was not sure how long the correspondence would last.

Now I can't imagine my life without it.

Everything you go through is important to me.

Again, congratulations.

Your friend,
Cobalt

*

Dear Cobalt:

Thank you for that last letter.
Your support means everything to me.
My first day on the bridge, we passed within a respectable distance to a black sun. It is not black even though it is called that. It is a whirlpool of light.
And I thought about how you said the stars were in my eyes. Truly, they are.
I don't miss the disks at the landing field, or the green-tinged fake moon of the port that is your indentured home.
But I do miss you.
I want to make a promise right now, no matter what, that I will always write to you on the wave. My life is full. Yes, I have friends and distractions. But when I am off-duty and go to my room and my personal screen there, I feel like I come home to you. You have been there for me for three years.
It means so much.
I am still coming down from the excitement of my promotion. Perhaps I will be for days. The boy you first met at Rory's is still inside me, but tonight my thoughts stream high over the stars, over the very universe itself, and I am something 'other'.

Your friend,
Liyan

Part Four

11. Third Meeting

He waited by the gate, the android with the blue-washed hair and a black silk coat with tails.

He watched the effervescent play of jungle-hued light from exhaust-swept, stale skies. The color today was belligerent.

The shuttles lined up in the coiled tunnel. The force-field ate green flame.

The diskships dotted the left side of the incoming coil, the triangleships flared to the right. Rockets rumbled, going right up through the middle.

The flight landing programs, intricate and precise, never allowed for collisions. But it often seemed the ships passed right through each other, taking up space and time for one where there were two.

Cobalt had written many haiku trying to describe this mirage. He felt he'd failed with every line.

Today he watched with only one thought. Which was Liyan's shuttle?

The flight was late.

People came and left. All strangers.

Finally a triangle landed. A flock of people emerged. One all in white.

Cobalt's heart leapt.

The hat he refused to wear hung from his belt. His hair shone, straight and thick, brown-green in the beaten tarmac light. He walked light on his feet and tall, not heavy as some passengers did after a long spaceflight. Among the group, he alone glowed. Or so it seemed to Cobalt's eyes.

This time Liyan did not approach looking lost, or grasp his hands, or hesitate. He simply moved upon him and took him, without a word, into a tight embrace. He did not let go until many seconds passed, confirming to Cobalt that the hug was authentic, a hungry connection, perhaps beyond mere 'heartfelt'.

Liyan smelled of intensity, electrical and sweet. His aura bristled warm and red.

When he finally stepped back, despite the confidence of his approach, Liyan stuttered. "I missed…I missed…I missed you!"

Cobalt laughed in a deep breath of release. He had no words.

"I like that you are laughing at me. It's okay," Liyan said, and his grin was a man's grin now, not a boy's. At 25, his features had sharpened, but his eyes were still round and young. His body was slender but hard, thicker in the shoulders and chest. He'd gained weight. All muscle.

The lieutenant first class of C&C Starlines met his eyes with confidence and said, "Where are you taking me to dinner this time?"

Cobalt replied, his own happiness no doubt showing far too much teeth, "The Riviera."

"Never been. I'm starved." Liyan clasped his shoulder as they turned for the exit that led into the port's small town.

"A lackluster meal again on your shuttle flight?"

"Most definitely."

It was as if they had never been parted since the last time Liyan had visited. Their ease with one another continued. A tremor of anxiety had haunted Cobalt for a few days as he wondered if they would meet more as strangers this time, both older, their time apart measuring in years. But their waves had only strengthened their bond. They both knew it. His worry had been only the result, perhaps, of caring too much.

Everything about him, even his thoughts, warmed in Liyan's presence. Liyan brought out powerful feelings in him, hope being one of the strongest. In a formerly bleak existence with no freedom, no rights, his future took on a different hue because Liyan was in it. Just one wave made his days better, lighter. Work was bearable simply because he had a friend.

They could've taken a taxi to the restaurant. But Liyan said, "I want to walk. I see lots of planetfalls, but it's never enough. When I am planetside or at a port, I always prefer to walk."

"Is the gravity all that different?"

"No. And yes. It feels different. And the ship is large but still confined. And surrounded by space. That's on the mind. I ignore it as much as possible."

Liyan had written little more about his fear in the past two years, but Cobalt never forgot his secret. He did not speak to his friends of his hollow, lost feelings. Navigation grounded him, he had said. Gave him target points of reference, headings, direction.

"I love the confinement of the ship. I love calling it home," he had written. That was all he needed to keep him going.

Now they walked at a brisk pace under the cankering afternoon sky of the old asteroid port. The force-field flashed occasional white lines overhead reminding them they were protected, safe. The toxins at the very edges of the field were what made the port sky green. The air they breathed was, in truth, filtered, considered clean enough by health-net standards.

"I don't miss this place," Liyan said with a smirk.

Cobalt said, "I hope not."

"But you, Cobalt, I will come here to see you any time I am close by."

"I know."

"I hope you know that. I come to see you. Only you."

A faint blush heated the skin at his face. "I am not a goddess with a crane hat rising from a lake."

Liyan laughed. "Well, I suppose not, but if I could see you more often, I would."

They spoke of easy things at first, the shuttle flight, health, their jobs. Then Liyan said, "I will make commander in six months."

That conversation lasted longer and carried on as they arrived at the restaurant.

"You sound confident." Cobalt knew he had been studying hard again.

"Oh, I have plenty of anxieties over it. Just like anyone. Maybe more so. When I feel them I make myself study harder, work overtime. Or I wave you."

"I hope my waves in return help."

"They do."

They were seated by a window overlooking lines of large, square buildings, white-lit from within. The station's hydroponics farms. They lit up the avenues they lined, squares of light that arrowed to a point in the distance until vision dropped off. The buildings shimmered blue around the edges giving them a tri-dimensional phantom shadow.

Cobalt's eye was not drawn to them, though. He could not take his gaze away from his friend. Not for a second. He meant to savor all the moments they had while spending this short weekend together. He wanted to memorize every curve and indent of Liyan's face, his lips, every eyelash, every reflection in his eye. His gaze traced down to his chin, neck, adam's apple, the edge of his chest, the broad shoulders still in the uniform of C&C with the little Pegasus logo on the cuff, just below the lieutenant's stripes. He studied the hands, long, and not so blunt as many men's hands were, the knuckles thick but well-formed, the flesh of his palms softly pale against the tea-hue of his skin-tone. The wrists were lightly veined in raised blue, a delicate tracery that hinted at both strength and masculine vulnerability. There lay life pulsing so close to the surface, a mortal power contained by the thinnest of veils, mere skin to hold it all at bay.

Like the force-field of a port o' call or the bulkhead of a ship, bodies were also merely containers protecting living cells from the battle-cold indifference of the void. What lay within was the mystery, the indefinable soul.

Liyan seemed to be observing him with the same fervor. He noted the man's eyes moved over him again and again, taking him in. They basked in each other's presence. It was a phenomenon of sublime pleasure.

They ordered steaks and wine.

Spoke of star-faring and navigation.

Philosophy and haiku.

They could not have been a better match.

"How are Lark and Tiri?" Cobalt asked. "And Sekina?"

"Loyal friends. Efficient co-workers," came the answer. "I wish you could meet them some day."

Cobalt bowed his head.

Liyan seemed to sense a rift and added quickly, "Lark teases me because we're going to be taking the commander test at the same time. He's not really competitive but he keeps saying to anyone who'll listen to him that his 'baby' is showing him up. Tiri will take the lieutenant's exam this year. Sekina is still well ahead on the path to getting command of her own ship. She's tired of the luxury liners, though. She's looking at exploration."

"That's all more toward military lines, isn't it?"

"Yeah. But they let qualified civilians in on the more science-oriented tours, including as ship captains. Between shifts, we all hit the online classes pretty hard. Sekina just got a Masters in Space Environment."

Cobalt tried to recall what that might be. He had a lot of downloaded knowledge, but not necessarily space-oriented. "What exactly is that?"

"She studies rocks. Asteroids. Meteors. Comets. Including the geology of planets sometimes, but it's more geared toward rock. Space rock. There is a branch of it that studies light, too, more physics than geology oriented. She's pretty smart about all of it. If I ever need homework help, she's the one I ask. Oh, and you didn't ask, but I'll tell you that her hair has peach stripes in it this month, and she's cut it so that it feathers all around her neck and shoulders."

"Last time you told me she was back to blue."

"It matched her eyes." Liyan took a sip of wine.

"Is she still single?"

"Single and driven to stay that way."

"Like you?"

Liyan's eyes drifted as he kept his glass raised, took another drink. "No." He spoke softly.

Cobalt caught his breath.

Liyan's hesitation showed in the lowering of his lashes, the withdrawing of his lower lip, the unsteady light flowing through the wine glass and making silvery shadows on his face.

Cobalt wanted to clear his throat. He wasn't sure if he'd caused discomfort or more depth of thought. In himself, it seemed a cool edge radiated through him almost defining itself as pain. He waited for Liyan to elaborate.

Liyan ended up emptying the entire wine glass while not answering.

Finally, Cobalt said, "Someone?" He kept his voice neutral.

Liyan shook his head, then said, "I don't know."

"Ah, a consideration, though."

"Yes." He took a deep breath and glanced out the window at the square lights of the hydroponics. "How many times...I forget...that Tiri and Lark have invited me...well, you know. I never knew how to write it. Sometimes I was overwhelmed or embarrassed, maybe? I'm not all that wild. So far. I've joked with them about it and stayed close with them everywhere except the bedroom. The teasing has lasted years." He smiled sheepishly, glancing back to Cobalt. "I might break one day. So there you have it. Not as dedicated as Sekina, only too shy and stupid to follow that side of my heart. Yet."

"You are ready when you are ready."

"I don't think so. Sometimes there are times when a person has to jump in, just so they can change the fear, or ultimately know it."

"Fear?"

"Of course. If nothing else, the third wheel syndrome. I don't want to be a toy." As he finished his sentence his eyes got wide. "Shit. I didn't mean it like that. Sorry Cobalt. This is why I've had trouble writing about it. I can't find the right words."

"No offense taken. I understand perfectly well what you're saying."

"Yeah, how could you not? But I meant, well, that's why I'm...um...maybe hard to get."

"Or maybe you don't like the games certain humans play."

"That's it exactly. I never have fit in that way even as a kid. Maybe I'm more cerebral or something."

"No. Cerebral is a cold word. You're not cold. I would say you're sensitive. That's all."

Liyan blinked at him, mouth parting. "Wow. Thanks."

Cobalt reached for the wine bottle and poured more.

Liyan said, "What about you?"

"Me?"

"You know. Someone else..."

"You're really my only friend." But his thoughts drifted to one other person. Someone who had been kind to him once or twice. But if they paid, it didn't count, right? He could never say that aloud to Liyan, though. Something stopped the words in his throat, or kept his hands from writing on the screen about anything extracurricular he did with the personal space of his body regarding Pel's requirements of him for financial gains.

"Surely you must have offers." Liyan seemed to blush as he made the statement.

Cobalt said, "Why?"

"You're...handsome."

"People don't know what to do with androids. Even if they had designs, where would it lead beyond a one night stand?"

"Maybe that's all some people want."

"I was talking about me. Where would it lead for me?"

Again, Liyan started to apologize.

Cobalt held up his hand. "I have no rights. My heart is not for sale, nor is it free."

Dark eyebrows narrowed, Liyan nodded. Then he leaned forward, elbow on the table, and rubbed between his eyes. "I know. Believe me. I know that. I didn't think before I asked."

Cobalt didn't like making Liyan uncomfortable in any way. "You can always ask me anything. What is between us, I think, allows for that."

"I'm just sorry it has to be this way. It's not right." He looked up, the brown eyes soft, so alive. "Your intelligence, your attention to detail and observation; you'd be brilliant in space. If only…"

Now Cobalt leaned forward. "That's why I value the waves. I go with you. Everywhere you go. And you describe it all and then I am alive and traveling with you. In your way, you have done more for me than anyone ever could. You have freed me."

All of a sudden, Liyan's gaze fogged over. He forced a smile. "But I want to take you with me." He stood, tossed his head as if to shake away the platitude, tense and swaying a little. "Are we done?"

"Yes, of course." They had wine left, but they'd already had plenty.

Liyan flipped a money card from his pocket.

"I'll pay for this one," Cobalt insisted, looking at his friend who seemed so distracted now.

"Sure. I'll be on the boardwalk."

Cobalt watched as Liyan, regal in his whites, exited the restaurant.

90

When he met him outside, Liyan was staring at the rusty, flashing sky, leaning against the guardrail at the edge of the asteroid itself where the green ceiling plummeted not only to the horizon, but beneath them as well. The ancient explorer Columbus was not needed to disprove anything here: their world was flat, tapered to a rock root bottom and free-floating in space.

Frayed and mildewed light outlined the human's form. A few people walked by now and again as false dusk approached.

Cobalt came up alongside him and watched the play of electric force-field flashes.

Liyan wiped a hand across his eyes. Cobalt had never seen him do that before. But he'd read about the times Liyan said he was overwhelmed, sad or even happy, and he might start to cry too easily, a trait within him which he self-deprecated, especially when discussing his future dream. Once he'd written, *"I'm still such a baby. It must be somewhere in the fine print when applying for the job, a prerequisite: starliner captains don't cry. I tell myself, 'Grow up, Liyan. Now'."*

He chuckled now, still embarrassed, still wiping. "I want to take you with me."

"Well, you can't."

He nodded and kept staring, cheeks shining.

A warmth pulsed in Cobalt's chest. He put his hand flat against the middle of Liyan's back. Liyan leaned into the touch.

*

12. Under the Stars

"I'm so impressed," Liyan was saying, holding the pocket screen in his lap.

They'd commandeered a couch in the lobby of the Grand Aurora. It was busier in the foyer, and by the elevators, but the lobby was always a peaceful place. So said Cobalt.

Liyan was still trying to get over his emotional outburst, which was really minor, of course, but he'd not wanted to deal with it at all. He'd switched subjects on their walk to the hotel twenty times.

Once they sat, Liyan had decided to broach the subject of poetry again. He said,"I know you write stuff you never show me. I want to see it all."

Cobalt replied, "I can send you all my files. You merely have to ask."

"On the wave. Hmm. Yes. But I want to see some now."

Cobalt had on him a pocket screen he worked with every day. He could access his personal files from it. He did so and handed it to Liyan.

Now they were discussing:

**a thousand hollow heartbeats
my life in secret
listening**

"You are an observer of life, but apart," Liyan indicated. "It makes sense coming from your predicament. But humans feel the exact same way. They are more privileged, yes, but they still have those feelings."

"Yes."

Liyan looked at him thoughtfully. "Ah, but then also there's your secret life."

Cobalt smiled. "If indeed the poem is even about me."

"Who else would it be about except the author?"

"Well…"

Liyan went on. "In your secret life you're listening. But you also have a life of your own. It's a secret, but it's real."

Cobalt rested his elbows on his knees, his chin in his hands. "It's a three-line poem, Liyan. That is all."

"No. It's endless depths of lines. And you know it."

"Then you would say the poem is successful."

"I'm not a literature expert. But to me it is very successful."

"Good. Because I wrote it for you."

Liyan sat back. "You listen to my waves. You memorize my waves. I'm glad. You can travel with me any day."

It was their spoken and unspoken understanding.

Cobalt lived vicariously through Liyan.

At dinner they'd been talking more about Liyan. Liyan had emotionally collapsed a bit. This was better. Now they were talking about Cobalt. To Liyan's delight. Cobalt was taking it all quite well. Did anyone ever give this man attention? he wondered. *No. Only me.*

Merely enjoying each other's presence, they lost track of time.

Finally, Liyan could not suppress the yawns. "I can't stay awake much longer. Meet me for breakfast." He did not voice it in a question.

When he fell asleep that night in the luxurious cottons and silks of the suite he'd rented at the Grand Aurora Hotel, where dark green light leaked around the edges of velvet drapes decorating the alabaster walls with underwater sea-haze shadows, he heard his own thoughts slur. They were saying, *"You can't fall in love with him. You'd always leave him behind."*

But he dreamed over and over of salt on his face, of Cobalt's warm hand brushing the center of his back.

*

The next day they went to the one college campus on the port and sat in the planetarium to see stars as the constellations they were once viewed from planet Earth when true-Earth existed.

"I never knew such a place to exist here on the port. I never visited the college," Cobalt said.

"I brought you so you can be surrounded by stars. For a little while at least," Liyan explained.

When the show was over, Cobalt said, "I don't want to leave."

Liyan leaned back, pleased with himself for this choice of entertainment for the day. "Let's just stay on for the next show, then."

"Don't you get enough of this in your job?"

Liyan laughed. "I work in a closed room half the time. I practically dream in numbers, formulas. On the bridge, mostly what we see on the viewports is blackness on top of blackness."

"And the occasional bearded dragon."

"*Very* occasionally!" He laughed. "I've never told anyone but you the whole story of that."

"You were space sick. No one would think it too odd since foldspace itself is still a vast mystery."

"Well, in any case, I keep the dream details of the event to myself."

"Afraid they'll take away your pin of valor if they discover you talk to space-dragons?"

"Hell, yeah." He grinned. Who would've thought his closest confidant would end up being an indentured android stuck on an island asteroid, a created human with such a great capacity of insight into a humanity forbidden to him. It never ceased to amaze Liyan.

They watched as stars sparkled overhead again, and were taken up in a swirl of light and an almost bored narrator's voice.

When they exited they were both hungry. They ended up at another boardwalk cafe decorated with orange lanterns and fake falls of trumpet flowers. Their waiter was grumpy, the wine sour. Neither noticed.

The afternoon was special for them both marred only once by a strange encounter.

As they left the café to walk back toward the center of town where the hotel imposed upon the tarnished sky, an older man with black hair pulled tightly back and an intense, cool gaze came up short in front of them.

At first Liyan thought he'd been distracted by something and just didn't see them, or perhaps he was looking for directions from them.

But the man's strange frown was directed entirely at Cobalt, and when Liyan saw the android's face tighten, the jaw lightly twitch, the throat flex, he realized his friend was having an emotional reaction.

That Cobalt knew this man was confirmed when the stranger said, "Cobalt, when did Pel let you out of your cage?" The tone could only be defined: unfriendly.

Stunned, Liyan opened his mouth to tell the guy to 'fuck off' (exact words and posture picked up from none other than the protective but imposing personality of Lark) but nothing came out.

"Hello, Juneau." Cobalt's voice came out stiff, formal.

"As you can see, I'm in town again and I've just been to see Pel about you. He said you were busy tonight. Now I know why." His crisp eyes flicked to Liyan. Suspicious. Maybe even…jealous?

Liyan stepped forward, figuring it would be better not to behave defensively. "Hello, I'm Liyan."

Juneau did not extend a greeting hand. He barely acknowledged him, except to say as if in passing, "He's a fine one for his kind, isn't he?"

Liyan did not know how to answer. Yes, Cobalt was fine. A fine friend and a fine man. "His kind?" he finally said.

95

But he knew. The man meant androids and it was a typical snobbish reaction to these toys of the ultimately rich, despite the fact that when it all came down to science, they were completely human.

The man shrugged. "Ah, one of those?"

The unspoken term was 'sympathizer'. Not a bad word in public opinion, but androids were so rare there was yet no organized militancy one way or the other about their rights. They simply were created to specification, then sold. And very expensive.

And the myths about them infused a belief that they were, in fact, less than human.

Liyan shook his head in confusion. Before he could say anything else, the man said, "I leave in the morning. But I'll be back next month. See you then."

He did not wait for a response. He moved away in his impeccable suit and soft shoes and rude air.

Out the corner of his eye, Liyan saw that Cobalt had become suddenly stiff, cool.

Liyan forced a smile. "Well, he didn't seem like a real nice guy. One of the hotel regulars?"

"Yes."

"Well, he didn't have to be such an ass."

Cobalt swallowed hard, then turned to look at Liyan. "Yeah, he is that, isn't he?"

"Definitely. And why would he talk to Pel about you? That's presumptuous."

"That's one way to define him."

"You've never written of him."

"He's not worth the words."

Liyan did not want to broach the subject further. But he could intuit there was a lot more between Juneau and Cobalt than mere 'hotel guest'. But he had to ask, "Pel's not looking to sell you off, is he?"

Cobalt reached out and touched him on the forearm. "No worries, okay? I'd tell you if I was leaving."

"I know."

But a discomfort grew in Liyan's stomach, a wave of heavy despondency for his friend.

Later, he thought about going to Pel. He'd never met him, and he wondered what he might say. *"Look out for my friend." "I know you own him but you can do right by him." "Oh, and by the way, could you keep that asshole Juneau away from him?"*

In the end he didn't do it. But that didn't mean next time he visited he wouldn't be so timid.

*

13. Departure

He decided the word for his behavior was babbling. Nerves, he guessed. And a strange, abject grief.

Breakfast. Pancakes. Steaming coffee in the hotel restaurant. Then another stroll under steaming, waste-colored spaceport skies.

Liyan talked (babbled) to fill the silence, to fill the air between them, and the infinity of space in his heart. He spoke again of the swan-boats. Foldspace. New theories in navigation not knowing if Cobalt even understood. He reiterated what he'd already said in his waves over the many years. To his credit, Cobalt patiently listened to it all.

In truth, he did not want to let go of these past two days. He didn't want to face the shuttleport, the tarmac, or the journey alone back to space.

But too soon there they were, standing before the double doors looking out over the field of blinking lasers, heat exhaust like ash against the moldy air, the old workshops where he used to wear heavy helmets, grubby overalls, and clanked around in safesuits for working on the stardrives.

He watched Cobalt's face intently now, the android's sweet smile. "I don't want to leave you."

"You won't," Cobalt replied, and his blue hair reflected peacock hues in the seasick light. "I am with you in the waves we send. It's our way."

"Our way," Liyan echoed.

"It makes our friendship even more special."

"You're an optimist," he accused.

"I can't be any other way."

Liyan decided it was true. A survival instinct. If Cobalt only saw the worst in a galaxy where he could not be free, how could he endure? For his own mental health he needed to see the best in life, focus on scenes of minor hopes one step at a time.

Liyan shrugged, then reached out and pulled him into a tight embrace. Cobalt smelled of all things desperate and longing, of cool flame and indolent hunger. An effortless breeze of ignited suns. He was summer in the northland where Liyan had grown up, where you looked at your submerged reflection in warm bays of saltwater while the inland farms basked in dry stillness and butterflies.

He remembered the silver hints of autumn around the edges of the air, the desolate structure of incoming night when everything stilled and stars lit and spilled their ash upon his skin. Cobalt was like that. In this moment. In this segment of his experience having visited dozens of worlds in billion light-year distances. The most beautiful memory of them all. Now.

Who could he write to about this?

Liyan's body wanted to smother and drown in that essence.

Their cheeks pressed, smooth skin, strong jaws. Cobalt's hair against his forehead felt like feathers. He breathed. And breathed again.

Kept him in his chest and, finally, turned away.

"I don't know when," he whispered, "but I'll be coming back here again and again. Whenever I can."

"Okay," was Cobalt's only reply.

He began the lonely walk to his plush and cushioned, first-class seat on the next departing shuttle.

*

Dear Cobalt:

One day apart and I already miss you. I have made it safely back to the starliner just in time to depart for regions far-away and grand.

The glitch in the air system was easily repaired at spacedock.

We enter foldspace tomorrow and take on passengers at Ursula. Nothing much there but teeming cities and hot air.

Sekina was first to greet me with a kiss to the cheek. She often holds herself back from affection, an insightful but inwardly focused person. But tonight she was so open, and she asked first thing about you. "Tell me about Cobalt and how he is. Tell me more about your relationship. An android is so unique! They should not be slaves but kings."

I couldn't believe her words. So we went for a drink in the lounge even though I was exhausted, where Tiri and Lark, coming off-duty, later met us.

I am fortunate to have such wonderful friends. Including you, Cobalt.

Now I'm sitting in bed silently writing this.

My mind pushes me to write on and on, pages and pages of mere nothingness just because when I write to you is when I feel closest to you.

I know I babbled this morning and you were polite to not point that out. But it was because I didn't know how else to super-connect with you, some kind of weird longing to fill a precious void.

I keep thinking, now and over the past couple years, what it would be like if you could be here, too, with us on the marvelous adventure, the fifth man in our group of four, the one who is the true wanderer sparking inspiration in us all.

I am falling asleep as I write this. My day has been long. The ship is steadfast, but in my serene and sleepy state it feels like it's wavering, pulling at its reins. The stars are more than beacons. They are tidal powers that pull us like a sea. Come out. Come in. We may be a mere (but large) cargo/passenger ship but we breach the folds of time and space to do the job. Isn't that just utterly amazing?

And the far-ness is like a journey toward the soul.

And yet I am also moving away from mine. From you.

I know you understand this. I can't speak of it well, it seems, when we're together. So this note is to assure you that for all our talks of wondrous things this depth in me, this priceless connection, this twinship/kinship we share is always forefront in my mind.

I wrote this several weeks ago:

what we are
after the spark
nova-voice

As I make my way through these years, I feel you with me. Even distance doesn't lessen the feeling.

I would write more and more and more, but my body demands I sleep.

Your friend,
Liyan

*

Dear Liyan:

Your beautiful words.
They greet me before sleep.
I moved today through my work mostly unaware. Not hearing properly when people spoke to me. Slower to respond. Maybe because your visit awakened me into an altered state.

And I am still reliving it.

From the moment I met you and you spoke of the stars and promised to write to me, I have felt as if I myself have traveled to them. Perhaps that is why my day went by in a haze. I am not here but more truly with you traveling between distant suns and folded space.

I felt no hunger or exhaustion when my day ended. I went straight to my suite and found your wave. I did not expect one so quickly.

Thank you for taking me to the old-fashioned star show. The constellations of true-Earth invoke a deep idea of a memory I can almost grasp. It is almost like déjà vu, but probably more accurately a 'racial' memory.

I still see you walking in your white suit to your shuttle and feeling as though I drifted beside you, boarded her, and went out through the force-field tunnel and into the dark.

Only half of me remains here writing to you. Only half of me inhabits this room, this life, this human-android suit. The other half is, in thought, right beside you.

Your friend,
Cobalt

*

14. The Robot Cliffs of Is

Dear Cobalt:

The stars are purple here. Something to do with the dust motes, like a perpetual fog, from the remnants of an entire system blown to dust. Some say war a billion years ago destroyed the ten planets and their yellow giant sun. The dust drifts on forever and the nearby system containing the planet of Is, where we are headed, is in the middle of that ageless war-cloud.

Coming out of foldspace we all saw purple dots on our viewscreens. Instead of spiking our water supply with sedatives, you'd think the captain had used hallucinogens instead.

Yes, of course I plan to see one of the great wonders of this galaxy, the gigantic and illustrious Robot Cliffs.

I will tell you all about it.

In the meantime, we work hard. This time in foldspace, which was unremarkable and dull, we worked on solving inconsistencies with reemergence from the event. We can travel the exact same route in foldspace from one firm point to another and with the same equations and still end up in a different area of space each time we come out. With no guarantees, we can come within range of our planetary destinations a day's journey away...or a week, or worse, a month.

We track and re-track our ways in endless quests to find a more steady path, a solidity to equations that drip from our fingers like wax and melt into the bulkheads.

This is because foldspace whirls ceaselessly. How do you track the actual patterns of a mercurial wind...or better yet, how do you predict its direction from day to day, week to week, year to year? You can observe general patterns, but the eddies and currents will still always come at you in varied shapes and speeds, each swirled imprint unique, never pre-destined..

Landing on a tarmac at the spaceport requires precision and is repeatable. Foldspace is like diving through a hurricane. We in nav can expect mostly chaos.

We soar with numbers. And I still work on the bridge four hours a day.

Tiri and Lark tell me to say 'hello'. I think perhaps I have talked about you to them too much...well, enough that they think they almost know you.

Your friend,
Liyan

*

Dear Liyan:

I commend your team for even trying to track something as elusive as foldspace.

When Pel brought me to the spaceport it was on a shuttle. The trip took two days. We did not use foldspace. I have never experienced it, but I long to.

When Pela used to play on her friends' starships I was never allowed to go. I remained behind as the wealthy took their 'yachts' to space for a day or two until they grew bored. Their navigators were mostly hobbyists. They did not breech foldspace.

Everything's still much the same here.

Crowds of travelers come and go. The fake moon rises and sets. The tedium of the hot green atmosphere is broken only by the fact that it churns and boils in its own sick borealis of ever-changing designs.

I made 38 cosmic fucks last night. Those are the purple drinks I was mixing the first time we met. It is still a popular beverage to order. I had one once and only once. It is a pure horror.

I prefer a glass of good wine and a table for two.
Wave when you can.

Your friend,
Cobalt

*

There were three regulars who paid to spend evenings with Cobalt once or twice a month.

Tomolo was dull and usually drunk. He was an overweight man who spoke little but used the android usually twice within an hour with never a 'thank you', only a soft grunt that bespoke a visceral pleasure.

Next came Saber, a jittery but kind man, the handsomest of the lot. He had fine medium brown hair, narrow features and beautiful teeth. He was the only one ever considerate enough to ask Cobalt if he was comfortable, or if he had any preferences to position.

The third, Juneau, with his hard eyes and untapped tension that fed a negative fierceness, was the man Cobalt and Liyan had run into on the street in front of the hotel. He was also the one who'd hurt Cobalt in the past. Juneau hated that Pel had threatened him with a steep fine (and hospital bills if it came to that) and still deliberately played as rough as he could get away with, turning physical battery into verbal abuse. He may have stopped leaving bruises most of the time, but he did other humiliating, distressful things including name-calling, spitting in Cobalt's face, yanking his hair and locking his hands tightly about Cobalt's neck as he used him.

He hated going with Juneau, who constantly threatened him and laughed about it. Because Juneau was wealthy, Cobalt could not be sure that one day Juneau might just kill him and pay for the privilege. Pel would not willingly allow it, of course. But Cobalt worried that Juneau had enough money to not care if a lawsuit resulted and Juneau lost.

Tomolo was a relief after Juneau, but forgettable.

But when Saber came he grew to not mind spending evenings with him. Saber was different. He enjoyed seeing Cobalt experience pleasure, while the other two didn't care.

Saber was also the only person he'd ever met whom he had found himself comparing to Liyan. The mouth was different, but they both had brown eyes, dark hair, but Liyan's hair was shinier, and Liyan's eyes were fueled by a deeper spark.

But the kindness Saber showed, and the respect for his feelings, kept reminding him of how easily Liyan had accepted him as a human, not changing his opinion after he discovered Cobalt was an android. That sweetness in Liyan, that fresh, young fervor that allowed him to see life, all life as beautiful and whole was dimly reflected in Saber. Saber, less sure of himself, not as quick-witted or far-seeing, was a dimmer mirror of Liyan. Cobalt definitely preferred him over the other two. In his cold and isolated life, Saber was a warm distraction. For that alone he allowed himself to smile in the man's presence, something he did not do for anyone else who rented him.

Sometimes he wanted to write to Liyan of Saber, but he always held back. He couldn't think of the right words. He decided it was best if this part of his job description remained an unspoken topic between them. He didn't want to burden his friend with that side of it.

Plus, Liyan's friendship, his letters made him crave something more from his life, a fullness and strength his star-traveling friend inspired.

He saw aspects of Liyan in Saber. And Saber treated him well. But all his feelings were for Liyan.

So Saber remained a subject to be avoided as well as his moonlighting job for Pel.

Now Cobalt sat back against his own pillows in his own room and looked for a wave from Liyan. Nothing yet.

Tonight had been a Saber night. He had not suffered at all. He leaned back against soft pillows and remembered the flash of Saber's perfect smile, smooth skin moving gently against his own, a quickening of pleasure. Even if he had enjoyed himself so many things were missing in their connection. Saber did not speak of travel or the stars. He did not have aspirations beyond his high-salaried job as manager of an investment firm. He was too calm, even bored. And he never blushed. Not even in the throes of ecstasy.

He closed his eyes and remembered his last meeting, face to face, with Liyan. How easily they fell into step with each other. There was a spiced scent of distance about the man, a wistful longing, brilliance in deduction and insight, and an innocent brightness of beauty unmatched in any other human being he'd ever met. All the cells of Cobalt's body hummed within his presence. When he was with Liyan, even the port's rotted skies became effervescent and fresh like a natural planet's eternal spring dawn.

As he drifted in loose-limbed satiation, his wavescreen beeped.

The message could not have been better timed.

Dear Cobalt:

No one knows where they came from. 20 stories tall they stand. Frozen in the pink cliff-top sands. There are no internal mechanisms. No gears or wheels or pulleys or intricate electronics boards or other technology inside them, so if the giant robots ever moved, or ever existed as the army they resemble, what controlled them?

The guidebook says there are 10,879 of them lined up over a hundred miles along the cliffs of Tremor Beach on Is. They are more than 20,000 years old. Some have fallen due to erosion and time and lie on the pink sands below, scattered, broken tin-men, metal islands in the crystal azure waves.

The rest stand atop the cliffs in a never-ending sea-breeze that wails a constant, lonesome dirge. The winds keep the sands from overtaking them completely. Over the millennia the cliffs have crumbled a bit here and there, but the giant structures remain mostly intact.

What a sight. The square angular heads with hollow, missing eyes, metal mouths set in straight lines of grim expression. Are they some artist's sculptures left for all eternity to gaze seaward and glint in the rusty sunlight as guardians of this long dead world?

There is no life on Is, although the wind itself seems empowered with a mystical presence. It seems to speak. Standing on those alien cliffs, my head no taller than the metal foot of Robot 1,391, the wind fiddles with my hair and scarf, washes through the humongous silver legs of the frozen form, air of iron-scent, salt-essence, pressing up and down as if it owns this eerie line of bipedal facsimiles. The arms are all bent in the same positions all the way down the cliff-line, the left arms straight down, five-fingers curved just below the hip, the right bent upward at the elbow, the hand

106

stretched out, palm down, as if reaching for something. All have the exact same pose, 10,879 arms stretched out, a gesture begun, never to be completed.

What it means no one knows. A chill creeps on my skin just writing this description.

You could look up holos of these enigmas and still never truly "see" the effect they have on the landscape, the view of them curving endlessly into the distance.

I found the trip to Is incredible and disturbing at the same time. It's as if they are a monument to lost souls, to frozen hopes and dreams, to an end of time.

I feel my words do no justice to the isolation I felt on this tour. Even though Lark, Tiri and Sekina all came along for this viewing adventure, the loneliness of the planet permeated my being.

I returned to the starliner depressed and antsy.

I wanted to wave you immediately. Instead I went to the gym and worked off my feelings of gloom.

It helped a bit. But now as I write, the atmosphere of that place returns.

I don't know if the others felt the same way. None of us spoke much on the journey. We didn't drink and celebrate afterwards. That says something.

(Later, though, Lark brought me black tea, hot. My favorite. He felt my forehead, said I might have a fever.)

I wanted something more, something else, or perhaps the view of this lost world simply made me miss some deeper meaning in my life. Something I can't define but need. A purpose beyond this career, some reason for being that I want more of. And yet, this career…it is everything to me.

Too many worlds! Not enough time! That is what we say to each other when we are all together in the rec room, or about to embark on a new voyage. We love our work, the alien places and spaces.

I wish you were here, Cobalt. It grieves me to say it but it is the truth. Would that you were not in this position of slavery. It is so unfair to you!

There are things I can say to you, talk about with you that I feel uncomfortable conveying to my friends. I suspect it is in part because of the distance between us. You are a safe confidant, someone who is motivated by wanderlust to hear me and appreciate the stories of my life because they are your stories, too, the stories you want for yourself.

Also, you are someone I am comfortable with. I feel I can say anything to you and not be judged. That my thoughts are of interest to you. That I am valued. The times we have met have confirmed it for me.

I am in the dark where you can't see me on a tiny speck of a ship in all the great backdrop of the universe. You are cast away forever on the shore of a jagged rock island in the middle of that dark. Our lines cross with a prickle of light.

It feels like you are beside me even though you're not. No one here understands that, not even my best or closest friends. Of course I don't speak of it in these terms, nor so intimately with anyone. But Lark knows how greatly I value your waves, how happy I am after receiving one, how I rush off to write you after any major event. Tiri and Sekina do, too, but are curious about you in a more intellectual way, and they are not as attentive to my moods as Lark, who sometimes seems like he is also reading my thoughts.

I quickly glance over this letter hoping it is not a complete disaster. But my thoughts are my thoughts even if they are confused or not always happy ones.

It's like those giant robots infected my mind.

Attack of the Killer Robots! But they never move. All they have to do is stand there and look ominous to send everyone running back to their starships.

Your friend,
Liyan

*

Dear Liyan:

I treasure every word you write, every observation of every world you visit, every emotional insight and discovery.

Sometimes, with your waves, it is as though I am seeing over your shoulder. If you feel me at your side, the idea of that is mutual.

You certainly communicate the desolation of Is and its majestic robot sentinels with amazing energy. Your wave is full of images I wish to contemplate more after I send this.

It has been awhile since your last visit and I still think of it as if it happened yesterday.

How I long to travel with you, and work aboard those fast ships.

I am fortunate that I have you to help me extend my reach beyond the stars. Because you are in my life, everything seems a bit more fair to me. Even my lack of rights, and my life of servitude.

For what it's worth, you are the one who gives it all meaning. I hope that's not too heavy a burden to bear.

The grief you feel will pass. Do not feel sorry for me. Do the best you can and share it with me and I'll always be fulfilled.

I had a dream of you once enfolded in a gathering of clouds and waving from the white horizon, smiling, happy. That is what I want for you always. It is what makes me happy.

Knowing that you are where you need to be and doing what you dream makes everything I do take on a new dimension of depth.

It is why I so enjoyed exploring the expressions of haiku with you. You were able to make me see beyond my every day existence here at the hotel even while remaining stuck forever here, working through the years. My status in life means nothing in the face of that. Nothing. Please read these words carefully. It is never necessary to define ourselves by what we do to get by, by what is required by the consequences of being living beings, no matter where or how we live. Our definition of self must go beyond that, or what is the point? I am no more a concierge or bartender than I am an android. Those are only words put onto me to categorize and define me in current terms of cultural recognition. But they mean nothing about 'who' I am and you have taught me that.

You follow your dreams. In my own way, now so can I. This very letter I'm writing would never have been written (nor any of the past haiku) had I never met you. All the philosophies we have discussed, our young ideas and our old fears would never rush around my mind as they do now, giving me new thoughts and vistas to ponder. You have opened the universe to me where I was once trapped.

Know this!

If the planet Is drenched you in gloom, then allow me to throw you a life preserver.

My heart beats because of you.

Your friend
Cobalt

*

Part Five
One Year Later

15. Koral

Dear Cobalt:

Working on the bridge full time as commander of nav (while Lark continues his work overseeing nav down below decks,) gives me opportunities to see and participate more in the actual frontline running of a starliner that transports both passengers and cargo.

Now I, along with Lark and Sekina, form part of the mandatory upper ranking crew line-up that greets all passengers as they come aboard through the shuttle bay. We take on 20 to 40 passengers per trip. They arrive all at once in two to three shuttles that land, disembark their passengers, and then take off.

I can't help but realize a sort of mirror to your own occupation. The starliner is an elaborate, moving hotel. We see guests come and go. Our job is to get them underway to where they need to be. Your hotel shelters them, mine shuttles.

I am sad to say that Sekina won't be with us for much longer. She's on the list to get her own ship. At such a young age, too, just turned 30! (The streaks in her hair are blue again.)

We're all proud of her. And we're all going to miss her so much.

Yesterday, a new list of passengers boarded. We get mostly wealthy tourists and rich, corporate businessmen with long-term visions in interplanetary business. Once in awhile we get families with children, those who are moving far enough away to a distant world that the shuttles are out of the question for such a journey. Most shuttles are not equipped with foldspace drives, so starliner transport is the only alternative. Passenger decks are luxurious and expensive when compared to crew quarters. Charging the passengers exorbitant fees offsets the cost of cargo shipping long-distance. But the amenities must also match the price, or people will feel ripped off.

In my early years of service, I avoided the passengers. My duties were elsewhere. They had their own decks.

But now...

For the first time I have met another android.

It was a shock, actually. An older woman boarded followed by a young, well-dressed man with gold and green hair. At first no one noticed his status. But his handsomeness stood out. Then it became obvious in the way he moved, how he responded to her voice, how she commanded him. He was no husband, son or even lover. He was her servant. He had a very cool gaze. Every move he made was practiced and precise. No mistakes. No sense of individual will.

I went out of my way to meet him. He did not seem to understand my greeting was for him, and kept stepping away to give room for me to greet his owner.

I said to him, simply, "Welcome aboard. I'm Liyan."

His bored gaze met mine. Or was it hostility? When I put out my hand as a gesture of good will he ignored it. He followed his female owner along the line, ignoring all greetings from any of the other crew.

The passenger decks are loaded with color. The walls reflect lavender, pink, pale blue. There are glass elevators and gold-railed viewports. Mirrors decorate various bulkheads to give more sparkle and light. In the center rec area is a vast, crystal chandelier. One corner has a burbling fountain decorated with wisps of baby's breath and green ivy.

Once a day, those of us in upper ranks are required one walk-through of the luxury deck, in uniform. This is for no other reason than to reassure the visitors, our guests, that they are well in hand. We are in charge, in control. There is nothing to worry about. This is especially necessary when in foldspace. If someone gets spacesick we report it and it's taken care of by the sickbay team.

Today I made my trek after my shift. I saw the android again. No one had ever given his name. No one seemed to care. But my own curiosity propelled me. I've never met another like you, Cobalt.

And I still have not. He was nothing like you.

When I approached him he turned slowly as if to face me but gazed past my shoulder as if I did not exist. I said, "Hello."

He did not reply.

"Do you have a name?" I asked. Silence. "Sir?" I prompted. "Are you all right?"

"Perfectly," he finally replied, and his voice came at me with a sharpness and iciness that bordered on rude.

"We met yesterday," I reminded him.

"Yes."

"My name is Liyan."

"You have a forward manner, Liyan," he replied, still never meeting my eyes. His eyes were green flecked with silver. He wore a tailored silk suit with a red satin tie.

"I know someone like you...back home..." I started to say.

His reply? "I'm not for rent."

That startled me. "I never meant to imply that." But I was embarrassed. His assumptions were quick and sure.

"My owner is Caxadia. Don't forget that."

"I was introducing myself to you, not her," I offered. I admit I was starting to feel defensive.

Coldly, he said, "I do not care. You will stay away from me or I will tell her bad things about you...Commander Liyan... and get you fired."

I couldn't move or speak for a moment. What he said was so threatening, so cruel. Stupidly trying to make amends, I said, "I was simply introducing myself, as I have with all the passengers."

"No. You were not." His voice came out in a sure and final tone.

"I have a friend like you," I started to say.

"He cannot be like me. I have no friends." Then he turned away, ran his hands through the small waterfall at the edge of the bulkhead and, water dripping from his fingers, headed down the corridor and disappeared.

Stunned and sad. That describes how he left me. I still never found out his name.

What was I thinking? That because I know you I know anything at all, in general, about androids? That I might empathize with how he thought or felt? I'm naïve at best, embarrassed to even be telling you this.

113

Cobalt, how can I be so smart and so stupid at the same time?
He had me shaking inwardly when I arrived at the rec room.

Lark sensed unease and poured me a beer. We talked until
Tiri called him away; he tried to get me to come with him. To spend
the night. He does this when he senses I'm upset.

I came here, to my quarters, to write you instead.

Your friend,
Liyan

*

Dear Liyan:

I hope you are not still upset about your meeting with
another android.

I can tell you that the way we are trained when we are 'born'
and conditioned promotes a self-preservation within that can seal off
unwanted emotion. Years of this behavior can lead to psychopathy in
a large percentage of my kind. Any violence is bred out of our
engineered DNA so we are of no physical danger to others, but an
android psychopath will cause unease if that is his goal. And his
manipulative threat to lie to his owner (or your captain) about your
behavior to get you into trouble is real. Do not go near him again. In
that regard, he is definitely a dangerous individual.

Because he has no empathy, he cannot see any overture of
yours as friendly, only a gesture filled with selfish motives on your
part. He does not know you as I do. That does not excuse his
rudeness. His owner is either unaware of his behavior, or does not
care.

My first owner, Pela, only wanted to show me off as a doll.
As a result, I was left in empty rooms alone for hours, days, with no
companionship, no interaction, and only allowed to use computers or
hand screens with permission. Pela was neglectful but not overly
cruel. She'd simply forget about me. I was not allowed any freedoms.
Any child might go crazy to never leave their home. I was lucky I did

114

have access, most of the time, to some social media, although forbidden to directly interact with others on the wave.

When I came to Pel I slowly integrated to the hotel life. It was a gradual process. I learned social skills by trial and error, but also I had some intuition and empathy to back me up. I don't know why I am so different from the android you just met, but there could be any number of reasons. Perhaps it's all in the specific childhood memories downloaded into our brains. Or perhaps he is very old (we do not age so you can only guess) and he's been ill-treated for decades. We can't know for sure.

Again, I implore you to stay away from him. Take his threat to destroy your career seriously.

On another note, I hesitate to ask this, but regarding Lark's invitation… This is not the first time. I cannot believe you have never once said yes?

If you don't want to talk about it, I understand. Tell me if I overstep myself in any personal area of our relationship.

Where are you headed next?

Your friend,
Cobalt

*

Dear Cobalt:

This will be quick. I have a long day of work assignments ahead of me.

Our next stop: Taraylia and the archangel ruins!

After foldspace we estimate a four day journey. Give or take a week.

I plan to see the ruins and spend the night there. I will write to you all about it.

Thank you for your insight about the nameless android I introduced myself to. There have, so far, been no further encounters. I plan to stay away from him.

Your question about Lark and Tiri I will have to answer at another date. They have a complicated and sometimes stressful marriage. I will go into this more with you, but not right now.

I'm sorry to be so abrupt. I'm already late for my shift!

Your friend,
Liyan

*

Dear Liyan:

It is interesting to note that the Archangel Ruins, though alien in nature and design, have been given an ancient, religious, humanform connotation.

Is it because they are so beautiful and large? Because the wings of the eight broken sculptures dwarf the bodies? Archangels were once depicted by human artists to have larger wings. This monument was not created by humans.

They are beautiful in holos I've seen, wrought of aurora marble, so their bodies shine with rainbow iridescence in their decay.

Do they depict the visage of citizens of a long lost civilization? The literature on this is endless, but all speculation. Who can know? Another mystery for you to witness, and surrounding the monument, endless tourist towns for you and your friends to explore. Will you stay in Cathedral? It's my favorite of the offerings. I read up on them all.

Another long day for me. I am about to get some sleep.

Good journey in foldspace.

Your friend,
Cobalt

*

Dear Cobalt:

We dropped off tourists and picked up 20 more.

I never made it to the archangels. It pains me that I could not see them in person.

During foldspace, we had a fire in the nav labs. No injuries. It has taken double shift work to make things right. No shore leave for us. Others of the crew were free, but not us. Not Lark or Tiri. Even Sekina stayed on to help, though it's not her area anymore, because she knows the ropes.

You may be pleased to know that no new androids boarded with this new group of passengers. I did learn the name of the one who was so rude to me from the passenger manifest. Koral. Not that that means anything to you. But I wanted a name to end the story of my encounter with him. And now I hope never to think of him again.

I am more exhausted than I can describe.

My eyes are blurring just writing this.

The damage has almost been repaired, and lost data retrieved. The fire began in a server system that got too hot. But the failsafe is there to prevent that. Somehow the failsafe itself failed. There was a lot of smoke damage and systems frozen or shut down that had to be repaired. The cosmetic work was left to the janitors who always do a perfect job. Repairs in space, instead of putting into port, are often necessary. The janitors who oversee all that are invaluable. Now you can't even tell there was a fire.

We enter foldspace again in two days.

I'll wave again before then.

Your friend,
Liyan

*

Dear Liyan:

I'm glad there were no injuries in the fire.
Running all over the galaxy, you may return to the archangels some day.
For me I have had several days of long hours. I am grateful to return at night to my suite. I find peace in composing three-line poems.

the dangerous moon glares
this unfinished life
awash in thick evening

endless yellow sky
unassembled years
where I wait

a panicked moon
rain
of silverships

all the tourists
in a hurry
all the green days

Safe journey.

Your friend,
Cobalt

*

Dear Cobalt:

Early this morning, before we broke orbit, I had a message to meet the captain in his office.
I arrived promptly.

He told me a passenger on the last flight had made a complaint about me. Improper advances.

Of course it was from the owner of Koral. I'm innocent, but I began to shake. Some commander I am! So rattled by this small event!

I explained my side of the story.

The captain said very little and dismissed me without further words. No reprimand, but no words of support. Many people know I have an android friend back 'home'. I'm sure the captain knows, too. We live in a small environment. There are few secrets. He must think it odd that in this rare case of hosting an android passenger I would somehow be involved in a small controversy regarding him.

I can't get the meeting out of my mind. All day my work performance suffered.

Later, Tiri told me Lark was upset for me. He wanted to go to the captain.

I went to Lark and told him not to say a thing. I don't want any further talk of this. Koral is obviously like a manipulative child, cold and perhaps angry. I don't know. I don't care. It's not worth the energy to take it any further. I was not reprimanded. No more action is required.

I was misunderstood by another human being who happens to be an embittered android. Misunderstandings happen between people all the time for all sorts of reasons. I'll get over it.

It feels good to write this all down here, as if I am talking to you, confiding. When I can see it all before me as a whole, it is a ludicrous story that will be quickly forgotten. I feel better now, getting this all down here, and knowing you will completely understand my position and my feelings.

I am grateful.

I love your poetry. It is sad and dark this time, but beautiful. And I love it because it is from you. I have not had any time for compositions of my own.

Maybe soon.

Your friend,
Liyan

*

16. Favorites

When Cobalt had not heard from Liyan for long spans, when the routines, the green skies, the long hours and the penthouse suite moonlighting wore him down, he would go through all the correspondences between himself and Liyan and find his favorites. He'd read and reread those waves, those beautiful letters until his mind eased and his heart slowed. He'd relax and bask in the aura of his friend who now fulfilled the rank of commander on a luxury starliner hurtling through space. Watching his friend grow and mature through an enviable career that took him to exotic places most people only dreamed of, became his single pleasure in life. But for a simple design of fate, he'd be there right at his side.

One of Liyan's more recent waves became one of his favorites.

Dear Cobalt:

In foldspace stars rush into thin lines that approach and veer simultaneously. The ship rocks in a star-net, both moving and static. From the inside it looks as if everything is churning towards us in a terrific storm but we are the ones hurtling through it all. The ship's drive causes ripples in spacetime. We dive the waves under. Over. Making temporary rips that fold back on themselves.

Foldspace is full of secrets. In between the ripples exists the holographic soul of the universe. Realities transformed. Blossoms of memory fields more vast than eternity. Our brains usually block this transcendent existence. Our perception is too small, too limited to contain it. However, we may feel a need to speak endlessly about varieties of God, or to sleep for days, or play games to distract from existential or philosophical discomfort. It's never predictable. We can't always control the pull of what foldspace will represent and present to us. Sometimes the brain stops blocking it all. A kind of self-preservation failure. You don't know when it will happen but it does. A space-sickness occurs. Sometimes it's minor. You sit and stare at a wall or forget to eat. Or you're compelled to write or paint or scribble equations in theoretical physics. It's like going manic, being drunk, drugged, inspired, energized. If you go too crazy you end up in sickbay strapped down and fed heavy-duty tranquilizers.

Mild tranqs are put in our food and drink by captain's orders right before the drive engages.

Most of the time it is sufficient.

It's part of the job description. We work through it. Everyone has good and bad foldspace experiences. Everyone. Even the captain. We all cover for each other, those who can taking the shifts of those who can't.

Mostly I handle it well. I've been severely spacesick only twice. The other hundreds of times I responded to the meds okay. If I feel at all jittery, I wait until I'm off-shift to do my bulkhead gazing, Or I try to put the whirlpool of images in my head into coherent language – a story, poem, letter to you.

Foldspace is like a drug. It's actually incredible. We all look forward to it. Inside the effect we all have a certainty we know everything. To make sense of this ultra-knowledge is another matter altogether. We've discussed before that there are some truly genius pieces of art, compositions in music or writing and theories in science that have come from foldspace altered states. But it is rare. Most of the junk is indecipherable. Nonsense. Blather. Like when you're in a dream and it all makes sense until you wake. And then the surreal aspects surface only to confound and confuse.

Only one time, so far, was I able to bring back something comprehensive and astounding from this tranquilized altered state. My navigation intuition helped us locate ourselves when we were lost. I met a bearded dragon.

It's the only time foldspace succeeded in accelerating my knowledge in a comprehensive way.

But I wonder if it could be done again.

What if we prepared not through taking tranquilizers, but through meditation? What if we concentrated on certain areas of thought, specific questions, and treated foldspace like a spiritual journey? What magic would we discover?

Of course there are cults who do exactly that. They discuss and even publish within their own ranks but remain on the fringes. Why? Public disinterest? Fear? Lack of depth of intelligence in the average human? Are most of us truly incapable of sustained imagining beyond the known? I wonder if there is something built into the brain that blocks us, makes us shut down like some overwhelmed computer system.

Cobalt, I am writing to you from foldspace – a wave I will send later.

There is a wind in the stars tonight. I can smell the forever fires of space. A flame-tinted breeze. Everything is burning. The void is singed by invisible ash.

Life is the beautiful obsession of this dark nature we find ourselves inhabiting.

This raven void.

It is mysticism itself, blue-edged on the very cusp of sleep or waking, always one or the other. I am either waking to my other self or sleeping to find it.

It is a muse and eludes. Beckons. Teases with the frustrating feeling of loving something more than being loved in return.

I am sitting in the common room writing this to you, Cobalt, wiping at my eyes again and again.

Lark comes in. He looks big. He crosses his arms, shakes his head. His gaze is drugged, the pupils huge making his eyes black.

I think he will make fun of me. Joke. But his voice is soft. He says, "Your heart is leaking gold stuff."

Then he tells me he was looking for me to invite me to a game of poker where the stakes are unusual verbs.

I tell him my verbs are tentative tonight and I can't retain enough of them.

He says, "Come play anyway."

So I end this now.

Your friend,
Liyan

*

Cobalt had read this wave many times. An attachment had been added later, after Liyan came out of foldspace. It contained a group of haiku poems, all numbered and placed under a single title: "Spacesick."

The title always made him smile.

Cobalt longed to experience foldspace for himself but knew he never would. He internalized Liyan's experiences with thoughtful introspection until it felt as if they were his own.

*

17. Sea of Broken Moons

Lark smelled of the nav labs, crisp, sharp but warm. He stood at the viewport, white uniform bright against all the black of space. The barest pinprick of stars sizzled over his head and by his left hand a butterfly-shaped constellation pulsed. His hair fringed his collar, coppery on top but a much finer blond at the tips.

He said, "Liyan. You keep running away from us."

Liyan leaned against the bench staring past him, watching the black. A longing uncurled in his sternum, a hollow ache. He could not deny Lark's statement.

He closed his eyes. Saw lavender eyes. Hair like a sea shining at dawn.

He opened them. Saw blond features, perfect posture. A strong silhouette. A best friend.

Tremors of fear crested his skin. He held himself back because of love. He stepped forward because of love.

Lark moved toward him. The heat of arms went around him, a whisper of breath against the hair at his temple. "Just come be with us. Okay?" Soft lips at the outer corner of his eye. The pulse in his chest increasing.

Liyan turned his face. Their lips met for the first time. When he pressed into Lark's strength, the pain in his stomach turned to pleasure.

He wanted him so much.

How had it come to this?

Lark's hand moved down his arm, the hotness of the touch seeping through his uniform shirt. Their fingers twined; they clasped palm to palm. He drew back and led Liyan by the wrist to the observation deck's exit.

Liyan moved slowly at first, drawing Lark's arm taut but not letting go of his grip. His chest expanded with deep breaths.

Lark's fingers tightened. He slowed his pace and turned his head to look at him with shimmering eyes.

Suddenly, Liyan remembered Davenda, lying in the black down on the back of a giant swan, gliding over a vast blue lake. He remembered the scent of sun-warmed, fresh water, the tickle of fine and delicate feathers, the taste of tears in his mouth. Lark had been watching him with such a serene smile. Everything was so graceful and smooth that day, the sky beaming and depthless in clear noonlight, and all the soft lapping of intricate breezes as the swan paddled effortlessly on its fairytale journey taking them with it. Lark had shaken his head at Liyan's too vulnerable expression of awe and said something about Liyan needing to get laid. He now realized that had been the first come on of many over the years.

He stopped in the middle of the corridor and all around them were gray walls, gray ceiling and floor, and the sterility of the moment couldn't have been further from that beauty of Davanda. But Liyan whispered through the flames of his throat, stunned at the utter heat of his skin, "Okay…okay."

"Okay, then," Lark said, tugging him onward.

They ended up in Lark and Tiri's double stateroom.

124

The sheet was cool against Liyan's burning skin, white and soft.

Trembles. Tumbles. Undulations. Bodies sliding. Lips to flesh. He didn't know where to hold on or what to think. He didn't really care. Tiri's affections were enthusiastic and understanding when it became obvious it was Lark who really quenched his thirst. She merely smiled in delight, nothing of her temper showing, no prelude to jealousy. It had been his fear that the "third wheel" syndrome would plague him. But for this moment he left his worries behind. He lost himself.

Now Tiri lay to his left, smiling in her sleep.

Lark, to his right, cupped his hand against Liyan's naked chest. The bigger man was still awake, his pale gold eyes sleepily watching him.

Liyan's breath caught. Blinking hard, he reached out and touched Lark's golden head. The intensity of what they'd just shared blurred his vision.

Again at the most inopportune times, he teared up. It was a goddamn hazard! He ducked his head.

Lark gave him a half-smile. He leaned forward, brushing his lips against Liyan's eyelashes, spreading the moisture. He pulled up and, still smiling, rolled his eyes as he murmured, "You sweet guy."

Unspoken between them: *I love you.*

The fluttering in his chest and stomach demanded he pull the man to him, wrap him close as Tiri's heat pressed his back. Lark let him.

But when he slept he dreamed of Cobalt.

*

The square bed stretched under a wide, curtain-less window. The view dumped straight down to Drebnot, the silver-stormed planet the station orbited. It was dizzying at first because you believed you were constantly looking down a huge drop-off to the world below.

Liyan got used to it.

The three of them, Lark, Tiri and Liyan, had bought the room for four days.

He wanted to write to Cobalt.

He wanted to describe the view.

But he wasn't sure what to say. He kept procrastinating, thinking too much, avoiding getting his waves.

What words would he use? He couldn't tell Cobalt about Lark and Tiri. It just didn't seem right to say out loud (or in a wave) what he was doing with them, how he was feeling. And what was he feeling? A longing that just would not abate? Cobalt would understand, of course.

Still, he was all tangled up inside and wasn't sure about anything. In the moment all he felt was ecstasy and warmth. But the loneliness inside him remained.

Lark could see it, could always read him. Now they were off-duty with a few vacation days to enjoy. The stars were behind them both at the moment. They had time to gaze into each other's eyes, feel what the other was thinking. Tiri had gone off for a swim. With her permission, they'd stayed behind to make love in the radiant light.

They lay in the aftermath of affection in a pool of red silk sheets, arms and legs tangled, facing the huge window, the black and silver view like a stark winter dream. Lark's chin pressed Liyan's shoulder, breath hot on his neck. His eyelashes swept down Liyan's cheek.

Lark put a gentle hand on his hip, warm and solid. He said, "Go on. Just write to him."

"What?"

"You want to write to him. You need to write to him. It's part of who you are."

Liyan stayed quiet.

"Cobalt is special. I accept that he's in your heart."

"We've met only three times." His voice came rough, small.

"Doesn't matter. You've known each other for years. You knew him before you met me."

"Only days before."

"It's everything. You may not have known it at the time, but he swept you off your feet and sent you into the stars where he couldn't follow. He's still doing it, sweeping you up with intelligence. With kindness. And all his words since. And he's an underdog. Trapped. Someone who needs a hero. Ah, how enticing."

Liyan rolled over and faced him. "But I'm not…a hero." He nuzzled Lark's neck, kissed him there on the heated skin. He smelled of salt, adventure, love. The muscles of Lark's upper arms pressed his own as they embraced, pale amber to tawny gold, and Liyan kissed him.

The stirrings in his body filled him up until he was overflowing with need. He pressed himself tight against Lark as Lark said, "You are a hero to me. You are to him."

Something twisted in his heart. He shut his eyes hard. "I've never been so happy, but I don't know how to say that to him when he's so alone, and so imprisoned in his status. It wouldn't be fair to him."

Lark's hand cupped the back of his neck. "You're a smart guy. You'll know."

"It hurts me to think it might hurt him to know…about us."

"You think his unhappiness means you have to be unhappy, too? That if you aren't alike in your oppression you're somehow less compatible, less friends?"

He opened his eyes and stared into Lark's swimming gaze. So soft. Passion-filled. Reverent. It was like he had just fallen through that big window and into the glittering, precious view.

Lark moved slowly, sliding against him, silky, sweet, and his arms curved under his back. "Tell him," he whispered, "that you finally got yourself well and truly laid. Man to man, how could he not understand that?"

He blinked up into his face. "He would understand. But this is more than…than getting laid." He pressed his lips tight together as he felt his eyes warm.

"Yeah?"

Liyan sighed.

Lark dug a knee between Liyan's legs, pulled him up until their lips brushed. "You. Hell. Just…come here."

Liyan clutched his back as their kisses melted deeper. The light and the sheets encased them in silver and red.

*

Dear Cobalt:

We took a glass shuttle through the Sea of Broken Moons. Me and Tiri and Lark…we're orbiting Drebnot, a roiling, boiling, storm-plagued planet. Yes, people live there but it's dangerous to visit, so we dump supplies via drone ships. A high percentage of those rusted old vessels burn up in the sky but at least you don't have to bury any bodies.

Liyan read the first paragraph out loud. "That's the beginning. Does it sound too cold? Too wordy? Lark?"

Lark was fresh from the shower, still drying off, shaking his wet hair all over everything. "It's fine. Just fine." He sounded bored.

Liyan went back to writing.

We're vacationing on a space station that orbits that massive planetary mess. Once, thousands of years ago, it had five moons. An asteroid storm took them out, breaking them up into a thousand moon-chunks. They litter the space around the planet. Orbiting forever. A million lunar pieces of junk. The Sea of Broken Moons. They glow ominously, giant crumbles of chalk and dust. Some are veined with ore deposits pulsing copper, carnelian and phosphor in the solar light.

128

"So I'm telling him about the moons, right? He always wants to hear about all the places I go."

"Yeah, it's good. All good." Lark patted him on the head as he moved beyond the bed to the bureau to find a shirt.

"But it's not about us."

"Yeah," Lark muttered. "There's nothing in there yet about you getting laid."

Liyan frowned, leaned against the pillows and turned back to his wave screen.

Did I say the shuttle was entirely transparent? It was amazing, like floating in space without a suit. It was actually terrifying at first. I'm used to the big ships, or enclosed shuttles. I worked on shuttles for years, too, but never saw a transparent one until today.

"Hey, Lark, were you kinda freaked by the glass shuttle? Did you feel sorta tipsy?"

"What, like throwing up? Hell, yeah. I hated it."

"It wasn't just me then." Liyan threw him a smile.

"What are you writing, that you wanted to puke? I thought you guys wrote poetry and shit to each other. Stomachs were rolling as we careened through the Sea of Broken Moons. Is that what you're telling him? Sweetheart, that is pure lyricism."

"Are you making fun of me?"

"Never. I'll leave that honor to Tiri."

"Sarcastic ass," Liyan murmured under his breath.

"What was that?"

"Nothing."

"Well, when you get to the good parts, read me those." He tugged on a pair of tight jeans.

Our room looks down on the storm-ridden planet; the bed is by the window. To sleep there brings dreams of falling. It's dizzying but lovely all at once. There is a device to darken the window but we don't use it. We all like the eerie, alien light. It's different from diffused bulkhead light, the constant living glow of the starliner's halls.

"Hmm, that's not good," Liyan said, reading over his words. "If I just say 'our bed' it's like springing information on him without warning, or as if I'm hiding something."

Lark said, "Tiri just messaged she wants pizza. Are you gonna take a shower?"

Liyan put his screen down. "Okay. I'm going." He got up from the bed.

Lark was fiddling with his own screen at a chrome desk by the door, but looked up as Liyan walked across the room. "And yes, you are hiding something," he finally answered.

Liyan said, "I don't want to hurt him…"

"I know that." Lark got up and came to him, putting his arms around him with a strange sigh.

Liyan leaned into his warmth. "But what do you think?"

Lark leaned back with a pained smile and shook his head. "My dearest friend, you don't want to ask *me* that."

*

Dear Cobalt:

This is my second attempt at this wave.
Why do I find this so difficult?
Here is my answer. It is because I love you.
There. Just like that. I've said it.
Now the equally hard part…I love others, too. Lark, Tiri, Sekina. But it is Lark and Tiri I have been spending all my off-hours with. I also sleep with them most nights but not all. It was a long time in coming.

You had asked me of this when we last met. My answer had been honest. I'd never accepted any of their offers to…share our nights. Not then. But now…

I find this difficult to speak of because I still think of you all the time, how we met, how you looked that last time I left you standing in the shuttle lobby in your beautiful long, blue coat with the tails and your eyes so full of my leaving, sparkling with my adventure that you cannot join.

I was so desperately lonely! And Lark…he's so good to me. Good for me. And Tiri and I get along so easily.

I long to see you and talk face to face again. I long for so much that we don't have.

I know you will write me back and say you understand. But my heart hurts still.

One day I will get my own ship. I will find excuses for detours to your out of the way sector, to the poison-sky asteroid of our beginnings. I will see you more often. I promise!

Believe me when I say it. I will have my own ship. Sekina is getting hers within weeks, maybe sooner. We all hate to see her go, but it's such a dream come true. And I will have mine!

And now, about Drebnot and the Sea of Broken Moons from the first letter which I started and aborted.

We rented a room with a vast window overlooking the storm-tossed planet from close orbit…

Liyan pasted parts of the first letter to the second. He did not read it to Lark. In fact, after returning from the space station vacation, he had gone to his own room to compose it in privacy and silence. He had seen a sudden pain in Lark's gaze that first day of their time off, after they'd made love, when he'd asked him his thoughts about keeping their love secret. It was then he knew he was being all-too selfish. Of course Lark would think dark thoughts he did not wish to speak. He might wonder if Liyan really loved him. Or if Liyan thought their relationship would never last.

Liyan's misgivings had always been there from the start. He'd spent years dodging the subtle and sweet seductions of Lark and Tiri. They were all aware of that fact.

Now, he didn't want complications. He simply wanted to ride the wave of bliss for awhile without over-thinking everything.

But of course it was not that easy. Life always came in tangles and knots and puzzles. Griefs and pleasures. Risks and frustrations.

He finished the letter. This time he signed it in a different way from his usual tried and true, six-year-old formula.

I think of you all the time, as if you are here with me, at my side.

Love,
Liyan

*

Dear Liyan:

I can't tell you what it means to me that you are so sensitive to my feelings.

But please relax. Please enjoy your life. You are years away from me, not to mention the obvious hundreds or thousands of light-years between us at all times.

Your waves mean much to me. All your waves. What would hurt me? If you could not speak freely to me, if you didn't write because you felt uncomfortable concerning my response, that would hurt me.

Never fear that I will judge or reject you. Not for anything.

I am entirely gratified to hear that your relationship with Lark and Tiri is so good for you. Believe me when I say it comforts me to know you are well looked after by people who love you.

I congratulate you on this new turn in your life.

Please just don't stop writing to me about anything…everything. If you must move on, though, I will understand. But I fervently hope not.

I had never heard of transparent shuttles until your wave. Magnificent! Proof of how an unfortunate cataclysm such as the destruction of a planet's moons and its subsequent life-condition alteration can also be looked upon as a site of accidental beauty.

You must have been in foldspace before this wave was sent, for I see it is dated weeks ago. Therefore I must ask, is Sekina now captain of her own ship? Did she get one of the exploration models she wanted or is it another cargo/passenger starliner? Does she still work for C&C? (I see in my research they have exploration vessels as well.)

*I have no reservations that you will have your own starliner one day. Of course you will **not** risk command to make false detours into my sector. But I enjoy the thought.*

Give Lark and Tiri my regards.

Breathe easy. And conquer those stars.

Love,
Cobalt

*

Part Four

18. Winterworld

Dear Cobalt:

Our last venture was to Arcturus which resulted in too much Azelfafage wine (which is a hideous shade of orange and tastes like soured water with a bitter, ashy afterburn) and Lark returning to the starliner wearing a too-small t-shirt that said: **BE BOLD, NOT BORING.** *The problem was nobody knew for sure that's what it said because it was in Arcturan, which no one reads anymore. He relied on the word of one vendor when he bought it. This was a vendor who sold him a size 2X that looked like a medium when it came out of the package.*

It didn't fit him. He didn't care. "I love this shirt," he insisted.

He was bold indeed, I told him, to even wear it. He decided I'd called him fat. I said, "You're not fat. That shirt's too small." He stopped speaking to me. That lasted five minutes.

I say the trip was uneventful because it was more of a tourist trap with nothing to see and endless shops vying to take your money, all carrying the same products. I don't know how these people make a living. Except Tiri helped the economy a bit. She bought lots of silver rings. One for every finger. One for me. One for Lark. And a lovely wide band for you. She didn't know your size so she bought one that adjusts. It will take months to reach you, but I've already sent it. It's quite nice. Pure sterling. Catches the Arcturan light like a mirror. I captured some of that light and put it in the box along with the ring. (No! Really! Wait until you get it.)

We weren't bold on this trip despite Lark's shirt. We were bored. Or maybe boring. I hate shopping. And the food was bland. Azelfafage wine is also not worth the price.

We also missed Sekina. She usually comes with us on these crazy jaunts. She's off captaining her explorer ship, the one she always dreamt of, the **Dar-alon**. It is a C&C ship but in a different division of the company. Their logo? A dragon with wings instead of a horse.

We all wave her often.

Love,
Liyan

*

Dear Liyan:

I cannot recall ever receiving a present before. I look forward to the ring. And the captured light???

Certainly, my owners Pela and Pel have in the past provided me with all I need, clothing, food, shelter, but I feel I have earned those things. They are not gifts to my mind. The tips I receive when I bartend are also earned.

When you have visited, the meals you bought me felt a bit like gifts. Once Pela bought me a silver bracelet I still wear. That is the closest I have ever come to the experience.

That…and the gift of your friendship, your waves.

Please tell Tiri I thank her for thinking of me. She sounds like a generous, amazing person.

On the topic of shopping, I only accompanied Pela a few times on excursions. It was nice to get out. She was not very picky and bought just about anything that caught her eye. Much of it remained forgotten in boxes in her vast closet space. If she ever bought me clothing, it was all chosen by her. I had no freedom in that.

Pel gives me more freedom. It would never occur to him to take me shopping but I have accounts where I can order what I need, and a yearly budget. Maybe that sounds generous, but remember I have no salary. I have never yet exceeded the budget. I like choosing clothing that is different but stylish, thus the tails on jackets. I like a streamlined style and something also somewhat formal for the hotel work. If there are gold buttons and dashes of color or brocade on *pockets, collars or trouser seams, so much the better. Tell Lark I have never owned a t-shirt.*

Believe it or not, we actually have a couple of bottles of Azelfafage wine at Rory's. Just in case anyone ever orders it, we can say, "Yes, we have that." No one ever has. The price tag is very high. Whether or not it is worth the high price is beside the point. Its rarity creates its value. But I think its color is off-putting even to the rich. It looks like dirty orange soda with a sort of radiant, hot glint. People do not even like to look at it.

But you can say you have actually tried it! That is one step further on your exotic journey.

I look forward to my gift.

Love,
Cobalt

*

Dear Cobalt:

Icehenge. The glamour of snow.

We put into orbit at Icehenge for three days, dropping off skiers and cargo.

Lark, Tiri and I went to one of the snow lodges for a day of skiing and a night of mulled wine and toasted marshmallows in the lodge lobby.

I grew up on a farm, flatlands with mild temps year round, the sea close by, and no snow. Of course at the station in our controlled environment there was never 'weather'. So I have never been skiing in my life!

Let me tell you. It is cold. It is wet. It hurts when you fall. And yet I love the snow. I love the glimmering of the ice, the graceful peaks and swells of ice cream-like snow so white you can become blind from staring at it. Icehenge has tidal waves of snow thousands of miles long. A winter planet with year-round glacial views. They have slopes for the daring and slopes (like the ones I used) for those who cannot slide more than a few yards without slipping and landing on their ass.

They do have seasons there. They have their storm season when the wind whips over the snow and changes the landscape so that all the inhabitants must remap their respective townships. They have a melt season when the snow becomes slushy and what little native wildlife exists is more prevalent. Those who chose to colonize this planet are certainly creative and imaginative. They farm indoors with grow lights. They fish through deep holes in the icy earth, or in the cold rivers that barely flow past the frozen waterfalls. It's a world of popsicles, parkas and permafrost. If you haven't learned to sled and skate by the time you're two, something is off.

I did love this world. I loved getting out into the crisp air, then coming in to the fire, sitting in a soft, big chair and getting cozy by a hearth. From icy winds to roaring flames, either way faces glow.

I passed two more tests in the past two months, both in command training. I'm slowly making my way.

Lark, though a front-line officer, never took his commander tests awhile back when he started to study for them, says he has no such ambition but I think perhaps he's simply lazier than I.

Tiri likes the pay raises but also has no desire to be the boss. Too much responsibility, she says. She likes to work, then leave it behind on her off-duty hours. She doesn't want the day/night worries of it all. She likes to think of herself as a goof-off, but she's damn smart at anything she tackles and always likes to lead.

I like challenges. And I have many ideas. I like to think a lot. Maybe too much. I don't mind asking people to check on data, research, new technologies. I already oversee a bridge crew of five. I like getting things done. I like having results go my way. It's such a satisfying feeling.

Have you received the ring yet? We sent it Star-express, but it can take up to six weeks. Or more. Mail is treated as non-essential and the mail ships do not travel in straight-forward routes the way passenger ships do. They may make many stop-offs and pick ups before reaching certain destinations.

Love,
Liyan

*

Dear Liyan:

No ring yet. I look for it every day by Star-mail. I have never received any Star-mail in my life, only local packages for things I have needed such as clothing. Your package will be an event for me.

I have never seen snow. My former owner, Pela, never took me on any of her further travels to more exotic climates than the city where we lived, and Pel never seems to go anywhere and if he did, he wouldn't take me with him. We have no relationship at all other than boss-subordinate on a master-slave level.

Icehenge sounds beautiful, serene, and very cold. What an intrigue.

Everything here is the same as always. The Grand Aurora Hotel does not change. It is merely a stop-off point between destinations. As you know. The guests come and go at an alarmingly quick rate. There are the usual dramas or melodramas. Most are benign. However, there was a fire on the fourth floor that did some damage. It was easily contained. There were no injuries. The cause: a customer with a homemade cooking device that exploded.

I am bartending more often now, about five nights a week for several hours. On holidays the revelry is anxious but the tips are good. The cash tips (not the credited ones) are the only money Pel has recently allowed me to have other than the account I have for ordering necessities such as clothing and toiletries. It is illegal for androids to have their own money but this is untraceable cash and Pel seems unconcerned. I save it all but I don't know what I am saving for. I will never travel. I will never need to pay rent. There is nothing I need that the hotel itself (and Pel) does not provide, including novels or movies for the days I have a few hours to myself that are not for sleeping. I suppose when the amount grows to a respectable portion after many years of collecting these frivolous tips, I could give it away to a charity of my choice.

138

Thinking about money causes me to realize that my life, though not truly my own, is at least not one of poverty. I have only had two owners and they, of course, have been wealthy since only the extremely wealthy can afford us. I have known only the best of accommodations, food and accessories. At the very least, I have never been cold. I have never starved.

I encourage you to continue with your studies to rise in rank. As I have always said, you have the aptitude to attain your dreams. You will do well in all that you desire.

Love,
Cobalt

*

Dear Cobalt:

No package yet?
Now I'm afraid the item is lost. It has been a long, long time.
I know you were looking forward to this mail. I have tracked it but lost it somewhere between Procyon and the Region of the Arm of Suns. The original supply boat was scrapped. All its contents were transferred to other liners. Who knows where it went from there? Someone didn't do their job in inventory.

It could still yet show up. It was insured but that's not the point.

Your last wave disturbed me some, I should admit. You stated you've not known what it is like to be poor. And yet you are not a free man. You must do whatever you're told. You cannot own a bank account. That is poverty, my friend. For a human being with dreams and feelings, it is unconscionable.

There is this division in my heart. I roam the stars. I have followed my own heart and gotten the position in life I dreamed of by studying hard and working hard. I love star-travel; the liner itself is a home where I have come to know every surface, every scratch and scuff mark, every scent from hydroponics to engineering to the cool tang of the nav labs. I have forged good, strong friendships of loyalty

139

and love. I see beauty, hear strange languages, taste new vintages and breathe in alien atmospheres. My dreams are slurries of green sunsets and giant swans and robot gods.

And yet...I feel I have left something behind. A part of myself. It is the part of myself that is you, the image you sent me to space with, the intelligent man standing behind the bar with blue hair pouring purple drinks for people who take for granted their rights and their freedoms. The man who longed as I do for possibilities beyond the stars, but who can only imagine them while I move among them. It is the part of me who is confined, trapped, and no amount of tugging sets it free.

Have I ever told you I sometimes dream I am an android? That I can't study what I wish or go where I please? That I am forced into labor of someone else's choosing forever? I wake sweating and scared from those nightmares.

I haven't told you the long hours of talks I had with my friends over the years, conversations about this very subject, the problem and how to fix it. None of us are lawyers or politicians. We have little clue how to even broach the subject on any world, let alone the galaxy as a whole, as to the rights of those indentured beings which should be automatic.

I haven't spoken of our talks because we never come up with any solutions. There is no point in talk when it is all only talk, when there is no workable answer to the problem. When we all just shake our heads and say, "It's too bad. It really should be different."

What is manufactured belongs, I guess, to the manufacturer. There are no loopholes to be gotten around. I've studied the problem from all angles and read the works of others who've studied it, as I'm sure you have as well. And the added hurdle is that this problem is underlined by the fact that it is created by and for the very wealthy. There is little hope, and no historical evidence, for fighting the powerfully rich (and I mean so rich the money cannot even be counted) and winning. It isn't done. It can't be done. Wealth and power always wins even if the little guy is in the right.

Thus, my nightmares.

And the division inside me.

I want you here. I think there would be a place for you on this ship, or any other. The destiny of the stars lies in your eyes. The last time we parted at the shuttle port I saw the glimmer there in your gaze, that great and anxious yearning, and there was nothing I could do but turn away and leave. It cuts me. It makes the ache in me to pursue my dreams all the stronger, and yet it never goes away because I keep thinking of that thing I left behind, that man, that part of me suffused with you in our simple exchange, our first meeting, when I promised to wave.

Well, I am continuing my studies when Lark isn't trying to sabotage me. He thinks I'll leave him and Tiri if I get command. But anywhere I go I'd bring them along, if they will continue to have me. Because I vow never to leave any friend behind. And if I could keep that vow with you, my life would be complete.

Love,
Liyan

*

19. Light from a Dead Sun, and Darkness

Cobalt printed the last wave he'd gotten from Liyan and kept it folded into a tight square in the back pocket of his trousers. He had it memorized, of course, but knowing it was there, feeling the edges of the square whenever he dipped a fingertip past the pocket seam and ran it across the silky paper made it seem like more than just a thought in a letter. It felt like hope. It was ridiculous, that feeling, but it gave him a sense of fullness of being he'd never had before.

He had the letter with him when he greeted hotel guests, when he mixed drinks at Rory's, and even when he met Pel's clients late at night in the top floor penthouse. His pants might end up in a chair or on the floor, but the letter itself was never far from him.

For days after receiving Liyan's wave, Cobalt's actions blurred. Everything seemed hazy, all his work, his thoughts, and the faces of the guests. Even their voices came to him as if from a distance, the tones and cadences of speech swimming in his head with nonsense until he often had to ask people to repeat their questions.

He became overly aware of color and scent. Bright reds stood out in crowds of otherwise blended pastel yellows, pinks, blues intermixed with black blazers, leather jackets, silver scarves. Outworlders were immediately identified by the dank, liquid scent on their skin and hair from the artificial air of the shuttles. Acrid hints of burnt metal identified the rocket yard workers who often came to Rory's to get drunk before bed. Whenever he saw them, he thought of Liyan. Maybe Liyan knew some of them, or they knew him. But he had said he'd never hung out with that crowd. And that first night they'd met, Liyan did not smell of the engines, or the vapors of their fuels.

Cobalt stood at the concierge desk in the lobby dreamily watching the people when one of the backroom clerks approached. He cleared his vision, catching the woman's still, green eyes with his own.

Zim had worked at the hotel for two years. They knew each other only by name and sight. Mostly, she stayed to herself, her brown bangs always hanging too long over her eyes. Her job did not require interaction with patrons and her social skills lacked sparkle. Now she came right up to him and set a package on the black desktop.

In her usual monotone, she said, "This was in the back room. It came this morning and it has your name on it. It's Star-mail. Aren't your deliveries always local? Does Pel know?"

Cobalt's heart skipped. He felt his stomach heat with the adrenalin of excitement. He took the package in his hand and looked at it. Without meeting her eyes again, he said, "Pel knows. I've been expecting it. It was presumed lost."

"Well, now it's found." Without anymore interest on her part, she turned and walked through a group of travelers passing toward the elevators, and went behind registration to the back rooms where she processed incoming and outgoing mail and bills on a small wave screen on a corner kiosk.

Cobalt held the parcel which weighed almost nothing but was heavy with meaning. This parcel had been touched, packed and mailed by Liyan, Lark and Tiri. He imagined he could still feel the warm imprints of their hands and fingers on the heavily banded, heat and cold-proofed cardboard box. On the front surface of the box were a dozen or so machine stamps stating when and where the box changed hands and traveled by different ships through different star systems until it finally found itself here in his hand. He saw a stamp for Arcturus. Azelfafage. Procyon. Mesarthim. And ship names: Kraken. Demios. Spacewitch. The package certainly had gone far astray. He saw the address label, faded, but printed in Liyan's careful script: Cobalt, c/o Grand Aurora Hotel, Asteroid 1191782, DiamondVoid XP.

He wanted privacy to open it. He knew he would not get it.

He opened a drawer, took out a pair of scissors, and clipped the bands. Then he slipped one side of the scissors into a sealed, side flap, pressing hard to get it to open.

A customer asked him directions to the hotel restaurant. He paused and gave the answer. Another came to inquire about outside local food establishments. Most of the questions he fielded were about food or drink or entertainment, all number one human concerns.

When the box was opened, he upended it and the contents slipped onto the desk. One was a thickly, tissue-wrapped item. The other a small, black plastic box. He opened the box first.

The silver band gleamed at him from its velvet notch. He took it out, held the smooth, cold metal between his fingers. It was an open-ended circle, which meant it could be

143

squeezed or pried apart to fit him. But when he slipped it on the middle finger of his left hand, it already fit him perfectly. It felt cool against his skin. He'd worn very little jewelry in his life, and never any rings. This one flashed brightly in the indoor hotel lighting, a curved design that tapered cleanly at the edges.

The next item felt heavier. He got the tissue unraveled while answering two more customer questions, and at last he held in his palm a piece of triangular crystal. It was fused with flashing colors of pinks, purples and yellows. He noticed within the tissue wrapping was a note. He picked it up and read.

The vendor on Arcturus swore this crystal came from the heart of a dead sun and is millions of years old. I thought it was simply pretty. I told you I'd send you light if I could. This is the best I could find.

Searching
in the tumbling golden galaxies
for the sky

Love,
Liyan

"Sir? Sir?" More customers came, lining up.

Cobalt glanced up. How long had he been staring at the crystal? Many of the faces before him looked annoyed.

He answered all their questions, gave them directions, maps, advice, and the rest of the day rushed by without note, but also without his full attention.

When the dinner hour came, he escaped to his rooms to immediately wave Liyan.

Dear Liyan:

The package has arrived. I received the ring and crystal intact. In fact the box, only a bit faded, had barely a scratch and bragged stamps from all over the galaxy. What a journey it must have taken. It's been over six months since you sent it.

I love the contents more than you can know. Thank you for the piece of dead sun. It is amazingly thoughtful, and a beautiful crystal, no matter where it's from (and I like to think it really is from a star.) Thank Lark and Tiri, too. The ring fits my middle finger with no need to adjust it whatsoever.

Your waves are everything to me, but with this package I feel I have received a piece of your journey itself.

This gift, and your last wonderful wave to me have distracted me from my work, but all in a good way since my life, lately, is highly unexciting. I intensely need distraction.

I'll treasure these gifts always.

Love,
Cobalt

*

Cobalt kept turning his hand up, looking at the ring even as he entered the elevator and came out on the top floor.

Everything gleamed, the elevator mirrors and lights just before the doors closed, the buttery penthouse sconces and lamps, the pink wine on the foyer table, but nothing so bright as his silver gift.

Juneau came forward to greet him, dressed impeccably in gray silks, scent intrinsic of sterile office spaces and stale compressed air. He lorded over an empire of investment conglomerates and corporations. Other than the flat line of his mouth and hard, cruel eyes, he was a handsome man, clean-lined, slender, tall. Clever, too. But as spoiled as they came with a sadistic leaning that spoke some lack of ego…or empathy.

"You're late."

Cobalt knew he was within a minute of the specified meeting time. He said nothing.

"You'll make up for the minutes, of course," he continued, moving toward the table, pouring two glasses of wine, the liquid ringing the crystal with little splashes.

Juneau insisted on routines, as if they added to his ability to control his surroundings. As if they were civilized. He liked Cobalt to come to him well-dressed, and fresh with a single brand of high-end men's cologne he provided. He paid for thousand dollar bottles of wine which he shared not because he was generous, but because he liked showing off. He ordered and controlled everything within his sight. He was not a nice man, but he was even-tempered. He had never hurt Cobalt out of anger. He did it because he liked to. Because he could.

He had never been happy after Pel had threatened him with fines if Cobalt ever turned up injured. He wanted to control even Pel, and there had been instances of rare fines that Juneau decided in advance he would pay. He told Cobalt he thought of the fines as part of the price of renting him from Pel, a price he insisted was far too high. "But that is the least of my worries," he'd told Cobalt once, "because I have more money than I'll spend in a 1000 lifetimes."

Cobalt often wondered why Juneau, with such immense wealth, didn't just buy an android to own, vat-grown and made completely to his specifications.

But it seemed, unfortunately, he merely enjoyed renting them out.

It was nothing for Juneau to pay for the treatment for a broken wrist one night when he'd twisted Cobalt's arm a little too hard behind his back. Or to pay for laser heat treatments on a couple of bruised ribs.

146

Cobalt dreaded these evenings with Juneau, glad they only came about once a month. But tonight he was in a better mood. The ring against the skin of his finger felt like wonder, awe, life. This was merely a moment contained within a span of vastness that diluted this scene, and Juneau was irrelevant. The folded letter in his back pocket and those memorized words seemed to surround him with a sort of protective veil. *I want you here. I think there would be a place for you on this ship, or any other. The destiny of the stars lies in your eyes,* Liyan had written. He was always able to go through the motions required of him but his real life, his reality and dreams as a living being flourished apart from all of this.

He drank the fine wine and it went into his system like warm fire. It was quite good. Even Juneau's mood seemed to lift as a result of alcohol.

The older man's dark hair glimmered. His eyes actually seemed to warm. The room flickered in soft rose light. Cobalt could smell fresh lilies by the door and the soft, alien cleansers used on the silk sheets of the newly turned bed. Despite tension, there was a beauty here in the wine, the elegance of velvet curtains and pillows, the sheen of the parquet floors.

And then Juneau was talking, which he rarely did, of a young girl he once knew in his early years, before he'd made a man of himself. "Lyra was her name and she had a way about her that made the rest of reality, all planets, systems, stars vanish when she was nearby, when I could hear her, smell her, when her palms touched my back. She loved to paint. She died of a sudden aneurism at age 21. Proof that the cold of the universe is all that suckles our souls."

Cobalt said, "You loved her."

"Love." Juneau's eyes half-closed as he shook his head. "A trick of light. A chemical reaction."

"You loved her and you don't believe in love."

"Exactly."

"But what you had was real."

"A wisp. A delusion. A nice memory. It can be manufactured. Put into a drink. Like this wine here."

Cobalt stared at the last pink tints in his glass. "Maybe the transitory feeling can be captured. But not the actual personality of a unique love."

He laughed. "What do you know of love?"

Cobalt didn't answer. All he thought of was that Juneau had somehow spiked the wine. Perhaps he used Enchantment, the same drug Tiri had used in a night club on one of Liyan's first stopovers on an alien world.

He could feel a heated rush throughout his body. He looked up with hot eyes at a man who'd lost so much at a young age from sheer chance, an unforeseen and tragic fate, and who compensated now by leaving nothing to chance, dispelling all emotion and trying to control every aspect of his empire.

This man had hurt him. This man had become an exaggerated character of the protective armor grief had given him. Nothing was left now but that armor. Their eyes met for a moment, locked. Cobalt breathed out slowly, forehead tensing. Juneau's lips twitched.

"Don't ever feel sorry for me, android. I have everything. I even have you for tonight. I can even make you want me as you never have in the past."

The ring on Cobalt's finger rested heavy on his skin. The barrier of the letter in his back pocket could not be denied. But he did not argue with his customer.

He got up. He went to Juneau. He leaned down and he kissed him full on the mouth. He tasted of the wine, and of emptiness. Some voids did not even have stars.

But the kiss was returned and a kind of false flame manufactured itself between them that defined a blush, a need, but nothing more.

Maybe this night would not be so full of resentment, or hate. Or lust for control. There would never be affection. But maybe there would be a kind of relaxation from the usual tension.

Cobalt carefully undid Juneau's tie, knowing the man liked everything neat and slow. He rushed nothing. Through it all, he demanded respect and/or silence.

More kisses. Never affectionate. They were about domination. About ownership. Cobalt had never initiated them before, but tonight Juneau encouraged it, no doubt his initial plan when he'd drugged the wine.

He liked Cobalt to undress him and neatly fold every article of clothing before putting it aside.

Cobalt did all that. And then it was his turn to be undressed.

A spycam might easily have mistaken them for lovers. But the time they took with each other, and the kissing, was all an act. Paid for. Previously rehearsed over the years. Despite their cold arrangement, they knew each other's bodies well.

Juneau, though well into his late 40s, had a fit, firm body, broader than Cobalt's, hard-edged, angular. He used his power, both mentally and physically, without hesitation. Cobalt's role was to submit to anything he wanted. Juneau, being a sadist, enjoyed watching another's discomfort.

But tonight seemed different. Maybe it was the drugged wine. Cobalt's relaxed manner. The pink, low lighting. Or maybe it was just a random mood. But Juneau fell back against the satin softness of the bed, the plush pillows, and pulled Cobalt to him as he never had before. A fever heightened his kisses. There was pleasure for both of them, a rare thing for Cobalt. They caressed in this manner for quite some time, easy, peaceful. Juneau did not act with his usual forcefulness or urgency. He lingered over Cobalt's body as if admiring it.

Cobalt decided it had to be the drug. Juneau had never once pretended to admire him except as an object to toy with.

Tonight there was more exploration, and a certain pleasurable, lethargic sensation.

Juneau said quietly, without looking at him, "You aren't that different." His hand ran warmly up Cobalt's thigh.

"From what?"

"From human."

"I am human."

"The legalities of that are...never mind." He kissed Cobalt gently on the side of the mouth as his hand stroked between his legs. Cobalt had never known him to do anything like this. While his body responded, a tension of mistrust remained deep within him. His heart beat a steady pulse at the bottom of his throat. Playing with Juneau, no matter how Cobalt responded, was never about anyone but Juneau. And their 'almost' conversations never led anywhere.

But a contemplative, dreamy Juneau certainly was odd. He spent the next hour bringing pleasure to Cobalt, oblivious, or perhaps simply unconcerned with the fact that Cobalt was incapable of relaxing with him. The fact that he responded at all came as a surprise.

The drug, of course.

In some ways it was a good change of pace for them. And yet, disconcerting. Still, it made it easier to give himself for Juneau's pleasure when the time came. He wasn't relaxed, so it still hurt, but he was suffused with a kind of liquid heat. His skin felt pliable, steamy. Juneau's body against his seemed to melt and there came wave after wave of shivering sweetness, like an awakening.

He closed his eyes and saw warm stars. Flung galaxies with octopus-like arms. Ships of amber, burning lights. Quasars of rainbow smoke.

In this whirlpool, his mind spun. Dizzy. Drunk.

Juneau laughed in a way that Cobalt did not believe could exist without cruelty, but it was light and airy this time, and he felt an echo of it in his abdomen filling him up, making him want to explode.

150

It figured it would take a powerful drug to make a man like Juneau open his heart against the sham of wealth, the legacies of grief, the disinterest of an unreal man, and the addiction of living for control.

At best it was comical if not downright pathetic.

Cobalt saw the stars dip and wheel. Flame caressed his back. Something quested within him. Turned him inside-out. Singed his soul. He cried out making Juneau press harder.

He had not felt pleasure like this...ever. Not even with the kind and patient Saber.

Juneau laughed again, body trembling, and when he was done he said to Cobalt, "I own you tonight." Fingers pressed a bit too hard in his side. "I've tried to buy you wholly but Pel will not sell."

Shock rippled through him, pulling him out of his daze. Though it was Pel who rented him for this with seemingly no conscience, he could not have been more grateful to the man in the moment for saying 'no' to Juneau. This had been an unspoken fear of Cobalt's for a long time now. Who knew how much Juneau might have offered? It would have been easy for Pel to pocket the fortune and turn his back on him. Perhaps Cobalt had made himself invaluable in other ways to Pel. To the Aurora. He hoped that was the case.

Juneau peered at him with tight eyes. The room swam with fuzzy light, the tinted lamps like candles, the fake moonlight striping the velvet drapes bronze. He smelled wine and salt and Juneau's spiced cologne. The satin pillows embraced him, everything a luxury, but inside a strange panic fluttered.

"Don't look so happy about that, android." Juneau's voice came low, steady but cool.

Cobalt did not reply. He could barely imagine the horror of being fully owned by this man.

Tense lips smiled. "Oh, wipe that look. You might like life with me. You liked this just now, didn't you?"

But there had been drugs involved. Veins on fire. Cobalt closed his eyes. The warmth of Juneau pressed against him but now all he longed for was a shower.

"Look at me when I talk to you."

His eyes opened.

"It's only a matter of time before Pel bends. Everyone has their price. It might not be money, but maybe something else they love even more."

"But why would you want...this? Me?" Cobalt asked, straining to keep his voice from shaking.

Dark brows rose.

"You despise me," Cobalt added.

"Despise you? No. But then I could do anything I wanted with you. To you. Anything." He bent suddenly and bit him hard on the shoulder. Cobalt jerked away.

"You little bitch. Don't flinch from me!"

After reaching an almost tentative compatibility it shouldn't have surprised Cobalt that Juneau would turn on him this way, threatening, controlling, cruel. There was only one way with Juneau. Submission.

"I'm sorry," Cobalt said quietly.

"And why wouldn't you want to go with me? I'm wealthy. I can offer everything. What, you can't take a little roughhousing? You're too sensitive for my whims? In an android, that's ridiculous. You don't really care...or is it that you'd never see your pretty friend again?"

"What?"

"That man you were with when I saw you walking outside...was it two years ago maybe? I didn't know Pel ever let you out. Is that pretty one special in some way? Does he rent you often? Well, he would be history, of course."

Now a different kind of heat shuddered through him at the thought that Juneau might be threatening Liyan.

"So who is he?" Juneau asked casually.

"I don't remember who you're talking about."

Quick fingers clasped around his throat, jerking Cobalt's head forward until their chins almost met. "Don't lie to me." The hand against his pulse tightened. "I can easily find out anyway."

A bitter taste climbed the back of his throat as Juneau leaned into the grip. The pressure caught at his breath and he realized the man was pressing against his windpipe. If he bruised him, Juneau would be fined. But to Juneau a fine was nothing.

"I can find him. I can do pretty much anything, you know. All it takes is money. And will." His hand choked him now, pushing him back against the cool sheets. Cobalt tried to gasp as he fell onto his back, knees bending.

"Anything could happen to your lovely friend, that young and shiny-eyed man. Maybe that would be Pel's price? Eh?"

Cobalt had his hands pressed against Juneau's chest now. The palm at his throat completely cut his air. In a moment the room would begin to spin. In his mind he saw Liyan smiling, trusting, greeting Juneau on the street as a friend. He thought about his friend's career, how faraway he was and yet, could one rich man's whim possibly stretch that far?

He tried to inhale. Only pain gripped him, and crushing weight. Using all his heightened android strength, he pushed Juneau back.

It was forbidden for an android to raise a hand against any human for any reason. Even self-defense. That was what he'd been taught. An android convicted of such behavior could be put down for good. But he couldn't help himself. He pushed hard, kicked with his feet, and Juneau went flying with a powerful yell off the bed and landed with a satisfying thump on the hard, parquet, penthouse floor.

Cobalt sat up, gasping, trying to catch his breath. He rubbed at his throat, coughing, leaning over the side of the bed and nearly throwing up. Groans came from the floor on the other side of the mattress.

Cobalt scooted to the foot of the bed, pushing himself onto his feet. He swayed, realizing that Juneau had possibly hurt him more than he thought. Lights flickered at the corners of his eyes. Beyond them encroached a heavy blackness.

He turned toward the table and his clothes. He needed to get out. But as he started forward, hands grabbed his ankles tripping him up. He fell hard, wincing and suddenly Juneau was on him.

"You could die for what you just did!" he hissed. He grabbed Cobalt's throat with both hands now, naked and straddling him. He pressed his fingers viciously into his neck.

It seemed a thousand thoughts passed through his mind in a single moment. Who would miss him if he died? Liyan? Pel? It would be an end to many things, slavery, longing, a humanity that was denied him. If he were gone, Liyan would not be in any position to be threatened by Juneau. Liyan had Lark and Tiri now. They would take good care of him. And for what he had just done, pushing Juneau, assaulting him, he could be tried and convicted, put down or imprisoned for life. The nightmare would never end. But now? Everything could end. The blessing of that could not be denied.

Juneau leaned down. "You are nothing. Never forget that! Nothing!"

His fingers curled into fists and he felt the cool, twinkling presence of the ring. A symbol for friendship, for freedom. In a strangled voice he could barely mouth any words. But he managed two. He heard them as if they filled the hazy air of the room in a fervent cry. Pleading. Decisive. "Kill me."

Juneau's voice seemed to hover on the word 'nothing' as his mouth twisted before Cobalt's fading vision. He felt his head wrenched back as he choked, trying, then failing to gain one more breath.

154

Everything went dark.

*

To Liyan:

You are one of the only people I can locate who may be a friend to Cobalt. I found your address on his computer.

If he means anything to you, you will want to know that he is in hospital as I write this. His condition is critical.

The story is difficult to put together, but he has been attacked and assaulted by a client of the hotel.

He is in good care on life support. The coma is induced to prevent brain damage. The end result is unknown. He may or may not awake.

I can supply updates at your request whenever you write to the address at the end of this wave.

I am very sorry for this news.

Pel
Grand Aurora Hotel
Asteroid 1191782
Diamond Void XP

*

20. Green as Android Tears

For the first time in his life he had gone far away, on a dark journey beyond the very stars where he dreamed to touch the slender night.

You could not touch a star. Its breath was a trillion condensed infernos. Its agenda: to consume. But somewhere in the back of his mind he saw himself holding a pink and bronze crystal that claimed to be one.

155

He came to rest in a windy void. In a distance of blue light dotted with black suns he was tossed and spun, neither hot nor cold. The sound of the wind crashed around him pulling his hair back, but he barely felt it. Sometimes the wind came filled with echoing voices too distorted to understand. He heard a pounding as if fists beat on a locked door. After an unspecified amount of time, he had a thought it might be his own heart. The sounds of life, it seemed, had followed him into death.

The void held no scent, only an electric flicker against his face, arms and legs.

At times the feeling of falling overtook him along with stabbing tugs of panic. He wondered if he fell forever would he eventually break up into a million pieces flying in all directions into infinity? He tried to curl his body into a ball, the screams in his mind accompanying his strange plummet.

Occasionally, the depthless blue light soothed his mind but most of the time the nightmare had full control. He swirled on the edge of sanity.

Off and on he would hear Juneau's voice. "You're late." "You're nothing."

A piece of folded paper pressed the back pocket of his slacks. He could feel the sharp corners, the thickness of the letter, the density of the words he knew by heart.

The last time we parted at the shuttle port I saw the glimmer there in your gaze, that great and anxious yearning, and there was nothing I could do…

He could actually hear Liyan speaking those written words, see him with that always errant fringe of bangs hanging low in his honey-brown eyes.

He was here in this turquoise space for a reason. To free Liyan. And to protect Liyan. To keep him safe.

From far off he heard whispers and shouts. Sometimes they spoke his name. "Co…co…balt…balt."

Even if he'd wanted to reply, he had no voice. The only sounds he could make were in his mind.

156

Sometimes he felt flutters, as if fingers touched his arms. Once he reached out into space and the gesture knocked against something invisible and hard.

No night. No day. He never remembered if he slept.

After a million years and some, a yellow crescent moon appeared growing slowly closer. Closer. When it bumped him, it wrapped itself around him cradling, rocking. It had a warmth he didn't know he'd missed.

He finally slept, woke, slept again. Woke to a voice saying over and over, "Take my hand."

He felt fingers interwoven with his own. A cool smoothness of metal twisted against his middle finger. The broken circle. The silver 'O' that connected him to longing, kindness, love.

He opened his eyes to a sting of light. He saw a familiar profile, strong chin, white-clad shoulder, hair the color of autumn leaves. His fingers curled against a warm hand.

No, he thought. *It isn't safe.*

But it was too late. He was still alive.

Liyan's head turned to face him, lips parting in a full smile but the dark eyes remained sad. "We almost lost you." His free hand came up to cup the side of his head. Cobalt felt the heat on his skin, the palm pushing back his limp hair.

He opened his mouth to speak but only air whooshed from his lungs.

"Don't try to talk yet. Your new voice box needs to settle in first."

His first question was 'how long?' Liyan seemed to read his mind.

"It's been a while, Cobalt. A long while. Pel waved me when you were hurt. It took me weeks to get here. I couldn't get away at first. Then I had to find a ship heading to this sector. There were none. My captain couldn't afford a detour. So Sekina came, her agenda being more flexible. You would've liked to see her hair. It was orange and pink stripes.

She brought me in her ship as far as the space station. From there I shuttled in. You've been in a coma for seven weeks."

Cobalt let that information sink in. Seven weeks. A new voice box. What else had Juneau damaged? If only Juneau had been a bit more determined. But of course he would not complete Cobalt's final wish. Cobalt had asked to die. Juneau obeyed no one but himself. Probably the fact that he'd asked to die had ensured he lived.

He glanced around, seeing the shining equipment, the clean, white walls, the green-edged sky beyond the half-open curtains.

"You're getting the best of care," Liyan assured him gently.

Of course he was. Juneau was paying for it as a part of his fine to Pel. He would have everything he needed to continue his life of servitude. And if it was Juneau's goal to buy him, one day he would succeed.

Cobalt turned to stare at the window where a pane of glass stood between him and the outside which was still a cage encased by a double force-field. He decided humans wore too many skins.

Liyan said softly, "Hey. You'll be okay."

But Cobalt didn't move. His vision misted. He closed his eyes. His hand in Liyan's grip started to shake.

He would never be free. Never.

*

The blue light void came back, but he woke from it more often now before slipping away.

Liyan stayed. How many days had Liyan been at his side? He was afraid to ask.

He began to eat again. The first words he finally managed to speak were: "You have to go back. To space."

Liyan stared at him for a moment, then said, "Good to hear your voice. Now shut up."

158

"But…how long have you been here?"

Liyan shook his head. "I've accumulated a lot of leave time so don't worry about it."

"Will there be a trial?" he asked.

"A trial? For Juneau?"

"No. For what I did to Juneau."

"What did *you* do to him? He's the one who nearly killed you! He should be locked up. Instead, he's merely paying restitution. And I've heard with his wealth that's not a hardship for him to bear."

Cobalt swallowed heavily. It seemed perhaps Juneau had not told the full story. So he would not be imprisoned. He would not be tried and convicted for raising his hand to a pure human.

Juneau's threats or Juneau's pride. One never knew which might win out on any particular day.

"I raised my hand against him," Cobalt said.

"From what I know, he never said that. Not to anyone." Liyan adjusted the cool sheet against Cobalt's waist, his eyes so alive in the silver hospital light. "Besides, if you did, he deserved it."

Cobalt watched him, the sure confidence of his solid, bronze hands, the way he breathed, calm and whole. Liyan filled out his uniform quite well. He was no longer the shy, skinny twenty year old who had embarked on a vast voyage nearly unprepared aside from some exceptional math skills.

Unlike the tourists who passed through the Aurora, Liyan did not smell of antiseptic shuttle air or the hangover sweat of the human rush through ports of entry, alien streets, chaotic hotel lobbies. He'd always had his own uniqueness. His skin shimmered with the sweet dusting of distant suns as it had before he'd ever reached them. If there was ever such a scent, Liyan smelled of freedom.

Voice almost a whisper, Liyan said, "Are you ready to tell me the whole story?"

Cobalt shook his head and glanced away.

"I missed you," Liyan said.

"You were made for bigger missions than this," Cobalt replied.

"Damn. I don't know what to say to that, Cobalt."

"You shouldn't have come." He refused to look in those shiny eyes now.

"Well." The pause came heavy in the air. "That's not your decision."

They sat for some seconds.

Liyan said, "Something terrible happened to you. I wanted to be here. For you. Is that impossible for you to understand?"

"Maybe."

"If our positions were reversed, would you have tried to come to me?"

Cobalt turned to stare at the gray ceiling above Liyan's head. He had his answer instantly, but he did not say it. The universe, without Liyan in it, would die an unjust and savage death. Or it would go on but on such a different frequency it would be like starting over. He didn't want to think about it. He wanted, instead, the comfort of his suite, the letters coming in from afar, the sanctuary of knowing the human he treasured most was wandering the realms of highest hope and greatest promise.

Now that human stood before him in the plainness of a hospital stall, the ivory of the fleet uniform a purity against the stark walls. It was all wrong, all out of place. He did not know what to do.

He should have died. It would have made things easier for all.

Liyan reached out and brushed the side of his face with his knuckles. "You need to come back to me. Who else will write me haiku from home?"

This rotting cess-pot of home, he thought, already composing. The place from which Liyan managed to escape.

160

this rotting cess-pot of home
where the air is
green as android tears

He turned away.

*

21. Shades of Green Light Layering the Windows

When he was very young, perhaps only a few months
fresh from the vats, he read the tragedies of Euripides,
Sophocles, Shakespeare, Anduloxmidan. The lesson? To learn
the risks of love which is a luxury afforded only by the free,
and even then mistakes and griefs and messes were made that
could never be undone. And for those for whom love was not
an option, or who were ordered to love a master with no
freedom or chance of escape, but who gambled it anyway, the
story always ended in despair or death.

Cobalt's arrangement with Liyan... the long-distance
wave communication was a perfect solution for his
predicament, the best relationship he could ever hope to have.
One that did not involve anything but very rare face to face
interaction. The complications were few. The risks
diminished.

He wanted to keep it that way.

From his hospital bed he learned that Liyan had been
home for two weeks. He had rarely left Cobalt's side, but
when he did need more than naps, and a long hot shower,
Liyan had a suite at the Aurora provided by Pel.

Now that Cobalt was nearly ready to leave the hospital,
Liyan wanted to remain another week.

It warmed Cobalt to think of another week with his
friend, but it also meant more complications.

"You shouldn't be gone so long. Don't you miss Lark
and Tiri?"

It was afternoon. Liyan stood by the window framed by beige curtains and an iron glow. For a moment he looked indistinct, phasing away on the sick light of trailing vapors from shuttleport starboats. A mirage perhaps in Cobalt's mysterious android mind.

Liyan's head bowed. "Intensely."

"Then why…?"

"They both wanted to come," Liyan interrupted, turning to look at him. Coming back into focus.

Cobalt was sitting up, dressed warmly in a thick, black robe. He'd just walked the floor, ten laps. He'd proven, to himself and his doctors, that his muscles were regaining their strength. He could continue his physical therapy on his own now.

"But," Liyan continued, "we couldn't all get away at once. I was so distraught they practically pushed me out an airlock just to get me to you sooner."

"I'm grateful, but…"

"Don't you see? You're one of us. Just because you can't physically be with us doesn't mean…" He breathed out heavily. "He'd never admit it, but Lark's still a little jealous. It's because he knows. He knows, Cobalt…how much you mean to me." He came to the bedside and reached out, touching the silver ring that still hugged Cobalt's middle finger. "This ring joins all of us, you know. But it is because of the bond you and I have. Understand that you can argue yourself out of the loop all you want, try to send me away, but it won't change the fact that you are my anchor, my conduit through space to a steadfast, unchanging constant, someone always there for me, waiting at shore for my return with unconditional appreciation." He hesitated. "And affection."

Cobalt himself would have used the tragic word 'love' but he felt suddenly too shy to say so.

All that aside, sometimes he did not want to be a 'steadfast, unchanging constant.' He wanted to be impulsive, daring, crazily jumping into foldspace and the crystalline atmospheres of planets unnamed.

But it was Liyan who was the type to pour out long withheld confessions. Not him. He remained mute.

"I'll always return to you no matter how long away. I thought you knew that. Cobalt, you're my home. That's everything to me."

Cobalt swallowed back a roughness in his throat. "Okay."

"That's all you have to say? Okay?"

Cobalt closed his eyes. He gave a small grunt. "It's so much easier for me to write."

"No it's not. Your letters so often feel held back. I understand, though. Self-preservation and all that. When we've gotten together in the past, we've talked half the night away. You were comfortable enough then to reveal yourself. We connected."

Cobalt took a breath. "I will admit it. Of course we connected." *I do love you.* "And you say Lark's a little jealous. Perhaps I am, too."

"Now we're getting somewhere."

Cobalt frowned, a slice of panic rising. "But Liyan, you should know now that it's possible Juneau will make things difficult."

"Juneau? He's been forbidden anywhere near you. Pel took out a restraining order. He's not even allowed inside the Aurora."

"Juneau is a powerful and rich man. And he's in love with me…well…," he tried not to sputter, "as much as he can be…in his twisted way."

Liyan frowned. "D…do you love him?"

He reached out, grabbing Liyan's arm and looking straight into his eyes. "I despise him."

"Then why…?"

"It's complicated."

"And you don't want to tell me the story. I know."

Cobalt shook his head. "It's ugly. And, yes, I don't want to tell it."

Liyan sat on the edge of the bed.

"He threatened you," Cobalt finally managed to say.

"Me? He sounds like the kind of person who manipulates others with loads of lies. And you believe them."

"You're not in my position. I have no recourse. I can't go to the law and say I do not want to be owned, let alone choose who owns me. He could hold promises over me you couldn't conceive of. If Juneau were to buy me, I would never see you again. And I'm sure all waves would be forbidden."

"Is that what he said? Is that why you're here? Why he nearly killed you?"

Cobalt's teeth dug into his lower lip.

Liyan's face fell in shadow, a blur. "I'm so sorry. Cobalt…I didn't know."

"Pel won't sell." There was a fluttering in his chest. He so did not want to burden Liyan with all this. Not now. Not ever. "But how can I know the future? What if Pel changes his mind for some reason? What if Pel dies?"

"I'm sure he has a will. He's not going to leave something valuable to a stranger."

"But what if the person who inherits me wants to sell? To a stranger?"

Liyan nodded. "I've been so stupid. Here I am, gallivanting off through the galaxy where everything's in flux, no two foldspace experiences alike, a universe of untapped mysteries a breath away where nothing ever stays the same… even our tourist routes are always in flux, and I am a moron, thinking you'll always be there for me, unchanging, thinking that this station and its facilities…its people…will always be there. I never forget your predicament, but I took it for granted that your predicament wouldn't change."

"I don't talk about these things with anyone."

"And I've taken you for granted."

"But I'm grateful. I've never had a friendship, not like this, not of any sort."

Liyan touched the top of his hand. "How did Juneau threaten me?"

"I never speak of you to him. He met you that one time on the street."

Liyan nodded. "I remember him."

"He remembered you being with me because I never go out. It was an odd scene for him to see me that way. He was instantly jealous. He couldn't know two months ago in the penthouse when he tried to kill me that his jests to harm you threatened my own heart. He simply guessed."

"What did he say he'd do?"

"He only said his power reached very far and that he could take steps to ruin your life. I would never, ever want to risk that!"

"But if he really wants you so badly, if he really wants to buy you, he could do the same to Pel…ruin his life."

"He did threaten Pel, in a way, and said that if money wasn't his price then there were always other things, things that humans valued beyond money, and he has ways of finding those things. He could force Pel to sell."

"I think he's full of hot air, that's what I think. He's nothing but a bully. He nearly killed you!"

Cobalt shook his head. "No, he's worse than that. I've tried to look into the extent of his wealth on the computer. It's boundless. He can back his words."

"If it's so easy for him, he would've bought you by now. Whatever's stopping him, we have to make sure it stays in place. I could talk to Pel."

"Maybe…"

"You can be there, too, when I speak with him. If you want."

Something about the light in the room changed in that moment with Liyan etched in bronze and the atmosphere somber, honest, shuddery with unseen currents and depths of open connection. Through the window came layers of copper, sage, iron-infused shades of green intermingling with the two figures on the bed. Liyan leaned toward him until his forehead touched Cobalt's forehead. Cobalt inhaled warm, star-spiced breath. Liyan whispered, "I'm so sorry, Cobalt. I'm so sorry this happened to you." He put his arms around his shoulders.

Letting go his reluctance, Cobalt allowed the light, the room, the arms to enfold him.

*

Cobalt had never seen Liyan look so strong, or so furious. That kid at the bar years ago had certainly grown up. He leaned over Pel's big desk, clearly blindsided but not letting it get the best of him. Cobalt had never told him all the truth about certain details of his life. Now he was discovering just what his friend was doing for years in that penthouse suite with men other than Juneau as well.

"You sold him by the night?" Liyan's voice rose.

Pel shrugged, trying to make light of it all. "Only to a few special clients. Only a couple times a month."

"A few clients? I had no idea this hotel was also a bordello. Does local law enforcement know?"

"It was strictly a private matter…only a few times…" Pel tried to defend himself.

Cobalt stood by, silent. Strangely, he was not feeling emotional at all. Maybe he should have been fuming, maybe he should be arguing, stating his own case. But that was not how he was programmed, not how he'd been taught to behave.

"I don't care. It's not about the amount of times, or anything like that. This is about giving Cobalt a choice."

"He's an android. He doesn't get a choice."

"Well maybe you could allow it. For once. Did he agree to work for you in this capacity?"

166

Pel nervously rubbed his palm against the edge of his desk. His limp, black hair hung in thin lines against his brow. "He didn't agree to be a bartender or a concierge. I told him I wanted him to do those jobs. He did them."

Liyan said, "Those jobs didn't almost get him killed. The other job is outright abuse. The point is despite his label you know full and well he's not a robot. He's a slave. You choose how to treat him. Maybe he has no rights, but you hold all the cards. You can choose to play them right."

Pel leaned back in his chair and seemed intent now on examining his hands. "I didn't know the extent of the abuse," he finally said.

"You knew enough to warn Juneau about fines and expenses if he damaged the merchandise."

"That's just good business. I didn't expect him to almost kill him. It never happened before. That's not my fault!"

Liyan raised his hands as if in surrender. Quietly, he spoke. "Tell us one thing, then. The truth, please. Did Juneau ever try to buy Cobalt?"

Pel nodded. "Twice. But he's not for sale."

"Why? You'd be a wealthy man for life."

"The truth you said?"

Liyan nodded.

Pel's lips curved in a half-smile. "I hate Juneau. That's all there is to it. One night a month…the money's good…I thought it wouldn't hurt anything. Cobalt never showed any reluctance. That's as far as I would go in giving Juneau what he wanted. It pissed him off, but he accepted the deal."

That was it. Pel hated Juneau. So simple. So elegant a reason, in a way. Cobalt stiffened.

Pel turned to him. "Cobalt, this was never meant to hurt you. I tried to make sure that the abuse would never happen again. You know this."

"This happened before?" Liyan asked.

"I told him Juneau hurt me," Cobalt replied.

167

"I'm sorry," Pel said. "I never condoned anyone hurting you. It's not how I run my business."

Silence, in its awkwardness, filled the room.

Liyan crossed his arms, inhaling deep. "So you're saying under no circumstances you would ever sell Cobalt to Juneau?"

"No. He's tried to force me. I have nothing he can bargain with, no family, nothing. And I hate the man. But his money was always good. I've said I'm sorry. I don't condone abuse or attempted murder, whatever you may think of me. There's a restraining order against him from ever setting foot in this establishment. And I've already decided I'm not going to send Cobalt to the penthouse any more. I didn't want this trouble in my hotel. And I'll make sure it never happens again."

"Cobalt deserves rights just like any other human," Liyan said with conviction. "The fact that he can't have them means his well-being falls to his owner. You. If you care at all, this means you are responsible for him, and in making sure he is treated right."

"When I inherited him from my sister, he came with papers that said those very words. Just like with any pet, there are bad owners and good owners. I tried to be a good owner but I didn't know what to do with him. So I gave him what he needed. Because I had no other use of him, I put him to work. He earns his board." He met Cobalt's eyes. "He never complains."

"He's trained not to do that," Liyan replied.

"He's a good worker."

"He's a good man," Liyan countered.

Pel started to speak, stopped. His eyebrows drew together. "Maybe I give him too many long days."

"Maybe you'll adjust those hours for him then." It was a command. Liyan didn't even hesitate to give it.

Pel nodded. "I'm not a bad man. It's hard to know what to do with a person who will never go their own way. A person you own who can amount to no more than an asset. I didn't ask for this."

"But now you know better. You know right from wrong."

Cobalt could not believe that Liyan was actually lecturing Pel, who looked both put out and perhaps slightly embarrassed.

"I've apologized. More than once. I'll cut his hours. What more would you have me do?"

"Oh, I can think of a few things," Liyan muttered under his breath. But he was clearly done for the day. He turned and headed for the door.

Cobalt stole a look at Pel who made no more arguments or defenses. He didn't look mad, but he didn't look chagrined, either.

Still, Cobalt counted this as a win. For Liyan. For him.

*

Layers of light. He kept seeing them everywhere, heavier than normal. They settled in gold on the parquet floor of the lobby, pinking against the plush sofas and chairs, spangling green-tinged in the lighted spaces and rising to burnt orange in the rafters leading to the second floor landing, the meeting rooms, the ballroom, the atrium.

It was a rainbow affect he'd never noticed before. Could the light of this toxic asteroid actually be beautiful if seen from the proper angles? Or was it just the drugs he was coming off of from being so long in the hospital?

Liyan's presence filled all the spaces of the lobby and halls with a kind of electricity he didn't even seem conscious of having. White-clad, confident as a king, he strode. "What do you say to dinner ordered in at your suite and a movie?"

He didn't order Cobalt; he asked. It seemed that as the years passed and Liyan grow stronger, wiser, Cobalt himself was diminishing.

Feeling tired after confronting so many troubles in one day, and still just out of the hospital, Cobalt worked to make his tone sound light. "That sounds wonderful."

The layers of colors swirled as they walked through the lobby, copper, russet, electric green weaving a path toward a better future.

*

During the week they spent together they went to the college again and looked at the stars. They walked a lot to give Cobalt the exercise necessary to regain his normal strength, visiting tourist shops, theatres and every café and restaurant the town offered.

Liyan walked the sidewalks as if they were air, as if he didn't even notice the gravity of them, or their crumbling squares. When he wore his uniform, he attracted stares. The stares would then land on Cobalt and questions would form on their brows. The locals knew him after all this time as Pel's property. What, they wondered, was an android doing with an officer of the stars?

At night they ate luxurious dinners. They watched ancient movies. They talked until the false moon went down. Afterward, Cobalt would send Liyan away to his own rooms. If they ever touched, it was by accident. If Liyan reached to squeeze his hand or shoulder, Cobalt would pretend not to notice.

But Liyan would smile at him from that beautiful and clear-eyed face with such a keen focus; the intelligence there was mesmerizing. And he would think: *Lark and Tiri have him. Lark and Tiri will take care of him. He is the spirit of the stars. And I will stay here and never change, be the steadfast companion at home.*

When they parted for good, though Cobalt hesitated, Liyan pulled him into a tight embrace, breathing deep into his hair. He could feel that starman heart strumming, rushing faster than light. The essence of Liyan transferred an electricity to his skin, the trembles of it running up and down his body, this man, this elixir dusted from other worlds holding him up, holding him, not wanting to say good bye.

Liyan kissed him warmly on the temple, his lips lingering. Then he whispered something so beautiful and amazing, like a secret hidden all his life only now revealed. "Cobalt, I promise, I will come back for you."

He was so overcome he never saw him walk away, never remembered how he got back to the hotel or in his room where he lay, all night, wondering about those tragedies he'd read, and if maybe he'd missed some. If there might be other stories where someone or everyone survived.

*

22. Return to the Stars

Lark's arms enclosed Liyan's shoulders. Tiri's circled his waist. Their warmth, their scents, their two golden heads…all so familiar to him. Their love sent surges through his brain and body that let him know he was desired, valuable, thoroughly missed.

"Welcome home!"

The greeting was immediate as he'd disembarked. The shuttle hadn't even cooled.

The spray of tears on his lashes was expected, and familiar to his lovers, but still embarrassed him.

Sekina had delivered him from Diamond Void, past Procyon, beyond The Fleet of Suns, to a repair station at the fifth moon of Rainfell. From there he caught a shuttle to where the starliner orbited Rainfell, still in the process of unloading passengers and cargo.

It had not been a long voyage. Maybe five days at most, though the foldspace part of it made it seem less.

He spent the day settling back in to ship duties, and answering the hundred or so pressing questions from Lark and Tiri about Cobalt, the hospital, the whole terrible ordeal until he couldn't keep his eyes open. His biggest worry now? Cobalt's obvious depression. They discussed the seemingly unsolvable problem long into the night.

"The only answer," Tiri whispered into the late hours, "is to steal him away and stow him away forever with us."

Liyan gave a pained laugh. "He still won't be free."

"And we'd all be criminals," Lark added.

Finally, he slept in Lark's arms with Tiri curled against his side, as always dreaming of blue hair and sad lavender eyes.

*

Part Five

23. Temples of the Falling Stars

Dear Cobalt:

So many light-years between us. The immensity. Of the mouth of space.

Am I a fool to keep going?

You urge me on. Lark studies with me so I can pass the captain's test. Even if it means I might get my own ship. Even if it means leaving them behind.

How many people in my life must I leave? Everyone I love?

I wouldn't, of course. As captain, if I had my own ship I would have recourse to pick my own crew. Or, at least, most of them. Lark and Tiri would always have jobs with me, if they wanted them.

I spend hours a night on the reading material, the practice tests. Doing homework. Writing star equations and space essays. Learning the organization of the big ships, both technical and social. I must know all the inner workings. I must know how to keep my crew happy and productive. I'm required to learn engineering and psychology. To date, I have a degree in both, completed in two years. I know the value and grade of every star-fuel. I know their scents...the best grade smells of oranges. I know the capacity of 60 different kinds of engines. It helps that I worked on engine repair as a teen. I know how to invent a working mechanism in the vast machinery of a star-drive, and how to solder it in place. I could etch the equation of its power fluctuations with its own vapor-ash on the white bulkheads of engineering.

I have clear eyes toward the stars. I can see their entropic paths.

It seems, Cobalt, I can do everything but bring you to my side.

I can't take the final tests until the end of the year.

I feel I am ready but I never stop studying.

Our next stop is a place I've never heard of. Transitore. A cratered world of lush valleys created when a meteor storm hit it five thousand years ago. The planet was pummeled from space, nearly destroyed, the human inhabitants dwelling underground for millennia. They have a whole religion surrounding the event. And the most glorious structures, some made entirely of nickel and iron ore meteor rock, celebrating the disaster are called Temples of the Falling Stars.

I have a day pass.

Tomorrow I will walk inside a fallen star. And I will tell you all about it.

I hope you are feeling well.

How I wish you were here.

Love,
Liyan

*

Dear Liyan:

I can't wait to read your report on the Temples of the Falling Stars.

Transitore. I looked it up. The pictures from orbit show an ovoid planet with layers of white and purple atmosphere that drape thicker at the more pitted and misshapen equator, and swirl out to space in wispy petals. The way the colors of the air engulf the world give its overall form a butterfly shape. It is amazing a planet could survive such repeated disastrous collisions with such a shower of space objects, some large enough to displace an ocean.

Enjoy your day.

I am well here, better with each passing month. Your waves always give me strength. I am back to working longer hours, but still not like I was. Pel has me on a reasonable shift, working approximately eight hours a day now. For months, as you know, I was still feeling exhausted from simple tasks, so Pel had me on four hour shifts. I get two days off for every five days I work. My off time is my own. I can do as I please, and I have permission to leave the hotel if I wish.

I read a lot. Thank you for sharing your lesson plans with me. I enjoy studying the subjects you are studying, even if I'm not doing it formally. You are way ahead of me, though. For one, I do not have a background in engine repair. And navigation confounds me. Despite my accounting experience, your gift for math is one I don't share.

On one of my days off I walked the length of this entire little flat world in eight hours. In the years you were here, had you ever done that? All alleys lead to the fenced edge overlooking the sparkling double force-fields. The further away from the ashy rocket yards you go, the clearer the air. It turns gold and rose, darkening to purple in the false nights.

I never knew that.

Love,
Cobalt

*

Dear Cobalt:

A large group of us went planetside, arriving at dawn on the main continent. I may travel far seven days a week but I don't always fully realize it until I set foot on another alien world.

From the main city of Dal Shihun, it was only a short hike through emerald sands to the Temples of the Falling Stars. We arrived well before lunch. Of course it was a tourist trap, but a stunningly beautiful one. The weather was cool but not cold, the sky clear as water, not a cloud.

The temples are carved from the leftover debris of the largest meteorite impact. Most of the meteorite burrowed itself in the planet's crust but huge sections broke off and flew in various directions. The temples exist within a small pile of that debris relatively close together.

Looked at from afar, it is a rubble of black rocks.

The temples are intricately sculpted on the outside with carved reliefs of animals, people, whole towns. The carvings tell myths and stories. The main one is, of course, the destruction of the cities and the mass exodus underground. Some carvings show scenes of war, others scenes of love both familial and erotic.

The black stone is hollowed out and you enter through an archway to an interior of dark walls much like a cavern minus the stalactites. There are curved alcoves where people leave offerings like candles and flowers. The theory is if you honor the star it will remain full and strong with no need to fall. Keep the star-gods happy and their anger will not be unleashed. That's the story of all religions, right? Appeasing the quick tempered supernatural beings. I'm not sure how happy it would make them to learn that one of the temples is now, in its entirety, a giant gift shop. Can't say I didn't glance nervously up at the sky before going inside that store.

Lark bought a t-shirt studded with iron-ore glitter guaranteed to be meteor sand. He changed into it immediately and glimmered and glistened in the sunlight on our hike back to the city, with me and Tiri snickering behind him because, well, his collection of t-shirts is taking over what limited closet space we have, including mine in my own stateroom where he now permanently stores some of his clothes. And he has only ever worn each one once.

He ignored us.

Then we all had lunch together with a few other friends at a place called The Meteor Pub that served mostly hamburgers and fries. And alcohol.

We caught the shuttle at twilight and ascended through a dark blue sky, home in time for dinner and the stars.

I was so tired but got called in the middle of my sleep period to repair a major memory conduit that was failing to receive star-data causing half the ship's consoles to go red.

Now it is late morning. My forehead hurts and all I see when I close my eyes are crimson squares pulsating. I feel like I'm writing this blind.

But before I sleep I'm sending this wave because all I think of is you.

176

Love,
Liyan

*

Dear Liyan:

The weeks go by in flashes. Mostly shades of green.
I have a lot of time now to read. There is so much!
Information exudes from the very air, it seems. I read until the
paragraphs blur. I peruse the libraries, the knowledge stores. I buy
information as if it is air. I believe I've overshot my allowance
several months in a row but Pel has never spoken a word about it to
me.

Of course I've had access to computer systems before. But
never had much time to study. I used to watch newsfeeds to put me
to sleep when I was amped up from working too many hours. Now I
ignore them. They offer no real knowledge. Just more human politics.
Nothing changes. Not for me.

Funny how I've tried to learn to read your math. And failed
miserably. I may be programmed for brilliance, but that subject is
your gift, not mine. But I like all kinds of sciences. I've read about
star-drives and the chemical compositions of star-hulls. I've read
about true-Earth and cosmic astrology. Oh sure, mysticism mixed
with physics. It's ridiculously absurd. But then again, the best
physicists courted both. It feeds my dreams. I'm not afraid of the
abstract. I read a book about the vat yards where I was born. I read
two on cloning. Full of myths, those. But they led me to less
nonsensical texts.

I'm no longer sad when I read or take my long walks to the
fenced edges of this world. But I stay away from the old planetarium.
I don't look too long at pictures of galaxies. Because I already know
you're out there, passing through all that spark and flame. I see it
always in my mind, your reflections in the burning, the scintillating
ships.

From you, now it is all about the words, the mind. Do you understand? I want to know the universe that way through your eyes only. Mine are not far-seeing enough.

So I don't look at star-maps. I don't linger on astro-images. For once the jade curtain of the sky that bars me from all star-fields is a welcome sight.

When you take your captain's tests at the end of the year, wave me as often as you can. I will be with you every step of the way.

Love,
Cobalt

*

Dear Cobalt:

I write to you in a cold light. I'm sitting on the observation deck and everything is pulsating blue/silver, blue/silver. My Pegasus emblem is dancing up the cuff to my sleeve. The tiny fluttering wings. He wickers. Call me Deep Cold he says.

I am not working. Not able. Not in this foldspace. Too drugged to subtract. Divide. Who knows if the stars are even really there? Falling apart in Lark's eyes. He laughed at me when I told him I saw you outside. Right outside. Standing on a fenced blue sphere. Watching our starship bend.

So when I went to the shuttle bay to suit up and go outside to get you, that's when they all came. And locked me in my room. When I cried for a view they brought me here to the lowest viewing deck and chained me to the bench. With a pillow. And a black Orion fur wrap. (I said I was cold.)

They gave me my portable wave screen in case I got cohesive and wanted something to read.

I know I am right. You are just outside these walls and to the northeast where I can see the warp-trails collide. It's possible. In foldspace everything exists close together. The speed of space is being everywhere at once. You're not that far away. If only I could reach out in the right...space.

I need to make notes on this but all I can see is your smile and the elixirs of your eyes.

I want to go home now.

I want to wrap up in the void and sleep and not awaken until I feel your hand on my face. There. I've said it. Iloveyou.

I cannot tap letters. I am trying to dictate and tap at the same time. It's stupid.

Sick on the cool floor and writhing. It hurts right here. Insert: my hand on my solar plexus. If you could place your head there and listen to see if I still have a heart I would appreciate it. I would owe you so many favors. Because I think I lost it somewhere out in Vega. Place your palm against my ribs. Let it sink into me. Tap your fingers. Make my heart form and beat again.

I am just lying here looking at this strange white ship from the inside out and trying not to hear the singing outside of the unstrung and jittery starlessness.

Shouldn't our engines be called unstar-drives? Because we are not moving through the stars right now, that is for sure.

I can smell the ozone of all this machinery.

It can't happen.

None of this is real.

O hell I think the black fur from Orion moved a paw.

This transmission is failing.

When I crashland I will still be thinking of you.

LoveLiyan

P.S. Coming out of foldspace and looking at the mess I made (a shredded black fur blanket is the least of it) and at this letter to you...I cleaned it up and then decided to send it anyway.

Tiri said, "Don't send it. Send him something nice."

Lark glared at her, folded his arms over his chest and said to me, "Why should you be embarrassed?"

Sometimes this is what it's like in space. Even budding captains get the loonies. No one's safe. Crewmates try to help, then look the other way and let you alone if it's merely a drunken wallow. And they lock up the suits and helmets and shuttle-bay doors real tight!

This has only happened to me bad four times in my career. Usually the tranquilizers in the water keep things level. But not always! Others experience the spacesickness more often or not at all. Lark seems practically immune. Tiri has had dozens of non-functional foldspace trips.

P.P.S. Deep Cold is back on my cuff and definitely not animated.

*

Dear Liyan:

Your letters and poems written in foldspace are among my favorites. Not that every wave you send isn't special. But this gives me a view of another side of you.

I should add that I'm glad you did not crash land.

Foldspace is an interesting phenomenon and I have finally had time to read some scientific treatises on the subject. It is still not well understood even by the best of minds.

The foldspace cults have written texts from the angle of mysticism. Also not well understood. Some call it Interstellar Halluci-gnosis.

It is not unusual that you would think, in the mind of foldspace, that you are ever far from anything. That is the nature of the travel, as you well know. It is designed to get ships to far places by the swiftest short cut. The fact that these short cuts even exist for ships to navigate gives a different idea and definition to the term distance altogether. You could probably do an equation all about it 500 pages long. You probably have. The math proves the condition. But it doesn't understand the mind trip.

I'm probably repeating everything you already know. But the subject is fascinating.

I know you are on the verge of taking your tests. Three days worth?

You will do well.

Then what? Do you wait for a ship?

I'm excited for you as if this is happening to me. It is because your waves are so colorful and candid. I can well imagine everything you are encountering, seeing, experiencing. I do sometimes dream I am there with you, Lark and Tiri.

Perhaps while you were in foldspace I actually was leaning against the fence at the edge of this asteroid. Thinking of you. Looking for you with my thoughts, my mind. Maybe we were very close to each other and if I could've reached out at just the right angle in space I could have touched the energy spark of your ship as it bent back upon the star-lanes.

Having the time to store up knowledge inside me makes me feel strong. More free. I am also healthier for my long walks.

For everything you have done for me, thank you. I am not the same weak, less fortunate man you left behind.

Love,
Cobalt

*

Dear Cobalt:

Yes, the tests. It's all I think about. Dream about. Talk about. Driving everyone around me mad.

Days away now. I can't sleep. When I pass out my dreams are loud, filled with light and echoing universes of numbers.

Yes, I will put in applications for ships after I am assessed (assuming I pass all the tests.) Then I wait.

I can stay with C&C or put in applications with other companies. C&C does not own me. But they have been good to me. And I know their company technology backward and forward.

I know you are anticipating this as highly as I am. It's great to have the enthusiastic support. I have the best of friends. My reputation is clear.

For a long time I worried about the incident with the android Koral. Not that I had done anything wrong. But I worried that he would somehow coerce his owner to sue me for some misperceived threat based on his strange anger toward me when I was only trying to be friendly. If you recall, the captain had dismissed the incident with little comment and I was afraid he thought there might be more to it and he just didn't want to know. But nothing bad ever happened. The captain treated me in the usual fashion, trusting me with sensitive systems in complicated situations. And much to my relief, we have never transported those two passengers again.

And Cobalt, I am so happy to hear that you are able to grow stronger, that your life feels freer. Knowledge is independence. But then that's easy for me to say. I was not born a slave.

Still, now you have the time to at least follow your mind if not your heart.

You are amazing.

Love,
Liyan

*

24. The Captain's Test, and The Windpoet

Dear Cobalt:

I cannot sleep.
I cannot sleep.
I can't sleep.

Love,
Liyan

*

182

Dear Liyan:

You'll sleep when you pass out.

Love,
Cobalt

*

Dear Cobalt:

An odd three days – the days I passed all my tests. We came out of foldspace on a Monday. I took them on Tuesday, Wednesday and Thursday. By Friday I knew the results. All this on no sleep and a hundred heavily sugared coffees.

Yes, I am drunk now. Yes I am waiting in all this darkness for my starship to come.

Tiri gave me a necklace of trillium to mark my success.

Lark just ruffled my hair…again. It meant everything.

Too much. So I went off alone to…get hold of myself.

I wandered onto c-deck, the lower lobby for the guests and it seemed one of our passengers, the famous windpoet Grfestielle, decided to give a public reading. It had already begun some hours before and his audience had wandered away. I was later to learn the performance lasted twelve hours.

It seems Grfestielle suffers from stage fright so he has programmed a yellow metal robot – one of the old kinds with a flat-screen head and pipe legs on squeaky wheels – to recite his…concoctions. The tinny voice was so amazingly annoying, quoting his words of weirdness and all his ghost-poems.

I caught an hour or so of it mainly because I was just trying to distract my jumping brain (and heart) before I could take no more. All I remember is that screechy voice and a lot of imagery of hands and buttocks. He described wonder as a rift of ages and I thought, well, okay. There was one I sort of liked about ghost-stars and iced tea. But not enough for me to stay. I left about the time the robot began droning the one where he took every 13th sentence of

Bradbury's **The Martian Chronicles** and put it altogether as a poemnovel.

In the rec room they threw a party for me and Tiri kept putting spiced gold drinks in my hands. I didn't even ask what they were…tasted of whiskey and cinnamon.

I had to crash early. Everything was spinning, gleaming. I couldn't stand upright anymore.

I'm lying on my side talking into this wave screen and the only light is the silver screen and a line of pink under my door leaking in from the outer corridor.

I'm going to send this now before I pass out completely.

I hope it goes instant and does not delay across the fields of the stars I have traveled.

Goodnight.

Love,
Liyan

*

25. An Aurora of Starliners

Dear Liyan:

There is no better news I can think of receiving than your last wave.

Congratulations on your success!

A captain now! I desperately wish I could be there to celebrate with you.

I believe the drinks you were given by Tiri are called Orange Pulsars. They are disgusting. If you must partake, mine are the best.

I don't think I need to say this but I forgot in my last wave to you. If you ever see me standing in the strange spheres of foldspace please do not ever try to go outside to greet me. Better to let me come to you. Please promise me that.

As I write this, I'm still digesting your promotion. Of course I had no doubt it would happen for you, but the reality of it is quite enormous. You were so very young and full of dreams when we met and now...this!

I can at least share the thrill, the anxiety, the accomplishment through you. After I send this, I will get up and take a long walk to the edge. I will look across the fenced chasm to the flickering force-field; try to see past the tourmaline shields to the star-vistas you inhabit.

And I will imagine you. I will imagine you all in white walking the decks of your own starliner, the crew looking up to you, the silvery space-paths the ship takes on your command.

I won't rest tonight. I won't be able to.

Love,
Cobalt

*

Dear Cobalt:

Under the crystalline dome of Spirika with the sun by day, then the stars by night hot against the ten foot thick glass, we rode tame, pink feathered dragons into misty caves where pale green water poured endlessly in great falls a mile high. All like a dream. Breaths like pink-tinged candy. The tastes of summer, of sweet rain. Dissolving sugared air stayed on my tongue two days after returning to the ship.

I never forget how fortunate I am.

I am on the list now. Applications are in for my first command.

My nerves. I don't sleep much. Lark has threatened to knock me out several times. It seems everything inside me is tense and made of tremors.

I will settle down, of course. Eventually. But I feel right now that I am such a smallness in such a vastness. The undertaking of running a ship, guiding it through expanses of nothing, finding planets like tiny gems on beaches of sand. I'm a navigator by trade and I still lose my stomach at the big picture.

Tiri says, "Focus. Start with the first number. The smallest of areas. An inch. A foot. A single mile. Don't look at the endless zeroes, the antiquities of the light years."

I'm a navigator! I know all this. But maybe I've lost my mind out here. Maybe it's just too big.

I think I want a science ship. Then I change my mind and hope for a cruise liner like the one I'm currently on. I'm also perfectly suited to captain a colony ship. Anything but a plain freight vessel, though I'd take that over nothing at all. C&C even has a line of more private transport vessels that ferry traveling circuses, performers, celebrities on tour. They go everywhere.

Your long walks…I am so glad you have the opportunity now to take them. I think of the serenity of your gaze and it relaxes me. You do that to me. Thoughts of your heart. Your calm insights. Your whispering haiku.

I'm the eccentric one. The weird one. The one darting around suns like a madman. There is something elegant about it all, though, and about you and me and our differing situations. How we came together, so alike, but live apart. Because I wouldn't be me if I didn't scour the space-dust lanes. And you wouldn't be you if you were just any ordinary human being.

I want you with me.

A voice in my head keeps saying, "Figure it out."

But I am no help to you.

These are the endless circles of my mind,

Love,
Liyan

*

Cobalt left his lamp on all night. When he looked up at the window on his nightly walk he saw it was pink, like a strange gateway and a comforting glow all in one.

In his head he started composing a wave. *"I am with you, Liyan, going round and round in the circles of your thoughts, my thoughts, and at the speed of space we're never really separate."*

But to touch and be touched. It was one wish that remained uncaught.

*

Liyan looked out the porthole window again and again at the sea of ships they were approaching.

He lay on his back, pillow against the bulkhead. He was alone. Tiri was in the middle of her shift. He expected Lark to come off shift any minute.

In space, the ships pulsed. Their auras tarnished bronze, old purple, glaze-green. First he could see the hazy mist of them floating in space, overlapping energies, more than two dozen of them creating a flickering aurora of starliners. Then as they drew closer, their gleaming hulls in focus, Liyan saw that twenty of them, the ones furthest out to "pasture," were those too old for foldspace though their bodies still shone in equal blaze to the eight new models. Twenty were sentenced to be scuttled but the final word for each had taken years, and would take years more. Eight beauties closer to the space station waited to be commanded.

The stateroom door opened. The living bronze light behind Lark spun through the ever-shifting fringe of his hair. In silhouette, he seemed bigger than life, and there were two crystals of light reflecting in his eyes. He said nothing but wandered to his bureau, taking off his white belt with the chrome buckle. He always hated the uniform belts, or any belt, never liking to be cinched into fancy clothing. He hung it from a handle on a drawer and it slid with a clatter disobediently to the deck.

Lark cursed under his breath.

Liyan's chest tensed over a quick needle-flick of pain that came just as suddenly as it was gone.

Still not speaking to him, Lark came over to the bed and sat on the edge. After awhile, he leaned up against the bulkhead, shoulder brushing against Liyan's. As he looked out at the ships past Liyan's gaze, his breaths came slow and shallow.

Five minutes passed that way.

Finally, Lark spoke, low and whispery. "Which one is yours?"

"Second from the left. The one with the bluest aura."

"The *Siren Song*."

Liyan nodded.

"She is gorgeous." Lark laughed, although it came from deep inside him echoing with a sort of aching quickness.

Liyan looked away from the porthole and up at Lark who himself was gorgeous with all the colors of the ships playing over his smooth face. He leaned into him, kissed the bottom of his jaw which was slightly rough. His breath heated the space between his mouth and Lark's neck. When he inhaled, he smelled the static sparkly scent of the nav labs one more time, a faint alien spice.

"After the settlement period, I'll make sure there are placements for you and Tiri aboard her," Liyan said.

"That could take up to a year."

It was a fact he couldn't argue. His heart skipped a little, then settled again. He said, "Then you have plenty of time to finally take your tests for commander. And I'll have a place for you at my side." He leaned his head against the inside curve of Lark's neck.

After awhile, Lark turned and pulled him into a loose embrace. Liyan turned his face and their lips met.

He could hear the breath of the ship in its walls, the soft, low tremble.

They got lost for a time. Lark had a slow mouth and warm, deft hands. Kisses that made the stars spiral.

And Liyan was going to leave him.

*

Dear Cobalt:

We came upon the fleet of ships, incandescent against a backdrop of velvet dark. The old ones looked still new. But they'd been stripped of working parts, consoles, systems, memory. They were hulks waiting for their deaths by fire.

*By far the most beautiful ship there, **Siren Song**, blazed forth like a silver-blue gem. An A-Class Cruiser. Bigger. Newer. A starliner for touring celebrities, musicians, actors, sports teams, politicians and royalty. And the very rich.*

My ship.

No, I don't own her.

No, I don't have delusions that I don't answer to higher orders.

But she is mine to command. And that's the most important part of it all to me.

I leave tonight.

Lark and Tiri can't go with me. Not yet.

It seems I'm too often in the position of leaving those I love behind. My priorities feel like a mess and yet I am single-minded. Is that wrong?

Am I a fool?

Of course now isn't the time to start questioning my decisions. I'll be making important ones all day, every day from now on. I can't appear in any way less than confident.

I will bring Lark and Tiri aboard when the time is right. They know this.

But it doesn't make leaving easier. Not at all. There is a weight of tension in my chest that was never there before.

My ship awaits.

I can't breathe.

Love,
Liyan

*

He watched the old starliners recede on the front screen.

His old ship with Lark and Tiri still aboard had already left, its bluish trail dissipating into the stars.

He turned to his crew. All strangers.

Liyan's pulse beat hard in his throat as he gave the orders and the heading for their first voyage. Only a shakedown cruise. No passengers. The crew wasn't sorted out yet. Everything was rough. But they were off. Stars billowing as if in a wild wind.

He looked around him. The console lights flared pink and gold. Silver-faced, square screens rose above each station. Black leather chairs affixed to the decks, steering, helm, engineering, communications and, most important, navigation. The woman who sat there was named Raen. He didn't know her. She came highly recommended. But he wanted Tiri. Of course Raen would not be unreliable, but Tiri was his confidant. Who would these new people be to him?

And of course he wanted Lark there. Exuberantly supportive. Quietly, but so intensely in love with him even when all Liyan could talk about was Cobalt.

He couldn't stop thinking of their good-bye.

The tight hugs from both Lark and Tiri. The salty kisses on his forehead, temples, both cheeks.

He trembled, seeing all the effortless functioning of the vessel's bridge under his power, his voice, his decisions. It was such a great advancement.

But the cost might've been too much.

*

Part Six

26. Siren Song

Dear Cobalt:

I am not sleeping well at all.
I am nerve-wracked.
I work 12 hours or more a day.
I am in love.
This starliner is so luscious and so new it still smells of fresh oil, disinfectant, cool wind. She is trim and graceful in her moves. They all are but this ship seems more so, turning her sleek body under the starlight as if to bathe in it, never jerking, never hesitant, humming her smooth song as she goes.

I command her and my heart feels too big for my chest. This is where I've come to land out here in the dark. I stand on the deck and ride the magnetic tides of this ancient galaxy. My own ego could overwhelm me if I let it. It's more likely I'm still in shock. This quick move. This grand adventure. And me in charge.

I miss you and Lark and Tiri so much, but I'm so busy I don't have time to be maudlin over it. Yet.

Right now I am working hard to bring them aboard...so much paperwork, so much shuffling, and analysis, a never-ending array of tasks that have nothing to do with standing on the bridge and giving orders, really, except to inform me all that I need to know about everything from the people who work here, from the tight schedules to the functioning of the ship's sewage system (which was apparently its only hitch on our first outing, fixed now, but could have led to disaster...don't laugh.)

I must make space for Lark and Tiri. It is a priority. In my most exhausted moments, lying on my bunk, I worry that they are arguing too much again, fighting but not making up like they used to. After I came to them, to their bedroom, things between them lightened up. I never heard them argue...maybe once or twice. The tension between them, and between the three of us became a different sort, a welcome sort. And even when it was Lark's attentions I craved the most, Tiri understood, she was never jealous, only welcoming, happier because now she had both of us. I always thought in our friendship, before we all got together, that I was like 'the third wheel', in the way, an extra fixture that is not yet needed. But I realize in hindsight that Tiri felt that way about herself even in the beginning by my and Lark's close friendship, that she was in the way, left out of our special rapport. I didn't realize that she knew all along Lark was in love with me.

And then there was the added complication of them (and me) not wanting to interfere with my feelings for you.

Some days I don't know what I'm doing. I'm in a spin. I can't stop wondering if I'm even now where I am supposed to be.

But if you love where you are, isn't that all right? But what of the loves you've left behind?

I still think about how you almost died. Every day. And when you got hurt I wasn't there. I came later, of course, when you woke, but so many weeks had passed before that in worry and frustration.

How selfish I seem to myself sometimes.

Love,
Liyan

*

Dear Liyan:

Do you think it is wrong to go after your dreams? To want what you want? Everyone makes sacrifices in life. Some people just seem to have a wider range of choice than others in that act.

Think about it. If you came here to live and be with me, you would not be 'who' you are to me, the far-journeyer, the seeker, the dreamer. Would I be true to love if I kept you cooped up, working with me in a hotel that is merely a stop-off in the hurry and bustle of daily life? To cage you, confine you, would that even work for any kind of relationship? For us? I would always think it was me who kept you leashed, my condition that made you hold back. My life is as it is. Written in code before I was born. But not yours. Is that fair? No. But would it be fair of me to put my limitations upon you? No.

I want you out there commanding your beautiful starliner. I want you working your fantastic math, having your foldspace breakdowns, navigating yourself through the mouths of quasar dragons, visiting worlds made of ocean or hiking through giant robot sculptures on a hundred miles of cliffs. I want you to see, smell, and taste all of it and then write to me about it so I can smell and taste it, too. I want to see the swan-boats, gulp the air of fairy tale alien forests, read of your graceful love for Lark and Tiri. It fills me up on a level I cannot define. It makes me whole.

I have no self of my own. I do live through you, in your every wave. That is true. But I am expanded for it. My own self is greater, stronger, happier these days. Do you believe me? You must. If you find yourself hesitating at all, remember that every journey, every life, every death is solitary. We are born individual and die individual. We try to connect with those like us along the way, and we feel great things about those connections, but the truth of the soul, I've learned in all these years, is to journey where you most need to go to become more than the flesh, more than just the name of who you are. I cannot do that. I am free only in my mind. But you are free in body and mind. You need to be where you are. I need to share in that with you. This is the only way.

You are captain of a big starship now. I can write those amazing words because they are true. 20 years old when you left. Now nearing 30. Look at what you've done in that period of time. I have shared in it all. It is not a movie or a novel, it is your life. And my life is richer for it. How could I ever thank you enough?

Love,
Cobalt

*

Dear Cobalt:

Our first passengers boarded today. Two casts of two different plays on tour. Three musical groups. A small traveling ballet troupe.

I put in requisitions for Lark and Tiri to join the crew. I don't see too many obstacles except the red tape. It could take up to six months for the transfer to be complete.

Your last wave means everything to me. Your words could not have come at a better time. Thank you.

Lark and Tiri also wave me often now. Knowing I have such good friends surrounding and supporting me gives me extra confidence in this.

I have not had any problems to speak of with the crew. A medic in sickbay asked me in a sarcastic tone, even though he had my chart in front of him and knew the answer, "How old are you?"

"My date of birth is on record," I told him. He gave me a little fake smile so I knew then and there my age could be a factor against me in learning to win the trust of all new people who do not know me, or each other, and who have never seen me work.

But really my biggest problem with the crew is keeping them fit. The boredom of space can be a hindrance. Many work only at whatever is requested and seek no more on their own. Some show up looking bored or tired or hung-over. A paycheck is their bigger concern. That is the way it was when I worked in the shipyards. I didn't notice it so much once I got stationed because I became friends with a group of more eager and active people not yet jaded by their jobs. In hindsight I can see that it was their passion for the work, same as mine, that led us all to be friends. Oh, and the fact that we all worked in nav.

But isn't this the most luxurious living? And our passengers are far from boring, all artists, all sought after, brilliant in their trades. We will be making so many exotic port o' calls. Davenda. Nod. Citron. And more.

What can I do to inspire my crew? Passion for the ship, the journey, the work as well as the play, the planetfalls, the voyage of

*discovery? We're more than a simple ferry-boat. They are all very
experienced, but over-experience can also lead to slogging routine.
Oh well, I'll figure it all out. Yes, most certainly.*

Love,
Liyan

*

Dear Liyan:

*I would tell your crew to go for long walks to the edge of their
town. Look at the streets, the buildings, the skies, the weather, the
lights. It helps. But since the ship is of limited space, they will not be
able to go very far. And they won't be able to look back and see where
they have been, and look at it from a distance in the varying hues of
day or night or false atmospheres of asteroid repair stations.*

*I think maybe an insistence that all your crew make as many
planetfalls as possible could be an option. Your waves to me soared
when you spoke of your off-ship ventures.*

*To see where the vessel they work within takes them should
be a requirement. They can then view how far they've come, and how
much further they're going even if they make return stop-offs to
planets and solar systems they've been to before.*

*It is also important to me, as someone who loves you, that
you have Lark and Tiri with you as soon as possible. You are where
you want to be but I dislike, after all this time, thinking of you alone
among strangers.*

*I realize I took a lot for granted in knowing they were with
you all the time, that should anything upset you they would be there
for you, take care of you.*

Please wave me soon. Tell me everything.

Love,
Cobalt

*

Dear Cobalt:

My first officer is, from my professional viewpoint, and in a language only captains should speak...so boring!

She likes to do all the numbers reports daily. They never pile up (a good thing) and uses a tablet hunched over in her chair for hours, forgetting to eat.

Of course the fact that she sends me the reports daily means that I have to deal with them...daily. Sometimes I do like a Saturday off in space.

I went to her with a read-out on my handheld, all those wonderful colorful numbers. I said, "This one here, so many colors. Look at it. It's an octopus swimming in a lavender cove beside a school of pink fish."

She looked at me so blankly I thought she'd passed out standing up, eyes wide open. Then she said, "It's not wrong."

"No," I said, "it's beautiful."

She frowned.

I said, "Good work."

She shook her head and walked away. Her name is Ydar.

I am NOT making the impact I wished.

I have this yearning to order her...and my entire crew...to present me with at least one haiku by afternoon tomorrow! It can even be done with numbers, I don't care.

I know I speak a different dialect from most of them, but I didn't think it was that different.

I am one of those strange people who think math is fun and looks like art on the page. I like the result but I like the journey, too. I need Tiri here to tell me her little stories. She would give me a report and on her recommendation it would say, "Sector 5 by way of 1.248695 degree-slant is optimal. Head for that spot on the readout that looks like a tiny bit of cool grass in the shade."

Our captain grew to like our enthusiasm.

Be well.

Love,
Liyan

*

Dear Liyan:

In the ancient science fictions, themes often postulated that science and technology might eventually (even fearfully) overtake the human heart.

In all its good and bad reflections, the human heart will be the last thing to die in any future, technological or otherwise…at least so far as you and I have lived it. You've proven it with your last wave, but some people believe their path to serious study and acceptance (success) is through grim struggle and dialog. Much sweat and furrowing of brows.

I am an android and I am smiling at that.

Uncover all of us and what are we underneath? Creatures who crave warmth as well as knowledge, comfort as well as excitation/challenge but above all, connection, love, and again love.

At least you command a ship that will always have interesting guests. Have them perform their plays and songs for each other and your crew, if they wish it. The option is there…like that windpoet only hopefully better.

Zim, whom I have mentioned before, may very much be a match for Ydar. She brought me the package from you, Lark and Tiri with the ring and the crystal in it. She works in accounting…more math. But I have never seen her make pictures with it, or light up in her sea-green eyes if anyone enters a room. When I see her around, which is rare, she appears half-asleep, sometimes even annoyed.

Once I thought to leave a poem on her desk. But I became strangely afraid. I thought she might think I was sick in the head and report me.

What sad paranoia is this that comes from simply wanting to connect with another being even if only with a scrap of words hoping to distract her for just one countable second?

You will do well in inspiring your crew, whatever motion you decide to make. I have no doubt.

Love,
Cobalt

*

27. Far Apart

Cobalt opened the package that had taken more than six months to arrive.

Zim watched him, a crease forming between her eyebrows.

All the pretty machine stamps on the outside distracted him for a moment, as they always did, announcing passage of it through exotic locales, Altair, Colcathar, Riza. The material of the box felt cold in his hands.

Inside was a holograph of Liyan, 33 now, and firm of jaw, his bright gaze seeming to see beyond the frame itself and right into Cobalt's eyes.

Zim said, "So he's that captain-guy?"

Cobalt nodded.

She tilted her head. "He's sorta handsome, I guess. You know. For a spacer."

Over time, Zim had warmed to him in her own way, which meant she actually spoke to Cobalt on occasion, after he'd left a scrap of writing on her desk. *Winter walking on the light shards of broken stars.*

She'd asked him the next day, "What's that from?"

"I wrote it."

She frowned, looked a little disgusted. Then she turned away and went back into her office, closing the door. Later, when she came out for lunch, she glanced at Cobalt through too long bangs and said coolly, "So where's the rest?"

"Well, it's like a game. I write one line, then you write one line. Like that."

She said, hands on hips, "It might not make any sense!"

He shrugged. "Who's around to care?"

198

"What would I say?"

"Anything."

"Anything?"

"Yes."

She didn't write lines of her own for him, she was far too shy, but she found occasional quotes, printed them out (she was too shy for waves as well) and set them on his concierge desk on some mornings.

Now Cobalt pulled from the package a black cloudy sphere and a tiny silver stand. Thin gold lines zigzagged inside. *"Lightning from Nod,"* the note stated. *"Guaranteed authentic."*

"That's Tamolite," Zim said suspiciously.

Cobalt just smiled. It would make a nice centerpiece amid all the other collectibles Liyan had sent him. The note was counter-signed by Lark, who had only last month finally passed enough tests to be officially appointed Liyan's first officer, and Tiri who headed *Siren Song's* nav department.

Zim said, "That guy, that *Siren* Captain, they say he has the fastest ship out there."

"He has the best navigation team. It's about cutting corners, not speed."

Zim scowled. "There are no corners in space."

"Not ones you can see."

"I read somewhere he's crazy. The quasar-whisperer."

"Tabloids?"

She shrugged. "Maybe... You know him. You tell me."

"What we have discussed in private stays private. But I can say the best leaders into wilderness territory know their territories well. All the nuances. The whispers of any changes in the air, the seasons, all the bumps and hills, the dangerous parts, the safe parts, when to go forward, when to turn back."

"There's only one season in space. Sub-zero."

"And then you introduce ships and synthetic moons and foldspace drives and maybe even a bit of war over the centuries, and what do you have? Something different in the mix and how you view it. For over a thousand years it's not a cold, unreachable void anymore."

"It's still void. It's nothing." Practical, narrow, xenophobic Zim. It was the expected answer from someone stuck for a third of her days in a cubical-sized back room on a backwater asteroid.

Or an android indentured to the confines of a hotel for life.

But not his answer.

Cobalt's eyes warmed and something in his solar plexus sparked. "No," he said. "It's everything."

*

Dear Liyan:

Why on this quiet night when the town streets and the shipyards are unusually silent do you feel further away than ever?

The other day I was counting how long it's been since we've seen each other. A little more than three years ago I was in the hospital and when I woke you were there. In that amount of time, so much has changed. For both of us.

I have saved every one of your waves. So many! I look back on them all, amazed.

I have no reason to write this wave. Nothing important to say, really.

But on nights like this when things are very still and I do not feel tired as I should, I miss you the most. I close my eyes and imagine the sparkle of stars dappling your ship's hull. I see you gliding away. My heart skips a beat. Then goes back to normal. It's all good.

Travel safe, my friend.

Love,
Cobalt

*

Dear Cobalt:

It must be a coincidence that I received your wave while we are in what I consider the darkest part of this galaxy. We are in what some call newspace, where the stars aren't as thick, along the edge where suns have not yet spread so far in their eternal entropy.

There is an orphan world out here discovered only two centuries ago called Lone, encircled by a ring of moons all haloed with bands of phosphor green, amber, orange like embers in deepest ash. The terrain is white tundra and jagged peaks and silver seas. When the wind blows it sings like chimes, like Pan flutes. Kai the military poet wrote of Lone:

a world
made of dogs barking in the distance
made of saffron wind

There is a huge scientific and training military base that operates here. Our performers get paid a lot to stop off and entertain. Most are brought by military ships, round trip. But for the first time we got a group headed out there.

In orbit, we met Sekina and her ship. She had purple stripes in her black hair.

And for Tiri it was not a first time stopover. She had trained on Lone for six months when she was only 18.

So far away, I know. And so many years. Yet we still connect. Sometimes when I get your waves it's as if you're standing right in front of me again, talking to me. I can hear your voice. I can see your polite, half-smile.

Instead, I'm on the edge of the galaxy poised to jump. The journey of this abyss scrolls on like endless credits in some crazy movie.

I want to plan a visit to your sector in the coming months. I must do this. I will find a way to fit it in.

Love,
Liyan

*

Right after Liyan had sent his six hundred and seventy sixth wave to Cobalt, Lark said in a soft, almost whispering voice he rarely used, "Sometimes I wish you loved us the way you love him."

They were in the captain's quarters. Liyan got up from his desk, the marginal tone and the words startling him.

His stomach heated, hardened. There was a flurry of panic like bubbles billowing in his chest. Could it be true? Was his heart disloyal? Did he even know his heart? Or was Lark just jealously making him question his convictions?

For a first officer he was out of line.

For a lover his behavior was annoyingly appropriate.

"It's not…" Liyan began.

"Don't." Lark held up a hand as if to block his words.

"But I…"

"Stop."

For a moment he was infuriated. How dare Lark accuse him of this! He was with Lark every night. He saw Cobalt…almost never.

The fury, like a blackness fogging his gaze, just as quickly dissolved.

Lark's ghost-gold eyes steadied him.

Liyan felt his own brows narrow. He took a breath. Strange, but he would remember that breath as if it were his first…so important. A stirring moment, so small but so huge, delineating 'then' from 'now'.

Then Lark gave him his beautiful trademark smile, the one that made him friends everywhere they went, a smile that gave long nights and shaded rooms a meteoric hue. He said, "No worries. Captain Liyan, I have always loved you." He turned and headed for the door.

A tide of urgency pulled Liyan at a jog across the room. He reached for the taller man's shoulder, coming around to face him.

Liyan's hand moved up, cupping Lark's smooth cheek. His voice came as if filled with gravel. "I love you. You and Tiri."

"Hell, I know that."

He breathed out two words. "Okay. Then."

A photon glimmer caught an edge of blue in Lark's stare. "I was scheduled to be on deck five minutes ago."

Liyan's palm pressed the firm jaw. He leaned forward and kissed him, warm and soft, lip to lip. A moment later he stood back, dropping his hands. He crossed his arms. "I won't keep you, then."

"Too kind of you," Lark muttered as he opened the door.

After he had gone, Liyan watched the shadows of the room reappear.

*

28. Spacewrecks and Other Anomalies

Orders were to wait at Lone for the acting troupes and performers to finish their obligations at the 14 bases located around the planet.

But a large ship, even a cruise ship like *Siren Song* orbiting useless for more than a couple weeks cost C&C too much in revenue. So they leased her to the base for eight weeks and Liyan took orders from a new commander. She was ranked as the admiral in charge of all 14 bases but Liyan never saw her in uniform. She always seemed to be between shifts when she spoke to him on the vids, and she always wore a blue fedora and a western style white shirt with silver buttons. She was in her 60s, had a fluty sort of no-nonsense voice, and when speaking was mostly distracted by something off-screen. He was never sure she even saw him at all.

For her first act, she had cargo delivered to him that turned out to be trash. "I'm not a dump ship," he muttered, realizing everyone on the bridge had heard him. But as commanded, they ferried it to the nearby coordinates specified and returned for more orders.

He took on marines being sent to a nearby solar system. They got in a fight and wrecked the ship's bar. Maintenance worked on it for two weeks while they hauled yet two more bays full of garbage.

He didn't complain to anyone but Cobalt and even then he was circumspect. One never knew when the military was scanning all waves in and around the area of Lone. He knew from Tiri and Sekina that the military, despite fedoras and distracted admirals, took itself very seriously. But he did manage in the midst of his frustration to send off a few distraught passages to Cobalt.

Dear Cobalt:

I'll be happy when we're off from Lone, beautiful as it is with its "saffron winds," to future unknown missions.

I'm tired of being the base errand boy. Sekina's ship works with the military but she's captaining a science ship so she gets the more exciting duties. New planetary investigations. Off-world rescues. Star-mapping. Even that last would be more exciting than dump duty.

Love,
Liyan

*

He stared at the three-d screen. This time the admiral did look at him. It was as if she were standing on the other

204

side of an open door or window in space and if she took two steps forward she'd be on the bridge. She frowned with her bushy, white eyebrows and said, "The anomaly in sector 69875 began emitting frequency green."

Liyan nodded patiently. He had no idea what that meant. And he'd never heard of a sector 69875 anomaly.

Then she frowned deeper. "Are you Captain Liyan?"

"I've been following your orders for four weeks now," he calmly replied.

"Huh. You look young for a captain. Anyway, we just need to launch some probes right into its mouth. But you need to be within sight. It moves, you know. You'll have to track it, set the launch codes with precision, etcetera. It's all in the wave I sent, all the details of the orders."

"We're not a science ship," he began.

"This is strictly a delivery. I know you're a bit fancy for that, but it must be done and my other ships are busy." She paused, looking down at something. "You have deflectors, don't you?"

"Of course. Not military grade." He knew impatience when he heard it. She wanted it done. He understood. His was a sleek starliner with titanium curves and triple lounge decks. The military ships were like ducks to his swan boat.

"They're laughing at us," Tiri had smirked one day.

He'd replied smartly, "We get better pay."

"Why do you think I left to work for C&C?"

"My point exactly."

Now he looked directly at the admiral who seemed to be not ten feet away from him. Her use of the word 'fancy' pissed him off but he was glad to do something other than haul trash.

Then she added, "When you get back we've got more level C cargo for you."

Junk. Discards. Waste.

The environmentalists for Lone allowed dumping of organic compounds only. Thus Liyan's beloved endless chore.

Where were the environmentalists for space?

He wasn't going to say, "Aye, aye." He wasn't going to call her 'sir.' He wasn't military. Instead, he forced a wide smile. "Fine. Liyan out." He cut off the communication before she could. As petty as that seemed, it made him feel good.

Lark came over to him and leaned close, smelling of amber. "I might have to relieve you of command."

"Huh?"

"You're losing it, Captain."

"Hey, I was polite."

"Not military polite."

Liyan smirked.

*

Dear Cobalt:

We'll be gone for a week. Foldspace is only going to last one day but the anomaly we're headed for messes with waves.

I can't say anymore about it. I've never even heard anything about sector 69875. But we'll be sending probes and taking holo pictures. I expect all will be highly secured, but if not I'll send you one. If, that is, there's anything to see.

In two weeks we'll be away from Lone. I don't care if the winds chime. I want out of there.

I never went into the military for many reasons. Tiri left for many reasons. And the androids there are owned for life.

I haven't seen any on Lone but Tiri remembers boot camp with some of them. Highly trained soldiers, guards, warriors. Males and females alike created in the vats with DNA programmed for less emotion, more brawn. She had heard rumors of entire secret ships of them headed off to secret moons to train for secret missions. If they vanish, no one's around to care. If they're never heard from again, no one will miss them.

Can you imagine? Breeding emotion out of a human? Doctoring the DNA so the feelings they have are minimalized, their humanity completely disrespected? And all done to military specifications.

It horrifies me. You are gentle and kind, Cobalt. To think of someone doctoring your genetic make up so you would be a better fighter, and taking away your beautiful personality angers me.

What if it were done to anyone? To Lark and his amazing charisma? To Tiri? To me?

We live in a brilliant and accessible universe. But there are hidden horrors.

I will write immediately upon my return to Lone.
Count on it!

Love,
Liyan

*

Dear Liyan:

Hidden horrors. Yes. But they've been around since the dawn of Mankind. The darker human heart (nor the good) does not become wiped away by technology, psychological evolutions, the increase in knowledge of the science of the mind. Future worlds, new knowledge, space travel...nothing replaces the final human heart. Not even mechanical devices within the human body. It is superstition to think otherwise.

To be human is to be flawed.

If nothing, it makes for good stories, right?

I look very much forward to hearing from you in one week. All about the anomaly.

Love,
Cobalt

*

Sensors had gone from pink-edged green to gold to red.

A shimmering line of what looked like jagged white static drifted across the viewscreen.

Like lightning in space, Liyan thought. He could almost hear the rain, and smiled at his ridiculous thought while knowing Cobalt would've liked it.

Sensors showed more oddities than they were expecting. Liyan and Lark had researched it. Not much to read, though. The files the admiral had sent them were slim, incomplete. All other probes had given back little information...or none. This new series of probes were better engineered, more complex.

Still, there were oddities on their sensors they had not expected.

Tiri was trying to configure the data when they all realized at once as the visual focus intensified, that they were registering shipwrecks. At least three of them.

"The admiral left that part of it out," Lark said, dismayed. "Why?"

One ship, a disk, was doing an endless, slow tumble around the anomaly, caught in the gravity of it like a lost juggler's dish.

"Why couldn't it break away?" Tiri asked.

Liyan felt the slow surge of alarm sting his arms and legs. He gave Tiri an abrupt order to direct the starliner up and back, their own tumble and veer course which shook the picture on the screen but which they barely felt.

"We'll launch the probe from here," Liyan said, though he knew the mission required them to be much closer.

No one argued.

And Liyan remembered his earlier conversation with the admiral.

"You have deflectors, don't you?" she'd asked.

He'd answered yes, but not military grade. She behaved as if she had not heard him.

"Did she say anything about the danger of this mission?" Tiri asked.

208

"Nope. Just a routine probe launch. That's how her paperwork addressed it," Liyan answered. *We're a garbage hauler to her, nothing more.*

"If we encountered these readings on a normal cruise coming out of foldspace, it'd be anything *but* routine," she said.

"Why'd she send us? I don't remember hearing any rumors that she's crazy," Lark said. He frowned at Tiri, as if Tiri might have some special insight having trained on Lone for several months.

Tiri shrugged, shook her head. "I was a grunt. Pretty much we're the last to know anything, including gossip."

She turned back to her instruments and her face changed. "Hey…"

"What is it?" Liyan asked.

"A weird signal." She gave a series of navigational figures. "It's another wreck. But this one's emitting an S.O.S."

"Is the signal old?"

"I can't tell."

Liyan reached behind him and settled into an empty helm chair. He'd taken minimal crew for this trip. Left the rest on Lone to finish their short vacations uninterrupted.

"Well, we can't ask. This thing, whatever it is out there, fries our communication signals."

"We can go back," Lark suggested.

Liyan thought about it. Another wasted week there and back. What if people on board the wreck needed help? Or what if the beacon was simply from an ancient, undying battery, leftover from the old times, a red pulse crying forever into the dark? How could they ever tell without going closer?

"What do you say?" Liyan commanded true, but he also always asked for opinions. That was what crew were for.

"Do you think the admiral overseeing the entire planet of Lone would really be crazy enough to send us here without proper defenses? She'd have been ratted out long ago if she were that crazy," Tiri said. "She can't know about the distress.

It's muted. It's a crap-shoot to send a signal around this thing. The anomaly is breaking it up. It's only by chance I saw it in the readouts. Maybe no one knows. Maybe this is old or new. But I think we have to check it out."

"I say we leave it to the bigger ships," Lark argued. "This was never a rescue mission. We're a glorified cruise liner."

"Which means we have the room," Liyan offered.

"Yes, we have beds. We can give medical aid. But we're made to avoid the icebergs, not head into them." The ancient reference was not lost on any of them. "Can you tell anything else about the ship or its signal from here?"

Tiri shook her head. "The anomaly is messing with everything."

"How much closer can we safely get?"

She rattled off a number.

Lark looked dubious. Later, he quipped, "The iron will of starliner commanders is a fact." He gave a wry smile. And Liyan knew that Lark was ready to take the risk in total support of him.

That was the moment, without warning, the anomaly stuck out an electric finger and jabbed at them as if their deflectors were nothing stronger than a net of gauze.

Damn the eccentricity of hermit admirals on planets called Lone.

Damn their own naiveté and the sparse records which told them virtually nothing about what they were headed into.

Tiri went flying across the bridge.

Lark grabbed at a chair but still went down.

Liyan whipped backwards over his chair and even through all that chaos, still the loudest thing he heard was the crack as his back broke.

Clamor and chaos. On emergency auto, the ship went into evasive maneuvers.

The anomaly, they now knew (a bit too late) was a cluster of gliding electrical bullets. Energy field meteors of such proportion that to even study it was suicide.

But old admirals liked notches on their belts. And they often didn't mind using disposable grunts or trash haulers to risk getting the job done.

After that hit, Liyan remembered flashes of many things. More hits. Or at least it felt like it. Somebody, maybe Tiri, shouting the stardrive was out. And the chain reactions were mini-storms destroying everything in their path. Ignitions. Flames. Fires. A computer muttered, "Destruction imminent."

It was a known conceit. Captains went down with their ships. But usually not on mad errands. Usually not for being careful, or doing nothing wrong.

He would not die a hero. But he didn't care about that. What he wanted more was for Lark and Tiri to survive this, live long enough to know old age. And he wanted Cobalt to know he wished the android's life could have been better, that he could've done more to contribute to a final freedom for him.

Smoke wafted over him, thick and black, burning into his throat and down his windpipe. Oxygen was burning furiously, the lights all at emergency orange to match the growing flames.

"Get up," said a harsh voice next to him.

But he couldn't move.

Then Lark was kneeling, coughing. "Can't you move?"

"Go to the escape pods," he wheezed. "You and Tiri. Get out of here. Program them for Lone or anywhere as far from this thing…"

"Not without you," Lark interrupted. Before he could argue, Lark hefted him up, yelling something to someone Liyan couldn't see.

He tensed against imminent pain from his back that never came and realized that was not a good thing.

He flopped upward, limp in Lark's arms as the man stood. Liyan gasped. Now there was pain in his lungs, his chest. Still nothing in his legs.

"I got you," Lark said.

"Let me go! I'll hold you back. You have to leave now!"

"Shut up," was the only response from his disobedient second in command.

He couldn't see much. He felt the strong arms, the running, the cooler air of the still-lit corridors where the smoke and flames had not yet reached. He felt himself slipping down Lark's body. His arms still worked. He grabbed onto Lark's shoulders and held on.

"Where's Tiri?" he asked. But Lark just ran and ran.

He heard the words again. "Destruction imminent."

Smoke stung his eyes. Burning metal, burning circuits, burning air. And the worst scent? The ash of dreams which were salt and bitters of a wine turned to vinegar.

They came to a passenger viewport, a long wall of black with centuries of stars looking coldly on as Lark held onto him, as Lark ran. He felt like he was falling.

Then there was the coffin. The green and blue lights running along its sides as if it were a holiday decoration. The antiseptic scent of brisk electrical currents as the auto-computers turned on.

Lark nearly fell getting him into it and ended up kneeling, making sure he was properly placed, strapped, and all while Liyan kept hearing the words. "Destruction imminent."

"Lark! Go!" he rasped. "Go!"

"I won't leave you to die with the damn ship like some storybook tale."

"But Tiri...?"

"Tiri's okay. She was right ahead of us. She's already in a pod."

The lid began to close, the straps to tighten and he felt the metal around him quiver.

"Lark!" he yelled. "Lark!"

The pod closed completely, began to move along the escape chutes and for a moment all went black. Seconds later the porthole (he thought of it as a tiny coffin window) revealed the universe of spinning stars as tranquil as always, and as deadly.

A shiver of fear ran through him.

He saw at that moment other pods spinning, turning. All safe so far. All headed fast away from the churning, lashing anomaly. Then his little view changed and the *Siren Song* came into vision range.

His lungs heaved as he watched, each breath burning, aching. The starliner somersaulted in space, a gigantic, magnificent creature caught in a heat sphere of total destruction. It buckled, toppled into itself, then exploded into an infinity of gold-white fireflies the same color as Liyan's tears.

*

29. Auto Delivery Fail

Dear Liyan:

I hope you are back from your mission by now and able to again receive waves.

Things continue as usual at the hotel.

Love,
Cobalt

*

Dear Liyan:

My last message hasn't bounced, but it also hasn't been marked as received. I hope you are simply delayed and all is well.
I look forward to hearing from you.

Love,
Cobalt

*

Dear Liyan:

Are you able to receive waves yet? Obviously, if I see an auto receipt fail message on this one, too, the answer will still be no.
I have scoured for waves of news of you and your ship. There is nothing. So I am assuming you are simply delayed either by the anomaly or by foldspace and you will be able to communicate soon.

Love,
Cobalt

*

Dear Liyan:

*Still no word. But also no official news of **Siren Song** or her crew. There is simply silence. Nothing. I do not even know who to wave about this matter. There is nothing on the nets from C&C. I have scoured the lists for lost ships, recent deaths. I am relieved to find, so far, no mention of you or your ship. But I am very worried. Please wave me as soon as you are able.*

Love,
Cobalt

*

30. The Death of the Siren Song

Space is velvet, he thought. *Space hurts.*

He floated in the pod in half-sleep, engulfed by billion year old night.

Over and over the after-image played itself in Liyan's mind. The starliner folding in on itself, collapsing, then exploding, copper blue flames licking long into the black until they vanished. Amber sparks dancing. Until there was nothing.

The bitter burnt smell of the air would not leave him. He knew it was an illusion. The pod circulated re-freshened air to him through filters.

He dozed and woke. Dozed and woke.

How long?

Average pods had life support systems that could last for months. The *Siren Song's* escape pods had systems guaranteed for a year. Plenty of time for rescue to come.

His pod was programmed for Lone. He didn't want to go there. He wanted to go to Asteroid 1191782, Diamond Void XP.

But he was too sleepy to even attempt a reprogram. If he tried to speak, his words came out garbled.

He dreamed of a school of pods, like minnows of the void, all shiny and bright headed to the nearest sun.

He dreamed of Tiri and Lark hurtling through space beside him in pods of their own, safe, alive.

In a sweeping agony of homesickness, he dreamed of Cobalt where so long ago he had left a part of himself, his essence, on that lonely asteroid, in that ornate Grand Aurora Hotel.

He turned and turned in his long sleep.

The starliner exploded.

His starliner exploded.

He was still a captain. None of it was his fault. And yet it seemed everything was lost.

*

When he finally and fully woke Lark was there surrounded by dim stars. Liyan blinked. He finally realized the dim stars were lights of a medical ward blinking, flashing. He couldn't move. But he could breathe. Deep. Strong.

He would live.

Lark's hand pressed against his forehead, warm and firm.

Liyan closed his eyes and spoke. "Tiri?"

"She's next door getting a bit of new skin. She had a few burns. She'll be all right. And the small crew we had with us survived. Sekina found us all."

"Are you all right?"

A quick nod was his answer.

"You disobeyed a direct order."

Lark's eyebrow rose. "To leave you?"

Liyan glanced away.

"Yeah, well, you ass, I'd do it again. So when you can you'll just have to write me up. After you thank me, of course. And if you were wondering, the admiral has gone into early retirement."

It felt as if something had caught in his throat. He jerked.

Lark took tight hold of his hand. "Just rest."

Liyan replied in a whisper. "I want to go home."

*

The surgery was complicated but the technology sound.

After days in a life-pod, Liyan was forced to continue to lie still for another week to let his new spine integrate.

Lark stayed by his side, joined later by Tiri. The drugs the medics gave him made him sleep over sixteen hours a day. He dreamed the death of the *Siren Song* more times than he could count. He dreamed he was a created human made of vat-grown, assembled parts. In this new nightmare, he knew he was a person with no freedoms. He would never go to the stars. An idea that he might be a starship captain trapped in an android body left him hopeless, helpless. An indistinct figure loomed over him, saying, "This one's hopelessly schizophrenic. It will have to be put down."

When he woke yelling, Lark's fingers were combing back his bangs, and he was saying, "Hey, hey…"

He saw through bleary, drugged eyes that Tiri stood on the other side of the bed. He felt her hand in his. When their eyes met, she said starkly, "A whole new spine and they still couldn't break out their best drugs. I'm having a strong word with your doctor. Right now!" She stomped from the room.

He looked around the room for Cobalt. Of course he wasn't there. He wasn't allowed to travel.

Lark leaned over him, forcing Liyan to look at him. "You'll get to see him soon enough."

"I didn't say…"

"You didn't have to."

Liyan reached up to grab Lark's arm. Lark reached back until they clasped hands. "Are you in pain?" he asked.

"Not right now."

"Good. Because day after tomorrow you get to learn to walk again."

"Can't wait to get upright."

"I'll bet. I had secretly hoped I could tell you what a rotten patient you are, but you've hardly even complained. I know you want to go home as soon as possible. My question is, can Tiri and I come with you?"

Liyan's breath hitched. He blinked. "I hoped you'd want to."

Lark squeezed his palm. "You ass. Of course we want to."

At that moment the door opened and Tiri's strong voice could be heard. "…something better for what he's been through. This one's giving him nightmares!"

Tiri came in followed by a sympathetic-looking R.N.

It was a gesture of love on Tiri's part, but Liyan figured he was going to have nightmares no matter what. For a long while, yet.

*

Dear Cobalt:

I am Liyan's friend and partner, Tiri. I know we have never communicated like this before, but now I am writing this for him.

We are so sorry your last four waves went unanswered.

There has been an accident. For now the details are classified, but rest assured Liyan is just fine. He is recovering in hospital. Do not be alarmed. He required a new spine and all is well. The surgery was quite successful.

I have little time right now, but want to say I am happy to answer any waves from you until he himself is able to do so.

He wants to come home to you when he can comfortably travel.

Would you be willing to arrange to put all three of us up at the Aurora… me, Lark and Liyan? I hope that is not a hardship.

I will wave you a timetable when I know more about the true length of his recovery.

Your friend,
Tiri

*

Dear Tiri:

Thank you for this wave. I would be lying if I said I have not been worried for many days now.

I saw your message and instantly expected bad news. Honestly, I feared worse.

I am so glad to hear Liyan is recovering well.

The three of you have open reservations at the Aurora whenever you can make use of them. No expiration date.

Please tell Liyan I am thinking of him. If there is anything else I can do, please let me know. I would come to him if I could. He knows that.

Your friend,
Cobalt

*

The physical therapy was annoying but efficient. Liyan could move around his hospital room with assistance after two days of beginning the therapy, but only for minutes at a time. Then he needed to rest. A hover-chair was brought in.

He still slept more than he was awake. He forced himself to sit up in the chair as much as he could.

He'd learned much in the last few days. Sekina's ship had brought them all to a hospital outpost. Liyan remembered nothing of that trip, or the rescue. Lark told him he had refused to allow Sekina to take them back to Lone. So she headed for a hospital outpost that was non-military, neutral. Apparently Sekina had visited him every day while he was aboard the *Dar-alon.*

"She held your hand and talked to you a lot," Lark said. "She had to leave after dropping us all here."

"Please tell her thank you. I'll wave her when I can."

"I will."

219

There was a lot more to catch up on, and Liyan quickly learned that the drama surrounding the death of his ship had grown into a kind of legal and panicky frenzy.

Lark and Tiri brought Liyan, in his hospital bed, documents and reports marked "classified"to help fill him in.

"How did you get these?" he asked.

"We all have clearance," Tiri explained. "We're part of the report."

Within one long document he saw the reason for all the secrecy. There were phrases describing the admiral overseeing the military bases at Lone as "unfit for duty." And, "the admiral, suffering from the onset of a rare brain malady could not make appropriate decisions regarding day to day..." etc., etc.

After the accident, the admiral had been put into a hasty retirement, somewhere safe where she could never again harm herself or others. In the official report, the blame for everything fell onto her. A lot of medical jargon was used to describe her condition and why it was she had ordered an expensive vessel of non-military civilians with a non-military grade deflector shield into a waiting death trap. And why Liyan and his crew had not been given the background files on the derelict ships, especially the one which still emitted a distress signal but had been adrift for years. If they had known about it, the *Siren Song* might have survived.

More psychological jargon was used to explain why it was not earlier apparent she was unfit for duty, why she remained in charge of one of the largest military contingency of bases for so long when her mental deterioration had been on-going for months.

Embarrassed, and perhaps facing both criminal and civil lawsuits, the military, of course, did not wish to go public with that information at all. Ever.

More reports came, amended.

When Liyan felt well enough he was interviewed by no fewer than three military investigators and four attorneys.

They told him what to say and where to sign. Failure to comply would result in prison-time, due to an old, outlandish law that mostly had to do with war-time secrecy.

However, if he complied, and signed their amended documents, he and the rest of his skeleton crew that had gone on the mission to send probes into the anomaly would be given restitution. The figures were somewhat staggering, given that the military could just threaten them to comply and pay nothing.

Instead, they offered money.

The official ruling for the disaster became one unfortunate and horrific word: accident. The cause, as told to the media, was part of an on-going investigation.

So it came that less than two weeks after his rescue, Liyan sat in his hover-chair in a cozy hospital office with a multitude of lawyers and signed off on a second 'official' report that contained nothing of what he'd witnessed. Then he signed a statement verifying that he would never speak to the press. He then gave permission for each of his affiliated crew-members to sign.

Afterwards, he was presented with a sizeable check. A settlement. Hush money.

The rest of his crew received payments as well.

The report did not accuse him or his crew of negligence. But neither did it vindicate him. The higher-ups at C&C knew the truth, but not the hiring bosses.

He would have a lot of trouble finding another captaincy. And he was legally disallowed from speaking of the accident to completely clear his name.

With Lark and Tiri at his side, it was time to go home.

*

Dear Cobalt:

May I come home for awhile?
I know Tiri has waved you. I'm sorry I could not until now.
I have quite a story to tell, but for once I don't feel like writing it in a wave.
I will tell you in person.
I am recovering well but still in a hover-chair.
Tiri says you have arranged reservations for us.
Thank you.
We will arrive soon. No hours-long shuttle voyage this time. We're coming in a big ship, close as we can, then taking the shuttle from there.

Love,
Liyan

*

Dear Liyan:

*Getting a message from you, **any** message, means I can breathe easier once again.*
Your room is booked. The best we have. The penthouse. I insisted. Pel did not deny me.
I look forward to seeing you more than you can know.
Be well.
I will be waiting.

Love,
Cobalt

*

222

Dear Cobalt:

*My name is Sekina. I command the **Dar-alon**. I will be in your sector on 29876 to deliver my friend Liyan into your care. Two more people will be accompanying him. You know who Lark and Tiri are even if you have never met them.*

My friend only wishes to come home and it is so little for me to grant him that wish.

I know you will treat him well.

Meet my ship's shuttle at gate 111 on the above date and time.

Sincerely,
*Captain Sekina, **Dar-alon***

31. Always the Distant Rumble of the Ships

He'd missed mucky green skies, emerald vapors, the distant glimmer of the outer force-fields.

He'd missed the ozone scent of the rocket yards. The constant hum of the ships.

But most of all he'd missed the android who'd stolen a part of his heart. And even though he'd had enough of himself left over to offer Lark and Tiri, that initial piece of his heart always ached, never allowing itself to be forgotten.

Cobalt met the three of them at gate 111. Liyan looked up at pale lavender irises.

The breath he took felt new and pure.

Their embrace was awkward because of the hover-chair, and because Cobalt looked fearful of hurting him.

Liyan stood up from his chair, then. He put his arms on Cobalt's shoulders, pulling him in. "I'm just weak. I need time and exercise. But I'm healed. You can't hurt me."

Cobalt laughed softly and they hugged tight.

When Liyan pulled back and sat down, Tiri stepped in front of him. She pulled Cobalt into a quick hug, then kissed him on the cheek. To Liyan's delight, Cobalt actually flushed.

"I'm so happy to finally meet you!" Tiri had never been shy. Now she looked askance at Liyan. "You never told me how handsome he is." Then she turned back to Cobalt. "He told us everything else but that!"

Now Lark stepped forward. "Hey, friend of my friend." Liyan watched as Lark politely embraced Cobalt, perhaps a little too quick.

Cobalt gave no sign that he noticed. He said, "Liyan has described you beautifully, but it's still nothing like meeting in person. And now allow me to escort all of you to the best hotel in this sector."

"We've heard the rumors of this grand hotel," Tiri said. "Now we get to see for ourselves."

The four of them headed for the exit.

*

The fake moon quivered, a chrome oval rising past the triangle window. The spaceport, usually quiet at this hour, spilled over with shouts of revelry. Virtual and real fireworks laced the double force-field shrouded sky. In a room on the highest level of the Grand Aurora Hotel, the android lingered by the silk curtains.

Cobalt turned toward the window, his coattails shushing the shadowed air. The moon of silver cast him in pale blue light which suited the aquamarine hair, the bronze features, the violet eyes.

"You should be down there celebrating, too," the android said.

Lark and Tiri had ventured out to explore the town, leaving Liyan and Cobalt alone.

224

They had discussed everything, that they would never leave him, and accepted that Cobalt was to be a fixture now at Liyan's side. Tiri had even read most of their correspondence. Lark had read only samplings. But through Liyan, they had come to love Cobalt as well.

The room lay in stillness, the gray shadows punctured every few moments by rainbows of refracted color from the blossoming pyrotechnics of the holiday. A new year approached like a new sector of space to be considered, entered, experienced. The old year waited to be left behind in stardust and vapor.

"Yes." Liyan replied. "It sounds wonderful." In truth, the fireworks of this day reminded Liyan only too well of the spectacular green and gold lightrise his dying ship created when it tore apart, ribbons of scarlet and gold littering the endless night while in his escape pod he hurtled with the rest of his shipmates in identical flocks of coffins spinning through the deadly vacuum.

The skin of his arms prickled uncomfortably at the thought.

Cobalt turned toward him and said, "I can take you down there."

"No need. I'm fine here."

Liyan watched his friend's face. Cobalt seemed to study him with real emotion.

Liyan gave him a small smile. "You know, I confess that sometimes I suspected during all the times we were apart and communicating only through waves, that your programming might merely have obligated you to respond politely, even cheerily to me. But whenever I came to port and saw you again, I knew how wrong I was."

"The myth of our kind is integrated into the culture quite efficiently."

"After Juneau, well, that was when I think it all sunk in. The word 'android' is such a disservice to you. It's an ugly word. It's the wrong word. After…after that I never questioned your humanity again."

Cobalt handed Liyan a glass of expensive Airielle champagne. "I know," he said softly.

Liyan clasped the drink gratefully. His hover-chair was soft but confining. He took a long sip, tongue caressing the bubbles, eyelids lowering to the mechanisms and lights of the chair-arms his elbows rested on, and the gentle step that kept his feet from dragging uselessly on the floor. He'd grown used to the easy maneuverability of the chair, but he couldn't wait to get rid of it for good.

The alien champagne was wonderful, but the effervescent air of it affected his vision with a stinging sensation. He did not want to look up and be seen as crying. He was a decorated captain. Thirteen years in space had made him strong, wise, decisive. People looked up to him. The story about the death of his ship still scattered across the intergalactic nets. Even now.

Some media articles he'd read ended with suggestive unanswered questions. Others were pure speculative fiction created to fill in the holes. There had been puffed up newscasts with rumor and supposition. Some blamed the explosion on the ship's engineering design, citing anonymous sources from C&C. Some decided human error was the culprit, and blamed the captain.

His hand quivered. Cobalt took the glass and set it aside. Then he knelt. Softly, he said, "You can relax here for as long as you need."

Liyan looked up and warm grief drew up inside him, a long ache that crept into his chest. Cobalt, in this moment, was more beautiful than ever.

He kept thinking everything had ended when really everything was beginning.

He kept thinking even Lark and Tiri were gone, but they were not. They were alive and taking in the few town sights.

"Thank you." All the dramas were behind him now, but he was crying anyway and nothing could be done.

Cobalt said. "And there will be more ships."

Liyan shook his head. "Maybe. It'll be difficult."

"C&C owes you. You take blame personally when you know there is none to take."

He had never said it aloud, but Cobalt knew. Despite all the official and unofficial reports and the admiral's negligence, he did also blamed himself. He blamed himself for not insisting on more research from the admiral. For not questioning her demeanor. He blamed himself for not taking even more severe and immediate evasive action as soon as he learned of the other wrecks, despite the ever-emitting distress call from one of them. It had been negligent of him to think he might perform a rescue in an area of space that had already wrecked three or more ships.

When the rescue squads of Sekina's ship found the crew and took them aboard, they patched him up for the ride home, but the real healing would take place here. With Cobalt.

This he had discussed at length with Lark and Tiri.

With their support, he had upon arrival, used the money of the settlement to buy Cobalt's contract from the soon-to-retire Pel. It had not been an easy deal. But it was the 'fix' he'd been looking for for thirteen years.

In Pel's office, Liyan, in his hover-chair, had turned his head to look up at Cobalt. "It's done. Now I'm giving you a choice in what you want to do with your life."

"But I have no legal freedom within the society itself."

"I want to make it clear to you I am only taking the responsibility to make sure you can make all your own choices now. I can provide any means you need to accomplish this. So if you want to leave here you can. You can do what you wish and I will facilitate that wish."

Cobalt had a hint of a smile on his lips when he said, "I wish to stay with you if it is allowed."

Liyan's skin warmed. "Are you sure?"

"Are you?"

Tiri, who had been standing with Lark toward the back of the office, said, "We are definitely setting a precedent here. In more ways than one. It might seem, Cobalt, that we three are together and you are the odd man out. But Liyan loves you. And we love Liyan." She elbowed Lark in the ribs and he nodded in agreement. "That's all any of us needs," Tiri continued. "That's all we need to know."

In the hours since then, Cobalt had never left his side.

The revelries outside stepped up. As the noise progressed and the fire displays superimposed themselves upon Liyan's memory of his dying ship with more color, tremor and explosion, Cobalt stated the obvious. "It's almost midnight."

Liyan nodded, swiping the back of his hand across his face.

"Have you ever wondered," Cobalt asked, "why we became such fast and immediate friends? A non-human and a human?"

"No," Liyan said softly, heart fluttering. "I haven't wondered."

"You haven't?"

"No. Because it is fulfilling. More than you can ever imagine. At least to me. I've never questioned how natural it was…is."

Cobalt's eyes glimmered with soft appraisal and maybe even a little heat. "Yes. I see you're right. And I can imagine. I have imagined. The fulfillment has been more than I could ever have expected."

"I know you're not just saying that because I own your contract now. You once told me you didn't believe in love. But our friendship is everything."

Cobalt stood motionless in an aura of silvers and grays. His shoulder eclipsed the moon. His words were almost a whisper when he said, "I'm the one who asked you the question. If I didn't understand our relationship in higher

228

terms, it would never have occurred to me to ask why we've remained friends."

"It's always been you. Always," Liyan confessed. "You know that."

"And that's why you bought my work contract."

They had already discussed some of this in Pel's office, but Liyan had saved one last detail about the ownership transfer for a more private moment. "Yes, That, and because I have always dreamed of being able to do this." He reached into his shirt pocket and pulled out a chip. "This is everything I've always wanted to give you, Cobalt. I was waiting until tonight to do it."

Cobalt took the chip staring at it, wide-eyed. "These are my ownership papers."

"Yes."

"Well, I suppose I could keep them for you."

"No. I wanted to surprise you and now's the time. I made Pel put your name on them. Not mine."

His eyebrows rose. "It's illegal. By law I am always to be owned."

"What is loved can never be owned."

Cobalt's eyes glistened, damp lashes quivering. "That statement would be rejected by a court."

Liyan shook his head. "What transpires between you and me is all that matters to me. I put your name on them. It's done. This is between us. For us. Of course I'd never abandon you to all the sticky legalities of it, but between you and me…it's done."

Liyan watched as Cobalt's fingers closed over the tiny disk. His hand was shaking.

How loyal Cobalt had been. All this time. And now, the fact that he could return the favor was a bigger event to him than even going to space and getting his own ship.

In his homeless, wanderlust heart, it made sense to Liyan now that with the ever-changing circumstances of his career and long before he had grown to love Lark and Tiri, he might instinctively and ultimately connect to the one being he could find who would accept him unconditionally and still love him whether or not he ever returned from the addictive, cold arms of galactic reaches.

And now that he'd freed him, Cobalt was truly his.

He felt shaken, like crying again. The lights through the triangle window shed tears of pink, orange, star-white and green. They were the colors of his ship, his memory, his travels.

He couldn't speak.

Cobalt said, "You bought my contract so you could give it me."

"Yes." He took a breath. "Yes," he repeated. The third time he said it, he nearly yelled the word. "I want you with me. Always. But only if you want it, too. I knew that only if you were free to make your choice would it be real between us."

Liyan stared past the curtains to the intermittent flashings of the spaceport and the even more beautiful darkness between those flashes. All that he was, warmth and blood, longing and human, sat recently so broken and still adrift. For the moment.

Horns. Whistles. Shouts. The noise increased. A fine scent of ozone tinged the air.

Midnight celebrations crystallized the man-made skies and strobe-lit the high room.

"Thank you," Cobalt said, mouth gracefully curving into a smile, as if he had never been free to do so. "I accept ownership of myself." He took a long breath. "You figured it out. And yes. I want it. Always. To be with you." He leaned down. His first kiss pressed Liyan's cheek. His second brought a gentle breath to Liyan's lips, all velvet and salt.

The thirteen year old ache in Liyan's chest turned to pleasure. He reached up to cup the other man's shoulders.

The fireworks had become falling stars reflecting endlessly the force-field that kept the abyss safely contained.

Through all that dark and night, Liyan had navigated himself right back to where it all began.

The kiss turned warm, more urgent. Liyan pulled back. "Come to bed with me, please."

"But Lark? And Tiri...?"

"We had a lot of time to talk during my healing. And then while coming here. They want me to be with you tonight. Tomorrow the four of us will talk. Together. As a team."

"I'd like that," Cobalt said. "I'd like that so much."

"I was hoping you'd say that. I don't expect you to accept them as...part of me...right away..."

"They accept me?"

"Yes."

"Then I accept. In fact, I always have since you first introduced them in your waves. I was so grateful you had such loyal, good people in your life."

"I know you always told me that. But it's different when you're face to face."

"Everything is different now. Better now. Because of you, Liyan. I never dreamed when I first met you, that young boy with all those stars in his eyes, asking me for a glass of ice water, that it would be him who changed my entire destiny. That you would be the one."

Liyan laughed and felt the entire room vibrate with the sound. All his emotions felt contained in that laugh. He almost couldn't catch his breath.

"Please," Liyan said. "Help me up."

Cobalt put his forearms under Liyan's shoulders. "Ready?" he asked.

Liyan nodded, felt himself easily lifted so that he stood as if on new legs. Cobalt turned him and put one arm under his shoulders and led him to the bed. Liyan sat on the edge, then slowly lifted his legs up and leaned back on the thick, springy, covers and pillows of the best bed the Grand Aurora Hotel provided.

Cobalt arranged the pillows for comfort, then took off his long-tailed coat and got into the bed beside him fully clothed. He pulled Liyan onto his side until they faced each other and said, "I lived thirteen years without you, with letters and gifts that were amazing and wonderful, but nothing like this. And now that you're here, I know I could never live thirteen more years or even one more day without you. Thank you, Liyan. For my freedom. For your love."

His throat tightened. He held his breath. He couldn't see through the tears for many seconds. Such an insidious habit it was, this thing with the tears he couldn't control. He said, trying to breathe, "Damn it, quit talking." He leaned in and pressed his forehead to Cobalt's. Their lips met again, tight, determined, then loosened and opened into a sinking caress of mouth, tongue, breath.

With the soft pink light, the diminishing outside revels, and Cobalt's supportive arms around him, he could finally relax for the first time after the accident. In Cobalt's arms, his body turned liquid and hot. There was no more holding back. No more suppression of love.

Cobalt's hand cupped his face, his fingers tangling in his hair. Lavender eyes, soap scent, the fine taste of his lover's mouth edged with faint champagne encompassed Liyan. All the words and confessions and letters that had flown between them through deepest shadows and coldest stars now gathered in one place for this moment, this reason for being.

*

Long after Cobalt had fallen into a restful sleep, Liyan lay awake staring at the carved ceiling as the candles burned low. The distant rumble of the ships shook the sky, that old, familiar background noise he'd grown used to so long ago.

He reached for the hand screen at the bedside table and brought it into the bed. Silently, he turned it on and began to write his final letter to an android.

Dear Cobalt:

I am home. Wherever you are, whenever we are together, that is the only real home I have ever known.

Love,
Liyan

****

Dear Reader:

Thank you for reading *Omega Untamed*: *The Omega Misfits Book 6.*

I hope you enjoyed Kee's story as much as I did writing it!

Next on my agenda is: 2 Omega Misfits novellas. One will be a Christmas novella. They will both be part of a multi-author giveaway, one in Oct. 2020, and one in Jan. 2021. To keep well-informed about these giveaways, please join my Facebook group or sign up for my newsletter (or both).

Newsletter: http://eepurl.com/cqDVcX

My Facebook group Wendyland.
https://www.facebook.com/groups/718074255203918/

In addition to the novellas, I have another stand alone Christmas story in the works, and a new shifter omegaverse series, **Endangered Alphas**, which will premiere starting in 2021! There will also be more intermittent additions to **The Omega Misfits.**

I hope you continue to stay with me on this journey where I continue my discovery of this wonderful omegaverse genre with many more books to come!

Happy Reading!

Love,

Wendy Rathbone

About Wendy Rathbone

Read Wendy Rathbone… where imposters and outcasts, princes and lost boys always find their happily every after.

I have written in all genres: sci-fi, fantasy, horror, paranormal, contemporary, erotica, romance. But I keep coming back to romance as the main focus. Gay romance. Male/male romance. The idea of two men falling in love is irresistible to me. It's all I write now.

All my books are available on Amazon and most are in Kindle Unlimited. So if you have the urge, go take a look. See what's on the shelf.

Male/male romance books by Wendy:

The Kingdom of Slaves Series (contemporary fantasy mm romance)

The Slave Palace
The Slave Harem
Master of Halloween (short story)

The Omega Misfits (Omegaverse mm romance)

Trust No Alpha
The Alpha's Fake Mate
Alpha's Embrace
Single Omega Dad
Omega Chattel
Omega Untamed ()

The Imposter Series (fantasy mm romance)

The Imposter Prince
The Imposter King

The Moonling Prince Series (fantasy, sci fi mm romance)

The Moonling Prince
The Coming of the Light

The Foundling Series (contemporary billionaire mm romance trilogy)

Rescue Me
Sacrifice Me
Remember Me

The Fantastic Immortals Series (fantasy/myth mm romance)

Ganymede: Abducted by the Gods
Zeus: Conquering his Heart

Stand Alone Novels

Sci Fi MM Romance

Solstice Gift (holiday)
Not Another Hero
Cocky Virgin Prince
Prey
Scoundrel
The Android and the Thief (Second edition coming May 2020)
Letters to an Android

Fantasy MM Romance

Lord Vampyre
Lace
Snow of the White Hills (mm fairy tale)
The Elves of Christmas (holiday fantasy mm romance)

Contemporary MM Romance

Romantically Incorrect
Snowfall and Romance (Christmas novel)
The Bodyguard's Valentine
Buying You

Contact links for Wendy Rathbone:

Come join my newsletter! http://eepurl.com/cqDVcX

Join my Facebook group Wendyland. I post updates, cover reveals, snippets, sales and other fun stuff every day:
https://www.facebook.com/groups/718074255203918/

Friend me on Facebook:
https://www.facebook.com/wendy.rathbone.3

Follow my Amazon author page:
https://www.amazon.com/Wendy-Rathbone/e/B00B0O9BMS/ref=dp_byline_cont_ebooks_1

Follow me on Bookbub:
https://www.bookbub.com/authors/wendy-rathbone

SINGLE OMEGA DAD
The Omega Misfits Book 4
Wendy Rathbone

My new financial guardian, Mathias, is a cold, self-centered, rude-ass Alpha and the son of one of the wealthiest men in the country. To him, I am a burden on society, only fit to live on a chattel farm.

It doesn't matter that I'm drawn to him, to his ominous presence and chiseled jaw, his muscular body in his fitted silk suits. I'm a single dad with kids and responsibilities --I don't have time for that rich bastard.

He keeps coming by the house so I can sign documents, fine. But then he's got cute gifts for my kids.

It's got to stop. I don't have time to fix him. Don't have time to fall in love with an Alpha right now.

A non-shifter Alpha/Omega love story with mpreg, a single widower Omega dad, an Alpha who cannot knot, emotional issues, two adorable identical twin boys, and an HEA.

Some characters from "Trust No Alpha" make appearances in this novel, however, this book is a standalone read.

TRUST NO ALPHA
The Omega Misfits, Book 1
Wendy Rathbone

It's a world gone mad. The Alphas are out of control. When you discover you're not who you thought you were, the nightmare begins.

KRIS
At age eighteen, life as he knows it is over for Kris. A secret to his nature he was not aware of has been revealed.

Now, kept as a prisoner in a locked room in the mansion of his wealthy father, Kris is at the mercy of Alpha laws and Alpha domination.

Things take a turn for the worse when his own litter mate threatens him, and his father starts behaving strangely around him.

Escape is his only hope. But where can he go in a world that allows him no rights?

THORNE
Marked as a dangerous Alpha, and living a secluded life alone and unloved, Thorne still grieves for the mate whose death he feels responsible for.

Years have passed, and he refuses to even try to function in normal society.

One day he discovers a young man on his property, disheveled, desperate, and scared. He acts like a runaway Omega, but he doesn't smell like one.

What is this boy? And why does Thorne feel an immediate need to protect him? To bond him? To make him his?

A non-shifter, Omegaverse love story of rescue, first time, fertility issues and an HEA. Standalone read. 65,500 words. (While Omegas are birth-fathers in this universe, there is no on-page mpreg in this book.)

THE ALPHA'S FAKE MATE
The Omega Misfits, Book 2
Wendy Rathbone

The Alphas think they own everything. Including people. Well, I'm here to say they don't own me, and I will never let one of those bastards touch me again.

The frenzy of their Burn cannot be trusted. I know from experience. My first time with an Alpha nearly ended in my death. And because of the laws which favor Alpha rights, and place a large number of unbonded, adult Omegas on chattel farms, my abuser can never be tried for his crimes against me.

Omegas are being hurt. Omegas are dying.

All Alphas are violent. Or so I believe. Until I meet Orion.

Ori is everything a guy could want in a mate. Six foot three. Beautiful brown wavy hair. Bright, dark eyes. Muscles like chiseled marble. He even says "please" and "thank you" at all the right times. He's got it all, except he's an Alpha.

Though he has given me a room in his home free of charge, and has signed fake paperwork saying we are bonded so I don't have to answer my attacker's claim, can I trust him?

But now I'm in danger. If I don't take a real mate, my life as I know it will be over. Can I believe in the goodness of Ori? Can I learn to love again?

A non-shifter, fake mate, Alpha/Omega love story. Rescue. First time. Omegaverse. Mpreg. Healing from sexual trauma. (All books in The Omega Misfits series are standalone reads and can be read in any order.) 61k words.

ALPHA'S EMBRACE
The Omega Misfits Book 3
Wendy Rathbone

I am Misha. My name was given to me at birth by the doctor who delivered me. I have never known my parents. I live in a ten by ten space with one window, a sink and toilet, a bed and a locked door. Once a day I'm taken to an outdoor exercise area. I am allowed a limited access tablet and tutored online by computer programs. I have one friend I talk to through a tiny crack in the wall. His name is Cedric and he has trouble keeping himself quiet. When he isn't talking to me about monsters and demons, he screams all the time.

Why is my life so isolated and depressing? Because I am a Sylph. Sylphs are the byproduct of illegal Omega to Omega matings. We are all beautiful, but 99.9% are born insane. The rarest of Sylphs, like me, show no outward signs of madness or brain damage, but we live in institutions because we cannot be trusted.

All of us Sylphs who have lived long enough to pass through puberty have hypersexual disorder which makes life even more difficult for us, let alone our keepers. It is like something Alphas call the Burn, a mating urge Alphas experience once every couple of months.

But we're Sylphs, not Alphas, and this Burn thing? We experience it all the time. It's a huge problem and why we are kept isolated. Most of us don't survive through our teens because of it.

One day, a handsome Alpha comes to interview and study me. He calls himself the Chief of Staff but his real name is Geo. Like magic, I fall in love with him instantly. I do everything I can to seduce him. He will have none of it because touch between an Alpha and a Sylph is taboo. But I have plans. No matter what, I intend to bond him and make him mine. Forever.

A non-shifter Alpha/Omega-Sylph love story of forbidden love, rescue, and HEA. Standalone read. No Mpreg. 58k words

THE SLAVE PALACE
Wulf and Locke
WENDY RATHBONE

Conquered. Captured. Sold as a pleasure slave.

After being taken as a prisoner of war, Wulf fights his captors and is sold as a One-Night Thrall to be used and abused, then put to death. He is purchased by a high ranking master of the famous Slave Palace. Why Locke buys him, Wulf has no clue, but something about this master is intriguing. Instead of abuse, Wulf is plied with luxuries he has never known by a man who actually seems to respect him.

Jaded. Looking for a challenge.

Eminent Master Locke takes on a bet with his best friend that he can't train and tame a dangerous One-Night Thrall in ten days. But something about this slave stirs him like no other before. All bets aside, Locke has the urge to keep Wulf, as well as save his life. But Wulf is fierce, unwilling, and his consent papers have been forged. If Wulf doesn't soon submit to his role as a slave, he will be sent to death as a prisoner of war.

A sweet, slow-burn love story taking place on an alternate contemporary Earth where owning pleasure slaves is legal.

LORD VAMPYRE
Wendy Rathbone

When Lord Neverelle becomes a guest at Cliffside Keep, Vanni watches helplessly as Damion, the young man he's grown up with and secretly loves, falls for the alluring and seductive stranger. Lord Neverelle is danger incarnate, and soon takes control of the household.

Not satisfied with Damion alone, Never uses a vampire trick called "the tempt" to compel Vanni, who is swept into a love triangle that includes fiery passion and nightly threesomes.

Now Vanni must ask himself, is any of this consensual? And what about Damion—does he really want to be with Vanni, or is it all a sensual play controlled by vampire compulsion?

M/M and M/M/M romance.

The Imposter Prince
Book 1 in The Imposter Series
Wendy Rathbone

His love for an enemy prince threatens his very life.

Dare does not mind serving the spoiled and cruel Prince Darius. Growing up with him, Dare does everything for Darius including homework, bed play demands, and even doubling for him as the prince grows too paranoid to face even the smallest of crowds.

But everything changes in a single moment when Dare, while posing as Darius, is abducted by the enemy.

A captive in a new and hostile land, Dare meets another prince who seems just as indulged and rotten as Darius—until Dare gets to know him, until they fall in love. Against his will, Dare must continue to play the role of Prince Darius for real, or risk everything: his love, his land, and his very life.

His only chance for survival is to keep a secret from the one he loves, a secret that is also killing him.

A male/male, enemies to lovers novel of mad kings, troubled princes, abduction, fevers, cold dungeons, warm hearths, comfort, wine, and true love.

BUYING YOU
Wendy Rathbone

It's one thing to be a beautiful cover model on billboards, buses and magazine covers. It's quite another to be sold as one.

Prized for his looks, Dane knows it's shallow, but he is on his way to having it all. It feels good to be gorgeous, smart and have top designers from around the world requesting him.

When he returns to his hometown to participate in a small Date-For-Charity auction, it seems harmless enough—until a hooded man walks in and bids higher on him than anyone else. Dane is intrigued but nervous when he finds out the guy has vanished after the winning bid, leaving only a limo behind to whisk Dane off into the night.

Enemies to lovers, opposites attract, and hot steamy nights that challenge two guys' trust issues along with their biggest fears.

SONS OF NEVERLAND
A Deliciously Dark Male/Male Romance
Della Van Hise

Set against a backdrop of contemporary culture, *Sons of Neverland* explores the universal questions of love, sex and death - the three most crucial challenges every human being must face. Stefan London is a grieving man, suffering through the loss of his young daughter. When he goes to a science fiction convention in the hopes of meeting her friends, he encounters instead a man who is dangerously seductive. Lured into the night, Stefan soon discovers himself in a world where vampires are real, and immortality is only a kiss away.

But the price of eternal life is high, and as his handsome maker warns, "Through my blood you will learn a secret that will compel you to live forever, yet a secret so sinister it will haunt you for that same eternity."

The secret will haunt you, too.

––––

A deliciously dark male/male romance. First time, slow-burn, enemies to lovers, love/hate relationship, HEA.

YEAR OF THE RAM
Della Van Hise

Only after Star Commander Morgan Diego becomes an exile as a result of a Galaxy Corps political blunder does he begin to realize how much he valued the companionship of his second in command - the mysterious Lucien, an Alfarian who is more elfen than human, with peculiar powers & abilities which begin to unfold as he, too, realizes what he has lost.

Separated by circumstance from his former life, Morgan is thrust into a world where he must survive by his wits. When he meets a peculiar little old man calling himself Kim Le, Morgan finds himself in a situation where he is required to master The Art - not only a form of human & extraterrestrial martial arts, but a way of living that will alter his life forever.

At the temple, he is introduced to his new teacher, another Alfarian man who begins to steal his heart - a heart which is already promised to Lucien. Torn and conflicted, Morgan struggles with the world he left behind and the world he now inhabits.

Beginning to believe he may never again return to his ship and to the friends and loved ones he left behind, he is all the more frustrated and heartbroken when a new Master arrives at the temple: a man to whom Morgan is immediately drawn both mentally and physically, a man who is strikingly familiar... yet utterly alien.